CONVICT'S CAPTIVE

Book Two

By

Paul Blades

Dark Visions Publications
darkvisionspub@gmail.com

Other books by Paul Blades:

The Maddy Saga:

CONVICT'S CAPTIVE

Book Two

By

Paul Blades

Copyright 2012@Paul Blades

Dark Visions Publications
darkvisionspub@gmail.com

Other books by Paul Blades:

Klitzman's Isle
Klitzman's Empire
Klitzman's Paradise
Klitzman's Pawn Parts One and Two
Klitzman's Predators
Slaver's Dozen- A Tale of Klitzman's Isle
The Taking of Cheryl Part One
The Taking of Cheryl Part Two: Slaver's Bait
Comfort Girl No. 4
Sacrifice to the Emerald God
The Blue Cantina: Anna's Surrender
The Blue Cantina: Down the Dark Ladder
The Warlord's Concubine, Books 1, 2, 3 and 4
Dreams and Desires, Books 1 and 2
Carmella Condemned
Carmella's Fate
Convict's Captive, Book 1

The Maddy Saga:

Vol. I	Maddy becomes a Ponygirl
Vol. II	The Training of a Ponygirl
Vol. III	Ponygirl Champion
Vol. IV	Ponygirl Summer
Vol. V	Ponygirl Love
Vol. VI	Ponygirl Season
Vol. VII	Ponygirl Gambit
Vol. VIII	Ponygirl Pleasures
Vol. X	Ponygirl's Choice
Vol. XI	Ponygirl's Fate

CHAPTER ONE

There was no question in Carly's mind that Blackjack Jackson, her captor, was a sociopath. She remembered studying about sociopaths in her senior psychology class. It was a form of mental illness. They couldn't help the fact that they couldn't experience empathy with other human beings. The normal feelings of guilt which most of us feel when we have injured someone are not felt by them. Other people exist only to serve their needs. It was, she thought at the time, unfair that they be treated in the same way as common criminals, punished for their crimes instead of sent to psychiatric facilities where they could be treated and studied. Someday, there might be a cure.

She felt much different about it now.

After enjoying the benefits of her body and being the recipient of her enforced, untrammeled lust, the man had locked up her body with nary a word to her, filled her orifices with offensive, degrading instruments, petted her like she was his dog or his cat, and then fell asleep as easily as an infant with a belly full of milk.

Although she knew she was barely more than a thing to him, she realized she had to be grateful he had continued use for her. When she heard it announced on the newscast that he had abducted her, she thought it was all over. And it almost was. But somehow his desire for her body and the services it could provide overrode his instinct for self preservation.

She knew that it was not just the sex. That was an important part of it, no doubt. He had spent 12 years locked up with hundreds of angry, cold, cruel and calculating men. He had undoubtedly been dreaming about having the use of a woman's body all that time. And now he had one. Carly was not one for false modesty and she knew that her body was much more than merely appealing, that her face was much more than attractive. She didn't let her knowledge of her comeliness rule her life, but having that self knowledge did provide her with a little more self confidence, a little more self satisfaction than if the opposite had been true. And she knew that the fact that she was what most people would consider a beautiful, young woman was a source of extra satisfaction to the man. It was kind of like hitting the lottery. Of all the females he could have captured, he had been awarded her.

But it was more than that which had motivated him to let her continue to live. It was the fact that he exercised complete and thorough control over her, that he held himself so superior to her, making her eat from the floor, keeping her gagged and bound almost all the time, playing with her body like it was his own private amusement park. He even insisted on washing her, as if she were his favorite toy that he wanted to take good care of. She didn't fool herself into thinking that there was any actual tenderness in his gentle touch. It was just that he perceived her as a valuable possession that needed to be carefully handled.

She was lying next to him now, on her belly, her face turned away, listening to him snore. Her arms were bound behind her and her ankles were joined. His body was jammed up against her right side. It was hot, large, unignorable. He was, as she was, naked. She had tried to edge her body away so that they were not touching, but the bed was too small. It was a double, not a queen. He was heavier than her and the bed tended to make her slide towards him. And every time she moved just a little bit, feverishly anxious that she not awaken him, within a minute or so he had moved too so that their bodies were back in contact. She finally gave up, afraid that she would fall off the bed. He would almost certainly awaken and would probably assume that her being on the floor was part of some plot to escape. He would beat her and then probably hogtie her in the bathtub like he had done before. He might even drown her this time.

Carly realized fully that her life depended on him viewing her as worth the trouble of keeping. This very morning, in the woods, he had had a pistol to her head, was a split second from sending her to eternity, but had changed his mind. Just thinking of it sent shivers down her spine and she was sure that if by some magic she was able to survive her captivity, she would have horrible nightmares about it for years.

One thing she was grateful for was the fact that she had been able to stop crying. When he had eased the thick black probe into her rear just before he bedded her down for the night, a terrible sadness had gone through her. He had used her there yesterday and he was going to use her there again. That was the whole purpose of the device, to make her ass more amenable to penetration. Well, maybe not the whole purpose. It was also, she was sure, for the purpose of accentuating his mastery of her, humiliating her, emphasizing her helplessness, and making clear her status as a convenience for his prick and nothing more.

It had hurt and had made her cry. She cried for about a half hour, silently, long after he had fallen asleep. She had thought that she might never stop. But she had finally exhausted her grief. Crying was so stupid anyway. It just made her humiliation and shame more thorough.

She was having trouble sleeping. Not that she wasn't tired. It was just that it was such a horrible thing to be the man's prisoner, to be living her life on the edge of a precipice. Dismal thoughts kept racing through her mind: dark thoughts about death, yearnings to be free, self pity for her abject helplessness, fear of what pain and misery the man would inflict on her tomorrow. But most of all, she thought about how he played her body like a violin, forcing ecstatic rushes of lust from her, bringing her to the apotheosis of pleasure and ecstasy.

She had never had fantasies that included being someone's sex slave. Well, maybe not never. As a young girl, her fantasies had included being whisked away by the traditional tall, dark, handsome stranger who would relieve her of all guilt and responsibility for her lusts, impose on her the vague but very real pleasures that she hungered for. But that was as far as it went. She hadn't had those fantasies for years. She had learned to take responsibility for her sexual needs, to satisfy them freely when she wanted to.

So what was wrong with her? Why did his use of her drive her to the heights of passion so easily? Every time he put his hands on her, her pussy began to burn. When his tongue entered her mouth, she felt compelled to kiss him, to feed on him. And when his cock was between her lips, and it had been there three times now, after she had gotten over her initial revulsion at being forced to suck it, she felt like she was being honored by its presence. She reveled in its soft textured hardness, its girth, its length, its heat, its power, even its taste, all the while experiencing shame at her licentiousness, her meek submissiveness, the humiliation of being used without consent.

Yet, in spite of how hot it made her, she felt repelled by his enforced use of her, her lack of choice, the callous way that he treated her, the fact that his manhood was rudely inserted within her body in this most personal way. It was just a hole to him, like her other holes. Each one brought its particular pleasures. And this one was, she imagined, the best of them all because it involved her total attention, her total focus, her total concentration on his satisfaction.

The man groaned. It startled her. Her body stiffened. She was so afraid of him. It was understandable under the circumstances. He was at least twice her size and he had spent 12 years with nothing better to do than bulk up his already powerful body in the prison exercise yard. But it made her feel cowardly that she did not at least mount some defense or protest against his abuses. And there it was again, that feeling of hopelessness and despair that brought on the tears. It made her conscious all over again of the penis like probe he had forced between her lips, the awful confinements her had placed on her limbs, and the fiendish object inserted so callously in her rear.

She started to sniffle and writhe once more in her bonds, testing them futilely, pulling at her imprisoned wrists behind her back, trying to force her ankles apart, biting down fiercely on the long, thick, cock-like probe in her mouth.

The door was only maybe five feet away from the foot of the bed. All she had to do was to somehow get over there, slide open the chain lock, turn the handle to the door and flee. If she was able to slip out of bed without him noticing, she might be able to hop over to the door.

Doing it quietly would be the trick. She might be able to stand on her tippy toes and, with her back to the door, take hold of the doorknob with her bound hands and turn it.

But how would she deal with the chain lock? If she stood near the door it would be about level with her chin. She could use her teeth, but her mouth was fully covered. Maybe she could use her nose. Yes, that might work. But she knew that she would not even try it. The likelihood of success was so low that it was not worth risking the whipping she would surely reap when he caught her. Even if she got through the door he was sure to awaken when he felt the cold air come flowing into the little cabin. She was in no position to run away with her ankles still bound. He would easily catch her and drag her back.

And she knew that he was always just a razor's edge away of getting rid of her. A foiled escape attempt would likely tip the balance.

It was hard to live under such a cloud all the time. As of now, she couldn't see any likely scenario in which he set her free. And if he didn't set her free, there was only one other alternative. She just hoped that it was swift and clean and not long and gruesome.

Something would happen though. She had to believe it. Somehow she would get away. Somehow she had to believe that she would be able to return to her life, albeit as a drastically changed and ravaged woman. She had to believe that or else despair would close in all over her and she wouldn't be able to go on.

She must have dozed off after that, for the next thing she knew she was springing awake. It was, as it had been since he had turned out the light, pitch black all around her. His body had moved. It had come closer so that his shoulder was over on top of her back. His arm had dropped over her. His hand was sliding down her bound arms. It passed over her useless hands and then crossed her buttocks, giving them a soft caress and then moved down over the backs of her thighs.

She held her breath, hoping that his contact was not a prelude to further abuse. Maybe he was just moving in his sleep. Maybe he would sink back into somnolence. Maybe he would leave her in peace at least until the morning. She made a little prayer.

His hand lingered on the back of her thigh. His breathing was deep. His body seemed at complete rest. She released her air, needing to breath, and in the hopes that the crisis had passed. She swallowed, causing her mouth to compress on the faux cock in her mouth. Her hands twisted in her bonds unconsciously. His hand and arm were hot against her skin.

And then the hand moved again. It slipped up over her arms and slid across her shoulders. It held itself there for a few seconds. Then she felt his body shift. The hand slid under her arms and began to caress her back. Her skin tingled at his touch. He had rolled to his side and come up against her. His stiffened cock was lying against her thigh. When his large, heavy, hot hand slid down and he gave each of her rear mounds a thorough, firm caress, her heart sank and her stomach rolled over. He was awake.

The hand kept moving about her confined body. She squirmed and whined unhappily. "Please don't let this happen," she called out in her mind to no one. She knew, though, that it was a futile plea.

All hope that it was just a rumbling of the man's dreams came to an end when he rose to his knees and moved behind her on the bed. He straddled her confined ankles and ran his hands, both of them now, up and down the back of her shins, her thighs and over her rump. She heard him release a long, lustful sigh. His hands moved up over her hips and up her torso, over her shoulders and back as if he was trying to awaken the cells of her skin all over her body. If that was his intent, it was working, because her body began to burn and she felt a pull in her loins.

"Noooooooooooooooo, please don't," she begged in her thoughts.

His hand, his right hand, dug into her hair at the back of her head. She felt him grasp it firmly. And then he began a slow, steady pressure, pulling it upwards. Carly had no choice. She raised her head and then followed the man's lead, moving her torso up, arching her back. His left hand slid under her, crossing over her breasts and guided her up. Between the pull on her hair and the hand across her chest, she was brought up to her knees. Her buttocks were resting on the back of her joined thighs. Her back was against the man's chest. He was so big, she felt like he was towering over her. She knew what was going to happen next and she asked the heavens to forestall it. But, as she had surmised, his strong, hot hands crept around her sides and seized her breasts.

He squeezed them gently. His thumbs ran over her nipples. His fingers took hold of her teats, pinching them lightly, tugging on them, pulling her breasts from her torso. Then they encircled her breasts again, massaging them, caressing them, conveying their heat and their passion to them. It made Carly moan with unhappiness and the genesis of lust. His right hand slipped down over her belly while he continued to stroke and caress her breasts with his left. His hand pressed against her belly, rubbing it all the way down to the 'Y' formed by her jammed together thighs. Then it slid over her thighs, caressing them, warming them, stoking her fires.

He was pressed up firmly against her back and she could feel his stiffened cock against her bound hands. She resisted a perverse urge to seize it. Everything was pitch black. The man had always seemed devilish, but he had never seemed more like a demon than now. He wasn't a man as much as he was a presence. He was all around her. His invisible, disembodied hands were tormenting her. Somehow, she had to stop it or she would go mad!

She whined and began to squirm in the man's arms. "Don't do this! Don't do this!" she thought desperately. She erupted into rebellion. She shook her head and her hips. She tried to bend over to escape his grasp. "Nnnnnnnnnnnnn! Nnnnnnnnnnnnnnn!" she called out in protest.

He didn't say anything. He merely reached up and took her teats between his thumbs and forefingers and began to twist them. She groaned from the pain, but refused to surrender. It went on and on. He twisted harder and harder. Finally, she could take it no more. She screamed, a sound that barely penetrated her gag, and became still. He loosened his grip. She issued a miserable, defeated whine. He pulled her torso straight again. She leaned back against him, sobbing.

It was as if he had a particular program to run with her and now that it had been interrupted, he had to start at the beginning. He began, like before, with a gentle caress of her mounds, then proceeded back through the other steps until his right hand once more was exploring her belly and the front of her thighs while his left hand continued to caress and stroke her breasts.

Carly's lusts recommenced their growth, as they had before, and she whined and her body shook slightly as if she could cast off the unwanted feelings, but she did not rebel. She knew that she shouldn't fight it. It was a waste of time. He would win. He always did. But she had to assuage her conscience by at least trying. Now that he had defeated her, there was no more reason to resist. She took a deep breath, emitted a long, deep sigh, and let her will melt away.

Her audible token of surrender had a noticeable effect on his ministrations as if it had been the sign he was waiting for. He gave both of her breasts heavy, lust producing squeezes and then leaned back. She felt him freeing the binding on her wrists. When they were separated, he took hold of them with his vise like grip and moved her hands in front of her. He lifted them up so that they were level with her neck and then pushed them together so that he could grip them both with his right hand. She felt him leaning over as if he was looking for something and then come back erect.

He hooked something to her left wrist. It was a chain, the 6" one he had bought the night before. He pulled on it until her left hand was forced to a position just behind her neck. She felt the chain pulled through the ring in the back of her collar. He then brought her right hand back and fastened the other end of the chain to it. He released it. Her wrists were now confined up above her shoulders, and out of his way.

His hands caressed her breasts and belly again and then moved to her back. He pushed her torso forward until she was bent over, her forehead touching the bed. He moved back, undid the locks holding her ankles bound to each other and spread her legs so that he was kneeling inside them.

He started to caress her back, running his hands up her spine to her neck and back down again. They sensitized her flesh wherever they went. He ran them down over her hips and over her rear mounds and back up. Carly just let herself revel in the soft, gentle contact. With her legs spread she realized that her pussy was now vulnerable to his touch and that mere fact made her lust grow. Soon he would put his hand on it and she would be off to the races. Her heart began to beat stronger and faster just thinking about it. He caressed her thighs and her rear, her hips and her back. Wherever they went, they left a trail of exhilarating sensation.

He shifted and placed his hand under her, between her thighs. He let it drift once, twice, three times over her smooth, hairless pudenda. Carly moaned. She expected him to continue, to delve between her love lips, to single out her little nubbin, to make her groan and writhe with need. But it seemed that his caress had been yet another test. He apparently had found what he wanted. His hand left and he placed it again in her hair, pulling on it just enough to let her know she should raise her head once more.

When she was up, she felt him lean over and straighten again. A moment later, she heard a buzzing sound. It only took her a second to realize what it was. It was the vibrating egg he had gotten at the porno shop the night before. He brought it around and began to let it run all over her body. He brought it across her chest and over her breasts. He drew it across her belly. He circled her loins with it. The buzzing sensation made her skin tingle. He placed it on a nipple and the vibration sent a flow of pleasure to her sex. He held it there for a while, massaging the breast with his other hand, and then moved to the other. Carly just closed her eyes and let the vibration flow through her. When he placed it over her clit, a wave of pleasure flowed through her body and she groaned.

The absolute darkness made what he was doing to her so unreal. Her mind was awhirl with sensations. He kept the vibrating egg firm against her love bud while her seized her breasts with the other hand, not gently this time, but firmly, roughly, dominating them, owning them. It made her gasp. A part of her knew that she should be resisting, but the feelings of pleasure were too intense for her to think of protesting. Some creature had seized her and was driving her to the extremes of passion before consuming her. It didn't matter who or what it was. Only the pleasure mattered. Only the intense sensations that drove out her thoughts of where she was, what was going to happen to her, what her life had come to. She wanted all of it driven away, at least for the moment, so that, in her confinements, in the deeds he compelled on her, she could be momentarily free.

He slipped the stone implement off of her clit and moved it down between her love lips. Carly sighed and moved her hips. The stone slipped along her lubricated gash, gathering her discharge. An unhappy thought crept into her mind. The egg was for her pussy. In a moment, she knew, he would put it inside her. And then, once that orifice was filled, he would turn to another, one that he had only used once, but seemed to enjoy. That she didn't want. That she wanted to say no to. That she wanted to prevent.

Although she knew that nothing she could do would, in fact, forestall it, she issued a whine and tried to put her thighs together to deny the egg entry into her fevered channel. But she was too late. As if he had sensed the beginning of her revolt, he slipped the vibrating egg inside her flush, moist tunnel. It went in easily and immediately began to transmit its vibrations to her needy crevasse. Carly gasped and then moaned softly, "Ohhhhhhhhhhh."

The man pressed the stone deep. Carly felt his hands reach for the leather belt around her waist. He unhooked the thin chains that ran along either side of her mons to the implement in her rear. "....eeeeeeeease...on't" she tried to say through her filled mouth. Her hands pulled at the chains that confined them to the back of her neck. Her body shivered as she felt him loosen the belt around her waist. "Nnnnnnnnnnnnn," she moaned again in meek protest.

He pushed her back over so that her forehead was down again on the mattress. Keeping one hand firmly on her back, forcing her down, preventing her from rising in protest, he pried at the thick probe in her nether region and began to slide it out. She expected it to leave her, but he stopped when it was about ¾ removed and began to slide it back in again. The mild abrasion of her small hole's delicate membranes sent a thrill through her that was unexpected. The vibration in her pussy continued and the combination of sensations created a synergy that made her moan.

He slid the object in her rear back and forth slowly again and again. Carly uttered a moan of futile protest, but it was more based on principal than on actual desire to have it end. The movement of the object was producing a feverish lust. She wanted to deny it, but it was all too real.

She was revolted at the thought of receiving pleasure from this penetration, but her unhappiness about it could not make it go away. If she had hands to use, she would have tried to push the man off of her, to do something, anything to stop the relentless, agonizingly pleasurable plowing of her ass. But like all else that had happened to her since that moment two days ago when he had seized control of her, she was powerless to oppose the man's iron will.

And then the moment that she truly feared came to hand. This time, when the probe was eased outward from her bowel, it slipped all the way out. She could feel her anal entrance gaping. The man shifted behind her. His right hand was still keeping her bowed over, her face jammed into the bed. His other hand guided his rampant meat towards her hole. She felt the bulbous head press against the flesh. "....eeeeeeeeeeeease!" she murmured in one last, desperate bid to avoid the inevitable. She shifted her hips back and forth frantically to avoid penetration. Her rebellion was easily foiled. With his right hand he reached under her, between her thighs and took hold of her clit between his thumb and forefinger.

He began to squeeze it until she moaned. She ceased her movement, her whole body cringing at the pain. He eased off a bit, but kept a grip on her love bud just firm enough to remind her of her duty to obey. He shifted his legs to the outside of her thighs and forced them together and then released her clit. He leaned forward. He readdressed his cock to her gaping entrance. She could feel the head probing at the distended hole. She bit down on her gag and clenched her imprisoned hands. The hot pole began to pass inside her. She groaned. And then it was in.

The man let it slide slowly forward. His hands took possession of her hips. His cock was slightly larger than the circumference of the probe which she had worn for so many hours and she felt her anal ring expanding. Suddenly, as if some strange drug she had been administered was taking effect, unlike when he had penetrated her the other day, she found herself passive and accepting. The vibrations in her pussy seemed to be echoing in her back passage, relaxing her muscles. As the cock slid forward, she gave out another moan. But this time it was a moan of pleasure and not of protest. When he was fully seated, his thighs pressed up against her rear cheeks, his taut belly against the small of her back, she gave out a groan.

His cock filled her in a way that was strange but wholly satisfying. It was like it was filling a need that she never had even known was there. How she had lived to date without experiencing it, she could not fathom. Why she had so fervently opposed it, she could not say. "Ohhhhhhhhhhhhhhh," she moaned. "Ohhhhhhhhhhh-hhhhh"

When he began his movements, her whole body thrilled. It was a sensation that permeated her consciousness at all levels, leaving no room for anything else but the pure joy of receiving it. Putting aside all pretensions of protest, she began rocking her body back and forth in cooperation with the man's thrusts. Soon, like an engine picking up steam, she began to rock frantically, needing desperately to reach crisis.

The man stopped his movements. She whined. He pulled himself from within her and gave her a mighty slap on her buttocks. She moaned and cringed with pain. He gave her another. She cried out. The power of it created a sting that pierced her whole body. He waited a moment and then pointed his cock again at her rear hole. It accepted him readily and Carly gave out a great moan of defeat.

He began his slow thrusts once more. Carly had received and understood his message. He would time their copulation. After all, this wasn't for her, although her cooperation and acceptance of her role made it much more enjoyable. No, it was for him, for his satisfaction. And her needs were nothing except to the extent that satisfying them brought him amusement or pleasure.

She ceded control to him. The abrasions of her dainty ring and the vibrations in her crevasse continued to send exquisite messages to her. Her need built stronger and stronger. She resisted the urge to accelerate her lusts by making any volitional movements. She waited for her passions to crest, if not patiently, for who could wait patiently for such a portentous event, but at least obediently. As it came closer and closer, she whined and she squirmed. It built higher and higher. Her breasts ached from hardness. Her mind was fevered. She wanted to call out her joy.

When it came, her pussy began a series of violent contortions. Her ring contracted around the meat that was rogering her. She groaned and moaned. His movements had accelerated and her pussy's spasms just went on and on, sending torrents of ecstasy through her body. And when her orgasm began to fade, there, in the background, she felt another one immediately begin to build.

"Ohhhhhhhhhhh! Mmmmmmmmmmmmmm! Ahh-hhhhhhhhhhh!" she called out. She bit down hard on her gag. The man was thrusting hard now, his thighs battering against her buttocks. He leaned over, his chest covering her back and his hands reached out and grasped her breasts. It was as if she had been swallowed by some beast, was inside it, and a thousand inner tentacles were probing her body, granting pleasure wherever they went.

The man grunted and groaned. He squeezed her breasts tightly. "Arrrrrrrrgh! Arrrrrrrrrgh! Arrrrrrrrrrgh!" he called out. Her pussy exploded again, celebrating the passion she had brought to him, her owner, her lord, her god. At that moment, she felt like she had no other purpose but to serve him, to receive his spunk, his lusts, his passions, to obey him in all things, to be owned and possessed by him. Nothing in her short life had ever seemed so clear. No one, she knew, could ever take her to this place again. No one! "Ohhhhhhhhhh! Ohhhhhhhh-hhhhh!" she cried out again and again and again.

When he had exhausted his forces, his thrusts slowed and then stopped. Her pussy's convulsions slowed, but it was maintained in a state of simmering pleasure by the still vibrating stone in her crevasse. He lay on top of her for a while. His chest was rising and falling and she could feel the beating of his heart against her back. Slowly, she began to return to her senses. She felt tired and worn and drained of substance. She felt him slip from her and then rise from the bed. Before he left, he clipped her ankle bracelets back together.

She heard him go to the bathroom and run the water, cleaning, she assumed, her wastes from his cock. He had flicked the bathroom light on and the rest of the room was set aglow, with long dark sinister shadows appearing like demons that had finally manifested themselves. They were the demons who had possessed her, Carly thought. They had driven her to madness. She had abjured her rights, her personhood, her individuality under their fiendish spells. She knew that she could not now take back her declarations of submission. They would haunt her all her days. And she would live only to be driven to those excruciatingly pleasurable heights once again.

He put out the light and came back to the bed. She had not moved. He reached under her and with two fingers, pried the vibrating stone egg from her purse. He lay down next to her and pulled her to her side. He released her right wrist from the small chain that had bound it to the back of her neck and slid the chain free. Pulling her hands to her chest, he ran the chain through the ring in the front of her collar and refastened it. Her hands were now posed in an attitude of prayer. He pulled up the blankets again and nestled into her back, placing his arm around her. This time, she did not shy away from contact. Within a minute, she could feel his chest begin to rise and fall in a deep rhythm. She timed her breaths to his and quickly succumbed to unconsciousness.

CHAPTER TWO

It was still snowing. Jack was sitting at the small wooden table in front of the picture window of the spare, 20' x 30' efficiency cabin. He had lifted the blinds so that he could see out. Everything was white. The car was under what looked like 10" to 12" of snow. The other cabins that he could see looked deserted. It seemed that he and the girl were the only ones foolish enough to try and make it over the mountain pass in this weather. Well, maybe not the girl since she really had had no choice in the matter, but at least him.

He realized that the delay was allowing the FBI to step up its search for him. He also realized that if he had iced the girl yesterday as he had originally intended, he would probably be somewhere in Texas by now. He turned to look at her. She was lying on the bed, her hands again locked behind her back and her ankles joined to them, her 5'7" frame folded up neatly. Her short, whisper blond hair was still mussed from her night of sleep. She had such nice pale, almost translucent skin. The red marks he had put on it were somewhat faded. She was looking back at him, her forlorn eyes peering over the brown leather of her gag. Was she worth it?

Last night he had finally broken her. She responded to her ass fucking like it had been her idea. And he had fucked her again this morning when the sun had just started peering in through the small gap under and around the blinds. He had been lying behind her, her ass butted up against his groin. She had writhed in her sleep and rubbed against his cock, waking him. His cock was already hard. It was a simple matter to bend her forward. It only took a few strokes of her pussy with his hand to make her wet. He slipped right in. She groaned and moaned while he fucked her and seemed to receive his spunk contentedly.

Afterwards, after his cock had slipped from her, she had turned to him, pressed her head into the crux of his shoulder and cried. He stroked her head in an attempt to console her, like you would any distressed animal, and she soon fell back asleep.

It looked like they would have to spend the entire day here. The wind from the storm was whipping around and raised other issues like what would happen if they lost power. They would have to go somewhere where there was heat or freeze to death. But where?

They had enough food and other comestibles. The small heater seemed to heat the room okay, although the place was a little breezy from lack of proper insulation. He had bought a couple of magazines and books yesterday so he would have something to read, a habit he built up from when he was in stir. The room came with cable TV.

It would be uncomfortable though sitting around all day with the girl. He wasn't used to such constant and close company. As a lifer in the joint he had been entitled to his own cell. He was used to spending huge blocks of time alone. And he didn't want to talk to her. The less he knew about her the better for when the time came. They had exchanged maybe a few dozen words since he had seized her and that was fine with him. Whenever he needed to communicate with her he had used a gesture of some kind when he could. He used her hair as a handle when he wanted her to move. He wanted her to remain an object as much as possible. The last thing he wanted was those big, baby blue eyes staring at him all day. But he had made provision for that too.

He had brewed some coffee when he woke up but had not made breakfast yet. There was something satisfying about lolling around the small cabin with nowhere to go and nothing to do. In prison you were always on your guard. Even he, who carried a lot of weight and had great juice with the guards, had to watch out. There was always somebody who wanted whatever you had, somebody who maybe was trying to prove something or to even up the score for some imagined or real slight. Or the higher ups, the captains and commanders, assistant wardens and, yes, even the warden himself, could decide to fuck with you one day. Today, nobody would fuck with him.

Although the storm had complicated his trek to freedom, it also kind of gave him a 'free' day. All the cops and robbers had to stay home when the weather was extreme. Nobody went out in this weather. Even the plows would be held back until the wind stopped blowing. It was like the fates had called a time out. For today only, he was not a fugitive from three consecutive life sentences, not wanted for 3 new homicides. He was just a guy holed up with his squeeze taking a short vacation from the regular daily grind.

He wondered if the girl shared his feelings. The thought of it made him laugh. There would be no vacation for her today as he fully intended to fuck the shit out of her. She might get to lay back and relax and enjoy it, but her orifices would surely be put to work. He hadn't fucked her yet this morning since he got up. But he soon would. Her mouth had been put on standby for a long while now and it was time to give it some exercise. But not just yet. He was feeling too lazy right now even to get up and cross the floor. And it was pleasant just to watch her pretty eyes shift back and forth, her hands stretch in her bonds from time to time, her ass wriggle as she tried to shift position.

Lighting a cigarette, he let the blurry, gray smoke escape his lungs and fill the small room. Sooner or later, they would leave the cabin, tomorrow morning from the looks of it, or maybe tomorrow night. He had bought one of those atlases that showed all the main roads all over the US. He hadn't looked at it to pick out a route yet. He knew generally how they would be going. He had gotten an Arkansas map at the grocery store yesterday. But he needed a Texas map to really plan out his route. They didn't show the kinds of road he wanted to take in the atlas.

He figured it was another 800 miles to New Mexico. He could make it in one day if they drove during the daylight hours. It would probably take two nights of driving to get there otherwise, especially by using the back roads. There was a phone number he needed to call. A guy he knew who wasn't a regular Rogue member, but sort of a fellow traveler. The cops never sussed him out when the whole chapter went down 12 years ago. No one ever suspected him as a co-conspirator so his phone wouldn't be tapped. He could hook him up with some safe private numbers of chapter members in New Mexico. Arrangements could be made. But what was he going to do with the girl?

She was a hot property. She wasn't like the runaways or crack addicts or stupid farm girls that they usually hauled in. Nobody cared what happened to them. They could just disappear. For them, the threat of immediate, disabling violence was usually enough to keep them in place. They had left nothing but wreckage behind them and more or less had nowhere else to go. Nobody was looking for them except maybe a distraught dad or a former boyfriend. And they had no juice, usually. Once a girl's trail ran cold, they were at a loss what to do. Sometimes a letter written by the girl under duress and mailed from some distant city would discourage them from looking any further.

But not this girl. They would be turning over heaven and earth to find her. Her face was on all the news stations. That station he had been listening to yesterday on the radio was from Omaha. And if Omaha had the story, the whole country probably did. No, this girl had to really disappear and the fewer who knew about it the better. So she had to go at the very latest when he made his connection in New Mexico.

And she couldn't be left lying around anywhere that she could be found like on the side of the road or some place like that. That would tip off the Feds as to where he had gone and cause all kinds of heat for the local chapter. But he was sure that they had their special spot where people went and were never heard from again. Once he made his connection to Mexico, he could just leave her with them. They would have some fun with her for a few days and then take her on a one way ride.

She whined and gave him a troubled look with her pretty, blue eyes. He realized that she probably had to pee. He would take care of that in a minute. It was a kind of a drag really that her life expectancy was so short. She had all the important qualities. She loved fucking. She was obedient and not rebellious. At the same time, she was proud and tough and bristled appropriately when she was demeaned. She was smart, which went along with being obedient. She had clearly weighed her options and decided to go with the flow, which made sense.

She knew how to keep her trap shut too, which was a definite positive. Even after almost buying the farm yesterday, she didn't snivel and complain, beg for freedom or mercy or anything like that. She knew just where she stood and how stupid it would be to make her life any worse off by being a pain in the ass.

And she was beautiful. She had a wry mouth that turned down when she was unhappy, which had been most of the time she had been with him. Her eyes conveyed fire and her inner strength. Her breasts were ample, firm and delicious and her pussy was tight and hot. And, to top it off, she gave a hell of a blowjob.

Yeah, he thought. It was too bad. Maybe he could figure out some way to get her into Mexico with him. He would buy a long chain and some shackles and keep her locked up all the time while he went out and earned. They would be just like a real couple, with her doing the cleaning and all and providing all the sexual conveniences. Yeah, she would be a treat to have in Mexico with him. But he would have a hard enough time negotiating his own surreptitious trip across the border. Even if he was a former, and the emphasis was on former, chapter president, he didn't have enough pull for them both.

He got up from his chair and lowered the blinds. It was unlikely anybody would be out and about today, but why take chances? He was wearing a pair of blue plaid, soft cotton boxers he had gotten in the army navy store. He had already done his workout. He was hungry. Breakfast and then a blowjob, he thought.

He went over to the bed and released the girl's ankles. Grabbing her hair at the back of her head, he brought her up and off of the bed and took her to the bathroom. She sat down on the toilet and peed, looking at him gratefully. She must have had to go real bad because her water made a loud sound like a fully open faucet. When she was done, he made her stand and wiped her coosh. Then he brought her out to the living area. He released her and tapped a spot on the floor with his toe. She knew what to do. She lowered herself to her knees, spread her legs widely and put her forehead to the floor right on that spot. Perfect. "See," he said to himself. "Smart."

His stomach rumbled. It was time to eat. He pulled from the fridge the pound of extra thick, honey cured bacon he had bought yesterday and the carton of extra large eggs. He had some bread for toast, butter and even some orange marmalade. Rummaging through the stand-alone, white metal dish cabinet, he found a fairly good sized nonstick skillet. He threw it on the stove at a medium heat and tossed ten slices of bacon in it.

The bacon began to sizzle almost right away. It smelled great. He poured himself another cup of coffee and sat at the table, waiting for the bacon to cook. One of the magazines he had bought yesterday was in a bag next to it and he took it out. It was called Motorcycle World. There were some great bikes in it.

First thing he would do when he got down in Mexico would be to buy a decent bike. He knew he would have to chop it up and redesign it a little, unless he was lucky enough to get a good used one. He had about 5 grand now, but would need a lot more. The thought entered his mind of maybe knocking off some more stores on his way to New Mexico, but decided it was too dangerous. Somehow, he would get more money, probably by running coke or being a bodyguard or something.

He got up after a while and turned the bacon over. He grabbed a coffee cup and poured most of the grease into it. He hated overcooked bacon and so once it got mostly browned he tossed a paper towel down on a plate and emptied the bacon out onto it.

Next came the eggs. He broke four into the well greased pan. While they were cooking, he dropped two pieces of bread into the toaster and got out the butter and marmalade. He came back just in time to flip the eggs. He liked the whites solid when he ate them and so he left them frying for about 10 more seconds. Then he slipped the greasy paper towel off of the plate which held the bacon and one by one slipped the eggs onto it with the spatula. He put the plate down on the table, buttered the toast, got some salt and pepper from the cabinet and sat down to eat.

Before digging in, he took a moment to appreciate the beauty of a plate full of bacon and eggs. It was stuff like this that you really missed. He looked at the girl. She was dutifully keeping her forehead to the floor. She was a looker, he had to give her that. Just seeing her there, all naked and bound up and ready for use was enough to make his cock twitch. But that was for later. Now it was time to eat.

He wolfed down his breakfast. It was greasy and hot. The egg yolk came out bright, golden yellow and he mopped it up with the toast. The bacon was so good!

He gulped down the coffee. When the eggs and bacon were gone, so was the toast so he had to make two more slices so he could have some of the marmalade. All the while, the girl kept her place, silent and obedient. He knew she was probably hungry and he would take care of that soon. But for now, he was taking care of his needs, needs he had waited 12 years to fill.

The marmalade covered toast was just the right touch to finish off his breakfast. There was a little bit more coffee in the pot and he poured out the last half cupful and lit a smoke. "This is the life," he thought. He could see himself in Mexico now, the girl obediently awaiting her own turn to eat after cooking him up a storm. He would have a heavy iron collar soldered around her neck and there would be a long, heavy chain connecting it to a ring in the floor. There would be a ring in every room so when he moved her there he could attach her to it. And he'd have a little cage he kept in a closet for when she was a pain in the ass to have around. It was a great thought. Too bad it would never happen.

He pushed out his smoke in the ashtray. A sense of total calmness and satiety came over him. He decided that it was time for his blowjob. He moved his chair so that it was facing the girl. Grabbing the fork, he tapped it on the table three times slowly and deliberately. She looked up. He unbuttoned the fly to his boxers and took out his cock. She looked at it and then looked back up at his face. She got the idea right away.

She shuffled over to him, her breasts jumping this way and that. When she was within reach, he placed his hands behind her head and unbuckled the gag she had been wearing almost constantly since he got it. He slipped the penis like protuberance from her mouth. "Time for a real one," he thought. She had the same idea. She inched herself a little closer, bent her head and sucked his already hardening cock into her mouth.

"Ohhhhhhhhhhh, yeah," he thought. This was just the thing to top off his breakfast. She glided her lips up and down his crank slowly, keeping them pressed hard against it. She swirled her tongue around the head when she got to the top and, on her way down, she didn't stop until his tool reached the edge of her throat.

He closed his eyes. His right hand was resting on her head. He let her go on and on. She must have sensed his desire for an extended performance since she fellated him unhurriedly. Every once in a while he had her stop and just kneel there with his rock hard prick in her mouth. If there was a heaven, he thought, it must involve getting a lot of blowjobs. If not, it made little sense to go there. He knew he was never going to heaven, but that was okay. That was the choice that he made. So he needed to get his blowjobs here.

He looked down at the girl. Her baby blues were looking up at him for permission to continue sucking him off. Her lips were pursed quite attractively and her cheeks bulged nicely. He leaned over, keeping his cock plugged into her mouth, and reached down and seized her breasts. He squeezed them gently, played with her nipples, pinching them and pulling on them until the girl's tits were jutting out from her body.

The worst part of prison had to be no tits, he thought. He could live with the rest of it: the brutality, the boredom, the lack of hope. But no tits? That was cruel and unusual punishment as far as he was concerned. If the law really wanted to calm the prisons down, it would make sure every swinging dick got a little tits and pussy once in a while. That was something you'd really stay in line for, cross all your t's, dot all your i's, mind your p's and q's. "No tits for you this month, Taylor," they would yell. "No pussy for you, Peters." He chuckled to himself.

Lots of guys, guys who had trouble getting it on the outside, would be breaking into prisons if that happened.

He kept massaging and playing with the girl's tits until her nipples had hardened and she moaned. It sent a nice vibration through his cock. She might have been faking it, but he didn't think so. He pulled her head off of his rod and reached further down until he was between her legs. He caressed her pussy and found it to be wet and hot just as he had supposed. He tickled her clit until she moaned again and then leaned up and, with his hand in her hair, positioned her mouth on his organ. She went right back to work.

His urge was growing. She pulled back her head and suckled on the end of his cock, running her tongue over the little slit. It made him groan. She lowered her head, pressing her lips hard against the stem of his manhood and then, spreading her tongue wide and holding it hard against the underside, drew her head back slowly. The abrasion of the rougher surface of her tongue sent a thrill through him. He wanted, needed completion. He began to thrust his hips up at her mouth on her descent and down on her return. He started going faster and faster as his heat grew. She matched his pace, licking and suckling. He gave a deep groan. He felt that little trough between excitement and explosion, that little delay in which your senses teeter tottered on the edge of rapture. He opened his mouth and took a deep breath.

And then he came. The girl's head was bobbing excitedly on his lap. His hands were gripping her tightly. He moaned and groaned as his cock throbbed and pulsed in her mouth. He felt himself emptying into her. "Ohhhhhhhhhhhh!" he moaned. "Ohhhhhhhhhhhh!"

When his ejaculations slowed, he sighed and leaned back in his chair. The girl kept up a slow, skillful, stroke of his cock, coaxing out every little spasm. When he was done for sure, she stopped, suckled the end just to give him one last message of pleasure and then, obediently, subsumed his softening tool in her mouth, awaiting his permission to release it.

He was in no hurry. Her warm mouth felt so good on his softened cock. His whole body still tingled with the vibrations of his climax. He closed his eyes and played with her hair. "What a shame," he thought. "What a waste." She was good.

Carly was fighting back tears. She was trying desperately not to cry, but, understandably, these waves of unhappiness kept flowing through her. She was looking up at him, watching eagerly for the sign that would allow her to slip his cock from her mouth. Even sitting, he towered over her. She estimated that he was at least 6'2" tall. The window behind him created a kind of ironic halo effect around his head, glittering off of his short, black hair. His face was rugged and even at rest presented an angry, malicious mien. His broad chest and thick biceps had a scattering of crudely drawn tattoos on them, some kinds of secret signs or logos she assumed. On his neck, on the right, was a two character Japanese ideogram. Carly assumed that it translated as something like 'don't fuck with me'.

All in all, he was built like a bear and twice as fearsome. She hadn't seen that big long knife he had carried with him the other night when he kidnapped her, but she was sure that it was around somewhere. And in the corner of the room, lying against the wall, was the 4' long, thin switch he had whipped her with the night before last. She surely didn't want to have to make friends with it again today.

It had been exciting to pay devotion to the man's cock. All those thoughts of how right it was, how powerful he was, how she deserved to be down on her knees to him, grateful that he deigned to enter her and grant her his ejaculant passed through her head while she was doing it, made her pussy hunger for his touch. And when he did touch it, she felt like she was going to faint. As soon as it was over though, when the last tremors of his cock were felt, when his manhood softened and shrank, these feelings vanished like the smoke from his cigarettes, leaving behind only their odor and ashy remnants.

As soon as she was done it all came back to her, how dreadful her captivity was, how despicable she was for receiving pleasure from what he forced upon her, how cruel and conscienceless he was, how dismal her future. Early this morning, when he had fucked her from behind on the bed, she welcomed his thick stiffness in her crevasse, craved the pleasure that he gave her. She felt like she had been honored when he pumped his spume into her. But as soon as the tremors of her pussy started to fade, she sank into such profound unhappiness that she turned to the only human being she had contact with for comfort, crying in his arms while he stroked her back into complacency.

No, she didn't want to cry now. She reached down deep and steeled herself. She wouldn't give him the pleasure of her tears. They would stay inside if she could help it. She shifted her knees and clasped her lips around his flaccid, reduced manhood. She had become uncomfortable once her passion had left her, but she certainly didn't want his cock to slip from her lips. She didn't want another beating.

During the long periods of immobility and inaction, she was able to rationalize away her behavior as a defense mechanism. She took pleasure from his touch, his cock, because the opposite was too hard to bear. It was the only way to preserve her psyche, otherwise she might go mad from hysteria. It was also a survival instinct. Each time she moaned in pleasure, she sensed him scoring it as a little victory. He had made the blond bimbo hot. It added to his pleasure and anything that added to his pleasure contributed to his desire to keep her alive.

Her stomach growled. It had been tortuous to smell the food that he cooked and listen to him eat it all up like she wasn't even there. He was a real prick, that was for sure. But she got the sense that he did it not so much to torture and abuse her, but to maintain the immense distance between them. He naturally got to eat first, drink the coffee, sit and relax in a chair, read a magazine. He didn't so much want to hurt her as he did want to enforce the natural order of things. She was barely above the level of an animal, a pet. Good pets learned to obey their masters, wait patiently for their beneficence, purr when they were stroked. She was a good pet. She did all those things and more.

His hand took hold of the hair in the back of her head and he gave it a subtle but discernable pull. Obediently, she raised it. He lifted it further and she rose to her feet. He sat her down in the chair opposite him. She spread her legs, like she had been trained, and sat up straight so as to present her breasts to him. She leaned on her bound arms behind her. He smiled, caressed her breasts briefly and got up from the table.

He turned his back to her and went to the refrigerator. She watched him as he brought out the eggs. "Thank god," she thought. "He's going to make me some food." He turned on the gas under the frying pan. When it had heated up, he tossed in a couple of slices of bacon and they started immediately to sizzling. She watched him crack a couple eggs in a bowl and swirl it around. He added a little milk and a spice that looked a lot like cinnamon.

He stood there pawing at the bacon with a fork while it cooked. Carly loved bacon, but rarely ate it. Too much fat and cholesterol. But that kind of stuff didn't matter much now. She would eat it and enjoy it.

She looked at the large window over the table. All she could see was the blinds. When he had it open earlier, she wanted to take a look out to see the snow coming down. She loved it when it snowed so much everything stopped. This was one of those days. And though she knew that he would fuck her silly today, at least she would not have to spend it on the road locked up in the trunk or worrying all day when he was going to pull down a dirt road and end her life. She would take a day of fucking over that any day, especially his fucking. She hated what he was doing to her, but not while he was doing it.

When the bacon was done, he flipped the pieces out onto a plate. He dipped three pieces of bread in the bowl, one at a time, letting them soak on each side. As each one was finished he tossed it into the greasy pan.

Within a few minutes, he produced three greasy pieces of brown and yellow French toast. Carly was surprised that he had gone to such lengths to feed her. And the cinnamon was a nice touch. But you might do the same for your dog or your cat if they had been particularly pleasing to you, sucked your cock and whatnot.

He cut up the French toast into bite sized pieces and broke up the slices of bacon, mixing them together in a bowl and tossing in a nice sized pat of butter. He surprised her again when he produced a small bottle of real maple syrup. He broke the cap and poured it liberally over the conglomeration. When he was done, he turned around and placed it on the floor.

Carly knew that she was expected to get down and eat it there, but she also knew that she should await the command. It came briefly thereafter when the man snapped his fingers and pointed to the meal. She leapt to obey and soon had her face in the bowl.

It tasted wonderful. It wasn't quite the way Mom used to make it, but it was close enough to be considered comfort food. She chewed each piece happily, taking her time to savor all the bad for you flavors. The man had sat back down in his chair and was smoking a cigarette, watching her. She knew that she was engaging in a performance for him, a kind of morality play. She cast him a dark look of resentment, but quickly let it slide. There was no sense in getting him riled up.

She took her time, savoring each piece. Her chin and mouth were getting sticky, but she didn't care. It tasted so good. She knew enough about nutrition to know that he was purposely starving her of proteins, the little bit of bacon he gave her aside. She knew that it would make her tired and somewhat lethargic. It was okay. She didn't have much to do anyway. And if it made her sleepy, that was good too. She welcomed being unconscious of her surroundings.

When she got down to the bottom of the bowl, she made sure she licked up every drop of maple syrup. It had been one of her favorite flavors as a kid. It made her think of her mom. She was probably going mad with worry. It was so sad that they hadn't talked in such a long time. She felt some tears coming on. She couldn't think that way. She had to put all that out of her mind. She could only think of this moment, this second, only about what was happening around her. She couldn't think about Randy, about freedom, about whether she would see another sunrise. She couldn't think about those things. She would go mad.

He saw that she was done with her food. She seemed to enjoy it. That was good. He didn't have anything against her getting some enjoyment from things. As long as they didn't endanger him or cause any problems. And as long as it didn't interfere with her principal purpose.

He rose from his chair, took a paper towel, wetted it and went over to the kneeling girl. He washed her face. Her look wasn't exactly thankful, but it was just a tad short of surly. She was pretty like that, all naked and angry. Some of the maple syrup had run down her chin onto her chest and he made sure that he wiped it clean. While he was there, he washed her breasts too, watching them appreciatively bounce and sway as he swept the wet paper towel over them.

They were too tempting to ignore. Putting the paper towel down on the floor, he knelt down on one knee in front of her. He took hold of her breasts, massaging and squeezing them. They were magnificent specimens. He leaned over and took one of her teats in his mouth, suckling on it, running his tongue over her areola. He wrapped his arm around her waist, holding her in place.

His other hand played with her other mound while he suckled on the first.

The girl didn't exactly struggle. She would know surely by now what would happen if she did, but her body seemed to squirm. He didn't mind. He switched breasts, switching hands in the process. He heard her release a whimper, like she was holding something back. He couldn't have that. He dropped his hand over her belly and seized her mons.

Her legs were already wide apart, a consequence of her training. He rubbed her clit lightly with his finger and then descended down the gap between her outer labia, and then up again several times. Her squirming became just a little more pronounced. He placed two fingers on her clit again and caressed it just a little more firmly, in a small circle. Her hips seemed to twitch. Her body seemed to draw in on itself as if she were resisting something. He delved his fingers down along the edges of her crevasse. She had moistened and he gathered up some of her secretion, spreading it over her love button. She whimpered again, breathed in deeply, and then moaned.

Having defeated her attempt at denying her body's wants, he removed his mouth from her breast. He looked into her face, only inches away from his own. She was looking at him with those marvelous eyes. There was an entrancing combination of arousal, resentment and fear on her face. Keeping his one hand buried in her purse, his other hand took hold of her hair behind her head. He brought his mouth to hers and merged their lips. For a brief second, her lips declined to open. He took hold of her clit with his fingers and pressed on it firmly, not harshly, but just enough to let the girl know what would happen of she rebelled. Her mouth opened immediately and he slipped his tongue in.

Her body seemed to melt as her tongue intermingled with his. His lusts were rising swiftly. For a moment he considered fucking her right there on the floor. His cock was pressing out from his boxers. Her pussy was wet, warm and welcoming. The aroma of her arousal rose from her loins adding to his excitement. She moaned again and her hips made a little circle in response to his ministrations "No," he thought. "Not here. On the bed, like I planned."

He had been thinking about how to fuck her all morning. He didn't want to spoil it by fucking her here. The other would be so much more enthralling for them both.

He broke their kiss and rose to his feet. The girl was out of breath. He pulled on her hair and made her rise and stand. She gave a little squeal and he slapped her for it. Not too hard, but enough to remind her to keep quiet. He took her over to the bed and made her get on it, kneeling and facing away from him.

After attaching her ankles together to ensure that she didn't try anything funny, he released her hands from behind her back. He had the small 6" chain that he had used on her last night and he used it to attach her wrists to the back of her neck, just like he did then. He piled up all the pillows against the headboard and indicated by a gesture that she should lie back against it. Taking a rope, he affixed the ring in the back of her collar to the headboard, locking her into position. She looked at him dolefully, wondering, no doubt, what he had planned for her. She was crying and he told her to stop it.

Stepping away from the bed for a moment, he retrieved two ropes from one of the bags he had brought in from the car and returned. He released her legs from each other and then tied one end of each rope to the rings in her ankle bracelets. He moved to the right side of the bed, holding the end of the rope that connected to her left ankle. He ran the rope through a hole in the headboard by the corner and then pulled on it until her ankle was in the air and pulled back and out, even with her hips. He tied the other one off the same way on the other side.

The girl's posture was that she was leaning back on the pillows, her wrists were confined near the back of her neck and her legs were pulled out and up, revealing both of her pleasure holes and making them vulnerable to his depredations. Because of where her hands were held, her breasts would also be readily available. Her fear of what was coming was clear in her frantic eyes. He smiled in appreciation.

In the bathroom, he cleaned off the gag, the vibrating egg and the thick black probe that had been used to expand her nether hole and then brought them back to the bed. The gag went in first, covering up her frown and her trembling lips. He greased the egg and then, after stroking her pussy back into wetness, slipped it in her crevasse. He inserted the probe in her rear after covering it with lubrication. She moaned and her eyes teared up as it re-expanded her hole. In his experience, it took at least a month of steady fucking to render the aperture permanently open for use. Otherwise, it usually retracted to its original size within hours. Still, with the probe in there doing its duty, it would be easier for him to penetrate her with his cock when the time came.

He turned on the vibrating egg on medium and then stepped over to the kitchen area to clean up from breakfast.

Carly wanted to scream. Her stomach was turning over at a hundred miles per hour. She was desperately holding back her tears in obedience to his command and she was trying to suppress any noise coming from between her lips fearful of earning more abuse.

He had slapped her hard across the face for whining when he lifted her up off the floor. He had pulled hard on her hair and it hurt even though she tried to cooperate. Her cheek still burned. It was just emblematic of his cruelty and strength. To him it must have seemed like a light tap, but his hand was so big and heavy, it rocked her teeth.

The egg was buzzing in her pussy. It was making it purr. She wanted desperately to stop it, but, of course, could not. The man was busy cleaning up the kitchen, totally oblivious to the torment he was causing her. She knew it was useless, but she tugged at her bound legs, trying desperately to close them, pulled at the binding to her wrists causing the chain to run taut but accomplishing nothing else. She bit down on the harsh intruder between her lips. The buzzing in her pussy was starting to drive her crazy. It felt like someone had put a live electrical wire inside her on low voltage. Everything down there was shaking. Her hands yearned to expel it, to stop it. If only she could just slow it down, that would at least be something. But it kept going on and on like a buzzer hardwired into her brain.

It was so unfair what he was doing to her, so unkind, so cruel. She realized that she was, to him, barely above the level of an animal, but didn't even animals have some rights? Didn't animals have the right at least not to be abused?

So maybe she was wrong. She wasn't just barely above the level of an animal. She was below it. More like a bug a little boy might torture. Or a character in a video game you could do anything you wanted to. And she knew what happened eventually to bugs little boys tortured. They stomped them out. And the characters in video games, well, when you were done with them, you turned them off. He was going to turn her off and he would have no more compunction about it when the time came than what he felt when he turned off the TV.

The moan escaped her lips before she even knew it. Her body turned cold with fear when she heard it. She looked at the man, ready to steel herself for punishment. He just looked at her and gave her a self satisfied smile. His plan for her, whatever that was, was working. And, apparently, moans and other expressions of pleasure, even if unwanted, were permitted, while protestations against abuse and expressions of pain or unhappiness, were not.

Her moan had the effect of a pressure valve, temporarily venting her buildup of lust. It didn't last long. About 20 seconds later, the effects of the agitation of her tender channel began to rise up again like yeast filled dough. She held her breath. She shook her head. She bit down on the gag. She couldn't stop it. "Mmmmmmmm-mmmmmmm!" she moaned, and knew she was defeated once again.

Jack was just finishing drying off the frying pan when he heard the second moan. He didn't turn around. He continued to finish cleaning up. When he was done, he lit up a smoke and came over to the bed. The girl's body was trembling and her eyes anxious as she tried to fight off another moan. She looked so pretty this way. Her pussy was glistening with arousal and the small circle of her rear entrance was pursed around the thick, black object that had been inserted there. Her upper chest had reddened as a result of her increasing lusts and her nipples were hard. Sweat had broken out across her chest and her breasts. They shimmered prettily. If it wasn't for the fact that later he would want to lie on the bed and watch TV, he might leave her tied up like this all day. Her lower holes were readily accessible and convenient for use.

He went back to the small table and crushed out his smoke. He drank the remains of his coffee. He came over to the bed, taking up a position right in front of her. Slipping his thumbs in the waistband of his boxers, he pulled them down his hips and off. His cock was erect. The girl looked at him with despair and moaned.

Kneeling on the bed, he positioned himself between her widespread knees. He ran his hands over her tender, pale white thighs. They were hot and trembled at his touch. He ran his hands over her belly and seized her breasts, pinching the nipples, squeezing the meaty parts, massaging and caressing them like little pet gerbils. He laughed at the thought of them squealing and squirming like two little furry animals.

It was true that they seemed to have a life of their own independent of the rest of the girl's body. They were so extraneous to any daily function and seemed to have been placed there by nature in their full shapes for the express purpose of sexual play. Most other female mammals had breasts that emerged only when they had offspring to feed. Women's breasts were available all the time. Their pleasant shapes and soft firmness made them alluring and exotic. It was no wonder women hid them away all the time. If not, it would be all men would be able to look at.

The girl's eyes closed and she gave out a deep sigh when he caressed her breasts. The vibrating egg had set her lusts afire and her skin all over her body was hypersensitive. He lowered his hands again to her belly, brought them across her thighs, moved back a bit on the bed and then lowered his head to her loins.

Carly stiffened and whined in protest as she saw him lower his head between her legs. She knew what he was going to do and knew that it would drive her into paroxysms of pleasure. His hands were planted on either side of her vibrating sex. She could feel his hot breath upon it. She closed her eyes and bit on her gag in frustration.

She found herself shivering in anticipation of the rush of pleasure the man's tongue was going to bring her, wanting desperately to immerse herself in the mind befogging bodily sensations it would bring. And yet, she cursed herself for her wantonness and wanted to push away the head that was hovering over her quim, to hold back the tongue that was going to caress her there, to close off her pulsing tunnel to its entrancing ministrations.

It was the point of his tongue that she felt first. It was faint, and at first she thought it was her imagination. But there it was, an undeniable presence just inside her blood engorged pussy lips. It moved slightly, tantalizingly. He began to flick it slowly as it gradually rose along her crevasse to the apex of her divide. When it began to tickle her stiffened nubbin, she moaned and twisted her hips. "Oh, god, I can't stand it!" she thought unhappily. "Please let it stop! Please!"

The aroma of the girl's arousal was dizzying to him. He had to resist the urge to plunge himself into it. Her cunt lips were spread wide, dilated, and the wrinkled interior was exposed. From her body's reaction, he could tell that the girl was highly aroused and that his attentions to her sweet fulcrum were going to drive her beyond endurance to a place she had never gone. "Good," he thought. That's what he wanted.

His tongue began to move more quickly, although its touch was gentle, just skimming the surfaces of her enflamed flesh. Carly groaned and twisted her hips again. "Ohhhhhhhhhhh!" she sighed. She had jettisoned any resistance to the acceleration of her lusts and wanted now, beyond all other things, for the man to let her come. She wanted him to devour her pussy, to go mad on it. His heavy hands framed her crevasse, drawing all of her consciousness to it. His thumbs and fingers worked the exterior flesh while his tongue glided over the interior. When his lips settled on her clit and he began a gentle suckle, her back arched and her legs pulled mightily at their confines. She moaned and sighed with delirious ecstasy.

The vibrations of the egg inside her continued, reverberating in her fevered canal and melding and merging with the ministrations of his lips and tongue. One of his hands slipped off of her mound and descended to her rear entrance. It took hold of the object that was implanted there and began to slide it back and forth, abrading the tender anal opening. The result was electrifying. Her need for release accelerated exponentially. "Mmmmmmmmmmm! Mmmmmmmmmmmmm!" she protested though her gag. And then, like someone had flicked a switch, it was upon her. Her pussy throbbed and convulsed. Her body cringed. Her thighs shook. "Ah! Ah! Ah! Ah!" she called out rapidly, timing her exclamations with the clenching of her sex. It became virtually agonizing as the tongue kept agitating her clit and the thick object continued to traverse her rear.

When her cunt's contractions began to ease, she took a deep breath through her nostrils, praying that the man would pause and give her some relief from the over-whelming sensations. But he did not. He began to lap his thick tongue along the hypersensitive interior lips of her pussy. The black probe continued to ride back and forth within her. The egg continued its fiendish vibrations. Her passions began to rise again. She shook her head and moaned in protest. "…eeeeeeeease!' she tried to beg. "…eeeeeeease!"

The man was relentless. He slid his abrasive tongue up and down her crevasse, plied it against her trilling clit, slipped it inside deep, to its full extension and slathered it over the sensitive roof of her chamber. His hand squeezed and fondled the outlying lips and then ran over her tender inner thighs, her belly, her breasts, igniting a hundred wildfires across her body. The other continued to plunge the thick, dark probe in her nether entrance making her whole body tremor.

When she came again, it was even stronger than the last. It was as if a thousand volt wire had been plunged into her hot tunnel. Her body jerked and contorted, her eyes rolled back, her bound hands clenched, her teeth clamped madly against the faux cock in her mouth. She moaned and groaned as the pleasure raced through her, her pussy delivering one heavy jolt after another.

This time, as her contractions wound down, the man took mercy upon her. He eased his attentions to her quim and slowed the pistoning of the thick object in her rear. His free hand caressed and squeezed her breasts gently, giving both of her teats a soft pinch. And then he stopped.

He looked at her. Her face was flushed, her hair was askew. Her body was covered with a sheen of sweat and she was breathing heavily, trying to recover from her ordeal. If he were a betting man, which he was not, he would bet that she had never experienced anything like that in her life. He slipped his fingers into her slit and removed the vibrating egg. She sighed gratefully. He eased the probe from her rear, putting it aside on a towel. Then he softly caressed her thighs, passing his hands over her vulva, cupping and then releasing it.

But he was not finished with her. He had played her like a virtuoso, but now it was his time. He slid his body up, leaned over her with one hand on the bed by her side, directed his rigid tool to her opening and slid himself in.

Carly groaned when she felt the cock find its home within her. She had known that he was not done, but had hoped she would get some respite. When he had risen on her body, towered over her, she had known what was coming. She wanted to oppose his entry, construct an impenetrable barrier to her womb. In her mind, she tried built a wall of concrete and steel, buttressed and reinforced, over her entry. She strained at her bonds, desperate to make it real. But her construct was shattered easily, pushed aside, negated, vanquished. She had no defense to his use of her. His member entered her as easily as a knife slicing through butter.

She knew what would happen when he began his movements. She closed her eyes and tried not to cry. When she felt him slowly slide his cock outwards until only its bulbous head was within her and then slowly descend once more, down to her inner depths, she released a forlorn sob.

He fucked her slowly and steadily, like he had all day to enjoy the moist heat of her crevasse. Long and slow, his strokes came. Carly's mind had stopped functioning. There was only the steady, thrilling abrasion of her inner tissues, the heat of the man's body between her thighs. She came twice, her body shuddering and shaking. The man took no notice of it, but kept on his course, focusing on his pleasure, his needs.

Jack felt like he could fuck her like this all day. Her pussy was hot from her fevered climaxes. He felt it when she came, her pussy clasping his cock, her body shuddering. After a while, he leaned back and bent his head, taking her nipples in his mouth, one after the other, suckling on them hungrily, pinching them with his teeth. The girl squirmed and moaned in response. Her pussy clenched again. Her hips shifted. He reached behind her head and removed her gag. Her lips were full and ripe. He pressed his own lips against them and began kissing her. Her tongue met his and they languidly intermeshed.

A swell of lust filled him. As if they had a mind of their own, his hips started to accelerate his thrusts. His iron like pole quickened its fevered journeys along the girl's welcoming tunnel. His heart began to thump in his chest. His breathing became deep. His balls were tight. His cock was sending him exquisite messages of pleasure. He felt his orgasm building. His hips moved faster and faster. His tongue's movements in her mouth became more frantic.

Carly was experiencing the propulsion of her lusts as well. The tongue in her mouth created a whole new dynamic to their fucking. Her hips began to meet his movements. Her thighs yearned to grasp him. Her hands yearned to cover his body with caresses. "Ohhhhhhhhhhhh!" she sighed. Her mind exploded with the joy of her body's enthrallment. "Oh, yeah!" she thought feverishly. "Do it! Do it! Fuck me! Fuck me! Give me your cum! Give it to me!"

Jack felt his cock's tell tale tingle and he knew it was coming. "Bring it! Bring it!" he yelled in his mind. And bring it he did. He groaned mightily as his orgasm exploded. His cock pulsed and jumped and throbbed, sending him stabs of magisterial pleasure. He was pumping wildly at her cunt, banging his hips against her inner thighs. She was coming too, he could feel it on his cock, and her body writhed and squirmed beneath him. She was moaning loudly into his mouth. He pushed his manhood deep inside her and held it there as the last two mighty throbs of his cock delivered exquisite ecstasy to him. He groaned, and then collapsed.

CHAPTER THREE

He lay atop her for a while. There was a comforting warmth running through his body. His cock felt like it had had a pleasing and beneficial workout, slightly tired, but anxious for more. When their mouths had separated during their mutual climaxes, his head had come to rest on her right shoulder, and her head on his. He could feel her still excited breath against his neck. His chest lay against hers and there was a slickness to it, their mutual perspiration mingling. The girl was still moaning slightly, as if she were leaking air somewhere. He rose and his cock slipped from her crevasse, leaving behind a trail of cum.

He rolled off the bed and returned to the kitchen. He lit up a smoke and took a deep toke off of it. That had gone even better than he had imagined it. She was such a passionate piece of ass, among the best he had ever had, and he had had quite a few. He went over to the refrigerator and opened it. There was half a quart of orange juice left and he opened the carton and took a long drink. It was cold and refreshing.

Back at the bed, he took in the picture of his captive. A small trail of fluid was leaking from her slit. She had recovered her breath and was staring back at him with a mixture of hate and awe. He had been right about taking her to a place she had never been. He could see that. She was, no doubt, trying to somehow harmonize her body's embracement of unbridled lust with the reality of being fucked against her will by a man of his coldness and callousness.

It made him laugh because there was no way to do it. It was one of those paradoxes of nature, a conundrum, an enigma. Our bodies are made of flesh and blood, and contain primordial needs, react to stimuli without conscious thought. Despite the thousands of generations that have passed since the dawn of human history, no system of thought, ethics, morality, philosophy or religion has been able to wholly suppress our animalistic natures. The spirit seeks self fulfillment, dignity, honor, integrity, and even pride, but clashes interminably with the part of use that wants to be rooting about in the mud, satisfying our baser, more fundamental needs, rutting like the animals that we are.

In fact, the compulsions of human sexuality far surpass in intensity that of most animals who rut only in season. Were it not for the gloss that culture and civilization put on us, we would be fucking each other all the time, every chance we got, mindlessly filling and stuffing every warm orifice and hole until we collapsed from exhaustion.

She was no different. When released from moral or ethical responsibility, made a forlorn prisoner who had no choice but to submit to sexual stimuli, her libido was liberated from the confines that culture had placed on it. Her body knew that instinctively. And so liberated, rejoiced.

He went back to the kitchen table and put out his smoke. He was about to start round two. Before he did that, there was something he needed to do. She had spoken and breeched one of his cardinal rules. That it was done in the heat of passion as a last, futile effort to retain the patina of self respect and morality that civilization had given her was of no moment. These little rebellions had to be stamped out mercilessly. And besides, it would make his cock hard again.

He retrieved the switch he had made the other day which was standing in the corner of the room leaning against the wall, and walked over to the bed. The girl's eyes spread wide when she saw it and then transited into a piteous expression. She moaned, "Mmmmmmm-mmmmm!" and her body shifted and strained at her bonds. She knew what was coming all right. And she probably knew that she deserved it. He would make sure.

He tapped the end of he switch on her exposed pudenda. She flinched and released a whimper. Tears were already flowing from her eyes. He decided that she didn't need a long exposition on her duty to obey and the reason for her upcoming torment. A few words would do. "This is for talking," he told her.

She whined in response and he could see that she was desperate to beg and plead for forbearance. Her body began to vibrate. She jammed her eyes shut, sending a cascade of tears down her cheeks and running over her lips. If he wanted to be fair about it, he would at least gag her so that she could give release to her moans and screams. But he wanted to see how disciplined she was, whether she was ready and strong enough to obey him in all things.

"I'm going to give you six strokes. If you scream or yell, I'll put in your gag and make it twenty. Do you understand?"

Her face contracted in misery, her lips trembled and her lips turned down into a piteous frown. She nodded her head dismally, knowing better than to give an oral response to his question. "See how smart she is?" he thought to himself. Contrary to popular belief, a good slave needs to be smart. It was the best defense mechanism she could have.

"Here it comes," he warned her.

He let it fly. It 'whizzed' in the air. It landed on the inside of her exposed, pale white thigh. It made a loud slapping noise. The girl's whole body made as if to rise off of the bed. Her lips were compressed firmly together and a loud hissing was emerging between them, followed by a series of forlorn whines. A long red mark had appeared on her skin. Unlike the ones he had given her the other day which were mostly faded by now, this was bright red and fresh. A body like hers should always have fresh wounds on it, he thought. They contrasted so nicely with her skin.

He let the second one fly. Its target was the opposite thigh, her left one. Her body cringed again, her legs flailed in their ropes. Her hands were tightened into little fists. The hissing was louder this time and the scream of pain that she suppressed was struggling to emerge. She closed her eyes and arched her back.

When her body came back to rest, he let her have the third blow, across the right thigh again. The first had been up by her knee. This one was about 4 inches down toward her crux. Her body leapt and writhed like the first one. She started to sob and her whines became louder. Without waiting for her to recover, he gave her the fourth, across the left, like its opposite, midway between her knee and cunt. She was blubbering now and her whines converted to loud groans, followed by peals of sobs.

The fifth struck her just south of the joinder between her thigh and her torso, only an inch or so from her pussy's lip. Her body shook and contorted. Her groan became louder still and was followed by a "p-p-p-p-p-p…," sound as if she was about to break out into a series of miserable pleas for mercy.

He gave her a few moments to recover. Her eyes opened and she looked at him, hatred pouring from them, unbridled hatred as fierce as fire. He grinned. She was a tiger all right. One in a million. Then he gave her number 6. He put a little extra in it. His aim was just a little off and he caught the edge of her left outer labia in the blow. It was as if she had become electrified. Her body stiffened and then she issued a long, loud wail. When she was able, she suppressed it, converting it into a mumbled cacophony.

It took her a while to recover. Her lips were clamped tightly together. She looked up at him hopefully. Was he a man of his word? Or was he a sadistic demon whose lust for causing pain had been ignited by her display of agony? That's what she was wondering, and hoping that it was the former. Well, he was a man of his word. And while he enjoyed the opportunity to occasionally inflict discipline on a defenseless beauty like her, he did not thrive on it like he had seen with some other guys. He liked it just enough to get his cock hard and needy like it was now. He tossed the whip aside.

She was looking up at him. She knew what was going to happen next. And she knew what was going to happen to her when he put his hands on her. Her lips were trembling and she grimaced unhappily when he got on the bed. She looked like she was trying to fight off her tears. He had told her no more crying and he meant it. He made an exception for when he whipped her. That would have been expecting too much entirely. But he didn't need to be greeted by waterworks every time he went to stick his cock in her. Besides, it was hypocritical by now. She knew that she loved it.

He knelt up in front of her and placed his hand on her mons. There was a little red spot on her right outer love lip where the edge of the whip had caught her. He leaned down and put his lips on it, kissing it. Then he knelt up and crawled close enough so that he could put his hands on her face. Using his right hand, he brushed away the small tear that had formed in the corner of her left eye. He then stroked her face, running his hand down the length of her cheek to her chin and back again several times, barely touching her.

Her lips were trembling and she was on the verge of hysterical breakdown. He could see that. That wouldn't do at all. He brought his face close to hers and brushed her lips with his. He then kissed her cheek lightly several times, moving from next to her chin up to near her nose. He repeated his kisses on the other side while stroking her hair. Then he brought his lips back to hers, brushing them lightly again, exhaling lightly so that she could inhale the heat of his breath.

He had had a dog once, a real junk yard mutt. It was already several years old when he got it. Someone had abused it terribly. Every time someone walked into the room, the dog would cower and go hide in a corner. Even him. But he worked hard on her. He petted her and talked to her, held her in his arms, fed her from his hand. He bathed her, brushed her, everything, all the while speaking to it kindly, murmuring sweet nothings. Eventually, he won it round. That dog would follow him anywhere and became fiercely protective. It was as close as he had ever come to being actually attached to another living being. The cops had shot it the day they raided the club and arrested the whole crew. It had gone after one of the cops and tore a big piece out of his leg. In prison, he often thought of it.

The point was that he knew how to give comfort to an animal when it needed it. It had nothing to do with real emotion. It could be strategic, as in the case of the dog. The point of all his actions had been to make it a faithful companion. Or it could be tactical, like now, where all he wanted was to have the girl calm down and not go off her rocker.

Carly sighed deeply. She hated the man for what he was doing. But she wanted some compassion, some tenderness, some humanity so badly that she was willing to accept it. She had been about to go over the edge. She had felt it. The beating he had given her for merely begging not to be abused had been just about the last straw. She had been struggling hard to keep things together. The constant bindings, the rudeness in the way he addressed her, the meals on the floor, the way he led her about by the hair, all of these things she had withstood. But the beating had been too much.

She knew why he didn't want her to speak. The less she spoke, the less like a person she seemed. She had read once somewhere that if you were ever taken hostage, you should do everything you could to show your humanity to your captors. Talk to them, tell them about yourself, your family, your parents, and, if you had them, your children. Hopefully one of them would see you as a human being and hold back from harming you, even protect you from the others. It seemed like the man had read that too and was doing everything to frustrate it happening.

And now he was kissing her. His tenderness seemed so real. He was really good. A manipulator. It seemed like he really meant it. He had kissed her pussy where he had hurt her. He was stroking her face gently. His lips brushed against hers. She could taste his breath. It was just what she wanted, just what she needed. She wanted it to be true, needed it to be true so much that she just threw away all of her reservations.

She knew that his rule was no crying, but just the thought of a tender moment was so comforting that she just broke down. She started to sob. She feared for a moment that he would strike her, but instead he just kept stroking her, shushing her quietly. He took hold of her head with both of his hands and made her look him in the eyes. He stroked away her tears with his thumbs. He kissed her lips tenderly, once, twice, three times. And then he withdrew. He spoke to her softly. "No talking. Understand?"

Tearfully, Carly nodded her head. He brought his lips back down to hers and they met. He pressed them against her. She felt his tongue and she opened her lips to receive it. It entered her mouth and she was lost.

He kissed her strong and hard for a long time. She kissed him back just as hard. It was a moment of absolute passion. She could almost believe that he meant it, that they were indeed lovers engaged in playing some kind of game, that he had compassion and love for her. She could almost believe it. His hand took hold of her breast and gave it a gentle squeeze. She sighed. It went lower, over her hip, then up her thigh, caressing her wounds. Then, sliding down her thigh, it crossed over again to her torso, came down her belly and fixed itself on her sex. It stroked it softly, gently. She felt her blood rising. She felt him stroking her clit, teasing it, running over it, tugging at it. She groaned. "Ohhhhhhhhhhhhh! Ohhhhhhhhhhhhhhhh!" And then she knew that she didn't need to believe it any more. Her lusts had taken over.

He kept stroking her quim until her moans started coming long and steady. Then he slipped off of her for a moment. The vibrating egg was still lying on the bed. He picked it up and, using the remote, turned it on. But this time, instead of inserting it into her pussy, he slipped it up to her rear entrance, held it there until the buzzing forced her to release a long, needy sigh, and then he slipped it in.

Raising himself, he addressed his cock to her pussy, rubbed the head up and down her slippery slice three or four times, and then, finding her hole, thrust himself inside of her.

She groaned deeply. He came forward and recaptured her lips. He sawed back and forth, driving her lusts. She kissed him back wildly. When he felt her body readying itself for an explosion of lust, he slowed his thrusts, cooling her excitement, making her wait. He did it three times in all. Each time, in a geometric progression, her sighs and moans of disappointment grew louder.

"Oh my god! Oh my god!" Carly thought. The vibration in her bowel was making her wild with passion. And his cock! His cock! It was going to drive her mad if he didn't let her come. "Oh, please! Please! Please! Please!" she thought desperately. "Pleeeeeeease!"

And then, she felt him drawing himself out. She gasped as his meat left her. She sighed with disappointment. Then he knelt back and, holding the towel he had used to place her anal probe on, he placed it under her rear entrance. "Give it to me," he said coldly.

"Give it to him?" she thought. "Give him what?" And then she realized. He wanted her to excrete the egg, the vibrating egg. He was going to fuck her there and he wanted the egg out. She could hardly think of a more humiliating task than to practically shit the egg into his hand. But if she didn't, she knew she would suffer. She looked at him dolefully. "Now," he said, his voice deeper and more harsh.

She grimaced, closed her eyes and squeezed her muscles. At first, it seemed too big. She would never get it to move never mind get it out. She tried harder and harder, straining mightily. And then it moved. She could feel it slipping along her bowel, still vibrating madly. She could feel it breeching her entrance. The idea of what he was making her do filled her with shame. She grimaced and concentrated on her muscles with all her might. She could feel her face filling up with blood from the strain. It seemed to be stuck on her anal ring and not wanting to leave. She knew that failure here was not an option. He would beat her brutally and then make her try and try until she got it out. She relaxed her muscles, took a deep breath and pushed as hard as she could. "Uuuuuuuuuuuuuuugh!" she groaned. "Uuuuuuuuuuuu-uuuugh!"

And then it popped free. He caught it in the towel. She gave a deep sigh of relief. She had never conceived that she would have to do something like that for anyone in her life. It was shameful, dirty, gross, perverse, and somehow wildly exciting. When he had put the towel aside, the man quickly took up position, probed at her loosened hole with the tip of his prick and sunk himself right in.

It was the reverse of the procedure she had just experienced. She had been filled, emptied and filled once again. She didn't know whether to laugh or cry. He began his movements, leaned forward, seized her lips with his and entered her mouth. She moaned with lust and kissed him back.

The abrasion of his cock along her anal ring was sending flashes of energy to her abandoned quim. He was giving her short, emphatic thrusts. His cock seemed to be filling her whole insides. She wanted to put her arms around him, to hold him, to force his body against hers, but was frustrated by her wrists' imprisonment. "Oh, yes. Yes! Yes! Yes! Yes!" she called out to herself. And then he moved away from her again, his thick cock still impaling her. Her slipped his knees up under her thighs and began a series of long, slow strokes. At the same time, his hand found her pussy, and after stroking it several times, settled on her stiffened, needy button and began to stroke it softly but urgently.

Her lust went off the scale. "Ohhhhhhhhh! Ohhhhhhhhhhhhhh! Ohhhhhhhhhhhhh!" she cried out into the small room. Her eyes rolled back. It felt like electricity was flowing through all her veins, overwhelming her body with sensuous, exciting sensations. She felt her climax coming. This time he let her go. "Oh! Oh! Oh! Oh! Oh!" she exclaimed as her pussy sent her wave after wave of thrilling, body wrenching pulses. Her clitoris was vibrating with pleasure. It was like he was generating some form of diabolic spell as he rubbed it, remitting to her through his fingers a torrent of passion.

His thick cock began to increase the tempo of its strokes. She could hear him straining, wanting, needing completion. Her orgasm had hardly slowed when it began again. The room seemed to be pulsing with the energy her pussy was emitting. Her body seemed to expand to infinity, filling the room, pushing out all the windows and doors. It subsumed everything else.

He came with a mighty groan. He pumped hard and fast at her rear passage. He left off the stroking of her pussy, leaned forward and took her mouth again, bruising her lips with his, scouring the inside with his hot, frenetic tongue. For Carly, it was a moment of pure joy.

She didn't realize when they stopped kissing or when his thrusts came to a halt. Her mind had ceased to record earthly events. When she came back to reality, he was breathing heavily atop her. His softening cock was still implanted in her rear. Her conscious mind began to return. She realized that she had just fucked royally the man who had just beaten her. "Oh, what does it matter," she thought lazily. He had taken her to places she had never gone and probably never would have had he not seized her. It didn't make up for it, certainly not. But it did add a certain piquancy, a certain strangeness to the whole thing.

She knew she could never fuck Randy again. Not because she felt unclean or ruined or anything like that. That, she thought, she could get over. But this? She would have to somehow forget it, like it was an impossible dream. There was no way on God's green earth that good old Randy could do for her what this man had done. Probably nobody could. If she lived, she would spend the rest of her life trying to recreate it.

The man slowly eased himself off of her. He got up from the bed and went into the bathroom. She could hear the sound of him washing himself. She looked over at the clock above the small sink. It was 11:30. There was still about 6 hours of sunlight left. She knew that this recent episode was merely a prelude to the rest of the day. Somehow, she would get through it.

Jack came out of the bathroom with a clean prick. He had also cleaned off the black prong, the vibrating egg and the penis gag he had been using on her. He put the prong and the egg on the table. He wouldn't use them for now. But he took the gag over to the girl and proffered it to her mouth. She sadly accepted it and he buckled it behind her head.

Although he was certain he would be back at the well later, his ability to rise to the occasion was temporarily at nil. For now, he just wanted to relax and maybe watch some TV. And he didn't want to have to deal with her for the time being or have her goo goo eyes staring at him.

He released her legs, letting them plop on the bed. He then released her collar from the headboard and, taking hold of her hair, brought her to her feet. He brought her near to the kitchen area and turned a chair so that it was facing the bed, about 6 or so feet away. He sat her down on it. She immediately placed her legs on the outside of the seat, spreading them so that her pussy was easily visible. Smiling at her compliance, he left her there for a moment and then returned with the ropes he had used on her on the bed. He tied off her ankles to the bottom of the chair so that she couldn't bring them together. Then, releasing her wrists from the chain that confined them at her neck, he brought her hands behind the chair and tied them off too.

She looked up at him dolefully. He smiled at her, caressing one of her breasts. Then he went and retrieved his little surprise. He had gotten it in the pharmacy section of the huge supermarket he had gone to. It was a padded blindfold, the kind you use when you're trying to get to sleep and every little bit of light bothers you. It was black with an elastic backer. When the girl saw it she frowned with dismay. She looked up at him as if to beg him not to seal her into darkness. He ignored her non-verbal entreaty, pulled the elastic around the back of her head and settled the blindfold over her eyes. It was soft and concave on the side that met her eyes and he pressed it down to make sure that no little spark of light could get through.

She waved her head about slightly and issued a small whine of unhappiness. He took her nipples in his fingers and gave them a little pinch. "Shhhhhhhhhhh," he hissed. She got the message and, after releasing a single sob, quieted down. Then he produced the *pieces de la resistance.* These were also from the pharmacy section. They were two little blobs of soft, sticky wax meant to protect your ears from getting water inside when you swam or showered. He rolled one into a ball and placed it in the girl's left ear. He packed it in good so that it covered the entire hole. Then he went around and did the other one. She whimpered and whined for real this time. That wouldn't due. It defeated the whole purpose.

Taking one of her breasts in his hand, cupping it from underneath, he brought his other, open hand down fiercely on the top part. It made a loud slapping sound. Her body cringed and she issued a plaintive wail. He did the other one too. She pulled and tugged at her bindings as she cried and sobbed. Then he pulled the wax from one of her ears and whispered into it harshly, "Shut the fuck up!"

He returned the wax to its former position. The girl's wails quickly wound down. She sniffled a few times and then became silent. Her body was shaking.

He looked at her for a few seconds. Despite his efforts, she was still exhibiting annoying signs of personality. It was maybe the shape of the head and her distinctly feminine hair. He knew what to do.

From the bed, he retrieved a pillowcase. He draped it over her head and pulled it down behind her so that her head was in a corner. The rest of the soft, white cotton fabric was bunched around her neck and then draped down her back, leaving her wondrous breasts in full view. He tied a rope around her neck, sealing it off.

Now that was perfect. Her whole personality had been erased. She was now just a set of tits and a pussy. Her face, or at least the prominence of her nose and her chin, were still discernable due to the tightly pulled pillowcase, but she looked more like one of those modern looking manikins they had nowadays than a real person.

He had seen pictures of them in magazines. It was a fabric covered face and could belong to a million other broads. "That's the way it should be all the time," he thought. He took hold of her nipples, gave them a little tweak and then went into the kitchen to make some more coffee.

Carly felt him move behind her. Since she could not hear or see him, she had to rely on the vibrations on the floor coming up through her bare feet when he walked. He had surprised her. Not the being tied to the chair part. That made sense. No, it was everything else, sealing her into darkness and silence. It was another horrible twist on her captivity.

In a way, it was like being buried in that hole she had been in the day before. She was alone in the midst of a vast universe. It was a universe way out of her reach. She was separated from it by a remorseless, intractable wall of darkness. It frightened her to be so isolated and removed from human interaction. She wanted to scream out her terror. It was like death. She was not alive in any real sense but for the fact that he heart was still beating, her brain was still functioning and air was still entering and exiting her lungs in regular intervals. But she no longer could affect any events in the real world. She was merely a floating, detached consciousness. She was in limbo, the space between heaven and hell, neither paradise nor perdition.

But, it wasn't really true that she was condemned to silence. The wax trapped the sounds of her body in her ears. The rush of her blood was like the rumbling of a volcano, deep below the surface. It was a noise that blotted out all external sound. And she could hear herself breathe, a strange, amplified rush of sound as if done through a microphone. If she swallowed, she could hear that too. And if she made a little noise, a whine or a hum, or anything, she could hear that as loud as if she had shouted it into her own ears. All of these sounds, silent or barely audible under normal circumstances now became her whole world, a perverse orchestra celebrating her powerlessness, her abjectivity, her dismal, low, vulnerable status as the dark man's slave.

Every fiber in her body wanted to rebel against her treatment, to scream, to pull and yank at her confinements, to roar with anger and hatred for what he was doing to her. She feared the man so desperately though that she cringed at the very thought of action. It had hurt horribly when he had slapped her breasts. The feeling of futility that arose from her powerlessness created a vibrating sensation of sickness that coursed through her. She imagined how she now appeared to her captor, a naked torso topped by an ill defined, silent, anonymous head. No part of her horrid inner turmoil would show through. She was like one of those ancient statutes recovered on some archeological dig, her arms and legs truncated, the head lost to antiquity, just a pale white trunk, cold and still, to suggest the human likeness that once existed.

But not entirely cold and still. Her breasts and belly and her fulcrum below them were still alive and warm. If she shifted her shoulders, her breasts shimmered. She could move her thighs and knees slightly. She could sway her head back and forth. And if the man placed his hands on her body, it would react as before. Her pussy would warm at his touch. She would sigh and moan as he suckled her breasts. She would cry and sob as he twisted her defenseless nipples as he had done so many times to punish her if she made so much as a little whine of unhappiness or protest.

She couldn't help it when the moan of unhappiness escaped. She immediately realized her error and truncated it. A fierce slap on the side of her head was the corrective he administered, one that made her brain shake. She didn't realize that he had been standing so close to her. It wasn't a punishment as much as it was a warning. Her body soured from her feeling of helplessness. She bit down on her gag harshly. "I have to be strong!" she told herself. "I have to endure! I have to be silent!" Whatever he did to her would only be temporary. Her current torment would pass. All of them would eventually pass. Until the last one, which would end her garish nightmare forever and grant her peace.

Jack watched the coffee pot perk a bit. He walked over to the TV and, using the zapper, turned it on. He flipped the channels until he saw a movie that looked good and then tossed the zapper on the bed. His boxer shorts were on the floor near the bed and he retrieved them and put them on. He turned and looked at the girl. She looked pretty like that, helpless and exposed. He knew that he shouldn't treat her so mean. She had been really cooperative and all. He just couldn't help it.

Her softness and weakness were just things that demanded cruelty. And he needed to make sure that he kept her as a mere object in his mind. It would be a lot easier this way when the time came. But as much as he objectified her, reducing her to her essential sexual elements, he still desired her more than any bitch that he could remember. Of course they were all years ago and this one was very much in the present. Nonetheless he sensed an attraction to her stronger than any attraction he had ever felt.

He had resolved to look in her wallet again to get her name straight, Carol or Christine or something, but he had changed his mind. It didn't matter what her name was. Fuckdoll would suit as well as any. Or Cunt. Or Bitch or Whore. Anything that would keep these feelings he was having from getting the better of him. He was going to Mexico. He was going to live wild and free once again. No cunt was going to ruin that for him by making him all soppy when he had to get rid of her.

But she was so delicious looking. He came up in front of her quietly and softly so she wouldn't notice. Her breasts were trembling as if a volcano of emotion was brewing inside her. Her vulnerability was so compelling that he had to reach out and take hold of them. Her body stiffened when his hands touched her. Her breasts were cool and soft and firm. He pulled gently at her nipples, tugging them out, making her breasts expand from her chest. She couldn't suppress a whine of unhappiness, but he let it go. He released her breasts and ran his hands down over her belly and across her widened thighs. She moved them, as if trying to move them from his grasp in protest. Her head bobbed and she leaned her torso forward, straining at her bonds. He gave both of her thighs three harsh slaps on the outsides, causing the girl to moan and sob in pain.

That was enough of that, he thought. The girl needed to be tied down more thoroughly. He got two more pieces of rope. He came back to the chair and first untied her ankles from the bottom of the chair's feet. He lifted them back, one by one, so that they were up off the floor and tied them off. Then he tied her knees firmly to the legs of the chair. She was now forced to sit on it like she was sitting on a racing saddle, like a jockey, but one without stirrups.

He took more rope, he was glad that he got the big roll, and tied one end to the back of the chair. He slipped the end over her shoulder and between her breasts, then around her back and up between her breasts again and over her other shoulder. He tied it off tightly. Her torso was now tied firmly against the back of the chair. Finally, he tied one end of a length of rope around the portion of the pillowcase that descended behind her head. He pulled it down, making the girl's head pull back, and tied it off to a rung just below the seat.

She could still move her head slightly from side to side, but not up and down. If she had been able to see, her eyes would have been pointed at the ceiling. He went around the front of her. Her posture made her breasts jut out appealingly. He took hold of her nipples and twisted them until she squealed and moaned. Then he released them, patted them gently, knelt down and suckled at them both while rubbing her thighs and then stood up. The coffee was ready.

He poured himself a cup, lit a smoke and went over to the bed. He plumped up the pillows and sat down.

The movie was an old John Wayne western, one of Jack's favorites. He was in the cavalry and about to retire but there was one last job to do, stop the Indians from going on the warpath. Jack watched it until the end. John Wayne was riding off into the sunset when they called him back to be Chief of Scouts. Everyone was happy.

During the movie, Jack kept looking over at the girl. Her nipples and areolas were staring back at him accusingly, like two little hostile eyes. He got up a couple of times, once to piss and once to get some snacks. He gave her breasts little tweaks each time he passed. The next movie wasn't so interesting so he started to flip channels again. He came across a news channel, CNN, and he decided to watch it for a while. There were a couple of stories about politics and a train wreck in Washington State. There was a big story about the storm that he was sitting in the middle of. It would not stop snowing until sometime in the night.

And then they switched to a 'major crime story'. A reporter was standing outside of a burning house, maybe 200' away from it.

"Thank you, Karl," the reporter said.

> "I'm standing outside the alleged headquarters of the Wausau, Wisconsin, Rogue's Motorcycle Gang. Authorities here have tracked the fugitive and

convicted murderer Blackjack Jackson to it along with his hostage, 22 year old Carly Walker. As it has been reported to us, a tense confrontation began when State Police officers attempted to serve a search warrant on the headquarters. The Rogue's gang has been cited by many as being involved in alleged drug activities, traffic in prostitutes and stolen goods, extortion and murder.

"When the officers went to serve the subpoena, shots rang out. We understand that two officers were shot, one fatally. A massive firefight ensued lasting over an hour. Three more officers suffered gunshot wounds and we have no reports on their status at this time. Police are unsure how many Rogues members were inside the headquarters. The house caught fire when the police shot tear gas into the building. So far, none of the Rogues have come out.

"Firefighters were called to the scene but have taken no efforts to extinguish the blaze due to the risk of gunfire from inside the building. It is feared that all persons inside the building may have perished in the flames including the fugitive Blackjack Jackson and his hostage. Authorities say they won't know for sure until the flames die down and fire inspectors can get into the wreckage. That is unlikely to happen until tomorrow morning at the earliest. Back to you, Karl."

"Yeah, that was her name, Carly," Jack thought. That was his first reaction. Then he felt a surge of pride for the way the boys in Wausau went down literally in flames. "That's what we should have done," he thought. It would have been better than serving 12 years as a slave. Well, he wouldn't go back this time.

Then he realized the significance of the news report. They thought that he was still back in Wisconsin! They thought that he had just perished in the conflagration of the Rogues' headquarters! This was terrific news! Apparently they had fallen for his ruse about traveling north hook, line and sinker. Some idiot had probably said that he saw him and the girl and the cops had concluded that he had gone to the clubhouse. Whoever thought that was an idiot though. Why would he go back to the most obvious place of all?

He knew that not everybody would be fooled. The FBI was a lot smarter than that. They would probably still be on his trail. And the minute they found out that he had killed that store clerk or found the girl's car in the parking lot in Kansas City, the idiots in Wisconsin and on the news would realize their mistake. Until then, though, the news stories would concentrate on him having been turned into a crispy critter back home. Joe Citizen wouldn't have his eyes peeled for him.

He got up from the bed. His blood was up. He went to the picture window and lifted the blinds so that he could look out. It was still snowing heavily. The car had almost completely disappeared. He couldn't see any of the nearby cabins. "Fuck!" he yelled out loud. If it weren't for this fucking storm he would be almost all the way to New

Mexico by now. And if he hadn't gone back for the girl yesterday, he could have beat the storm over the mountains and gotten away. He could've been in Mexico maybe tomorrow or the next day. "Shit!" he yelled. He was missing a golden opportunity.

He turned to the girl. "It's my fault for wanting this cunt so bad," he thought madly. She needed to suffer. He would make her suffer.

The switch he had used on her before was lying on the floor next to the bed. He picked it up. He approached the girl. She was totally oblivious, breathing in and out as best she could, silent as the night which enveloped her. Some spell she had put on him had made him foolish. He was thinking with his cock not his brain. All he had to do once he had gotten the new car at the airport yesterday was to keep going. He had wasted at least two hours going back for her and digging her out. And he had been greedy too. He didn't need half the stuff he had bought. Instead of fucking around in a supermarket, he should have been making a beeline for Mexico.

Rage overwhelmed him. He struck out at the most obvious target. The thin switch cut through the air making a whirring sound, a sound that his victim could not hear.

There was no warning. Once second Carly was trying to puzzle out what the man was doing standing around her and the next a fierce fire erupted across her breasts. Her body stiffened and she howled into her gag. "Oh my god! Oh my god!" she called out in her mind. Another blow fell, just as harsh. She hadn't been ready for this one either. The pain shot through her. She sobbed and cried out and tried to twist and turn her confined body, but to no avail. Again and again the pain came. She knew that it was the switch he was using. But why? Why? What had she done? Before this, he had punished her mostly when she had done something wrong. What had she done? What?

These frantic thoughts went on in her mind on a level beneath the part that was absorbing the excruciating pain from the blows and desperately trying to think of a way to avoid them. A line of fire crossed her belly. And then another. And another. Then he was back to her breasts again, making her scream the loudest.

There was a pause. A long pause. Had he stopped? Was it over? The pain still reverberated through her and she could not stop crying. Her mind exploded as the harshest blow yet struck her breasts. She screamed until she ran out of breath and then screamed again.

Then they stopped. Or at least seemed to stop. Thirty seconds went by. Forty, a whole minute. Then, sensing that it was indeed over she let her body relax and collapsed into a torrent of tears and forlorn sobs.

The last one had been the hardest. He had been saving it up. Her breasts and belly were covered with angry red stripes. He could hear her still howling. His heart was pumping a mile a minute and his breath was coming heavy. He realized that he had lost control of himself. He didn't like that. He needed to be in control if he was going to get away. He tried to understand why he had gotten so angry.

Tossing the switch aside, he went to the bags with all their stuff in it and drew out the bottle of Jim Beam. It was still more than ¾ full. He unscrewed the top and took a deep swig. It burned as it went down and felt good as it seemed to spread warmth all over his body. He took another swig. He was starting to calm.

The alcohol was soothing him. He was grateful for it, but wary. He hated guys who tossed back liquor like it was mother's milk and lost control over themselves. It made them think they were big guys, invincible. He had seen too many of them make foolish mistakes and either die in terrible accidents on their bikes or get into stupid fights over nothing and end up getting a knife in their belly. He knew he had to be careful. He didn't want to become one of those. But the sour mash sure tasted good and it felt good to have it rushing through his body.

He sat back down on the bed, bringing the bottle with him. The girl was still moaning and crying. He would let her go on for a while and then he would tell her to stop it. She was entitled to a little crying. He had really done a job on her. Offhandedly, he hoped he hadn't done anything to scar her. Then he realized how foolish that thought was. It didn't matter how much he scarred her. She was as good as dead even now. She had no future in which whether her tits were scarred or not would matter.

It occurred to him, as he thought of that, where the origins of his rage against her had come from. It was the terrible tension between wanting the girl and knowing that he couldn't have her. There was no scenario in which he could keep her with him. And as much as he had abused her, he wanted her so badly that he wanted to kill the world. But he couldn't kill the world, so there were only two people he could harm and he wasn't about to harm himself. That left her. And she had caught it all.

It was ironic that she had to suffer because he had grown to care for her. No, maybe not care for her. That was too strong a word. He admired her spunk. He treasured her beauty. He was enthralled with her passion. The smell of her, the warmth of her body, they way she looked at him cockeyed kind of, her head slanted to one side, her mouth awry. Her pussy was a soft, hot morass that was comforting when he was in the mood for comfort and impassioning when his lusts were on the burn.

He took another swig of Jim Beam. He lit a smoke. The TV was still on. He had blotted it out and hadn't realized it. CNN was doing a story about some business scandal. He flicked the TV off. He didn't need it. Leaning back against the soft pillows, he blew a cloud of smoke towards the ceiling above him. Mexico. Two, three days at most. He would get there. It was too bad the girl had to go.

CHAPTER FOUR

Yeah, it was too bad she had to go. He shouldn't make her suffer too much before then, he thought idly. She hadn't done anything wrong. She was just who she was. He wouldn't treat a dog this way. That didn't mean that he didn't have to be strict with her. Like now, all tied up and silenced and cut off from all sounds. It was good she see that all that she experienced from here on out came from him. Without him, she was just a mass of flesh floating in the silent darkness. He could turn the world off and on for her. It would keep her obedient and besides, like he had said to himself earlier in the day, he didn't want her spending the day making goo goo eyes at him.

He put out the smoke when it got down to the filter. The booze was making him a little woozy. He had been thinking about Mexico and how great it was going to be there. But he had to get there first. And somehow he was going to have to make contact with the guys in New Mexico. The FBI was probably watching them like hawks. He couldn't just ride up to their clubhouse. Then he remembered the cell phone he had bought. There was that number he could call, the one that the Feds almost certainly knew nothing about. He would have to call it.

Before he knew it, he was waking up. He had drifted off to sleep. Looking at the clock, he saw that it had been for almost an hour. He hadn't meant to sleep, but it had felt good.

He got up from the bed and rummaged through the bags by the kitchen table. The girl was moaning softly.

He looked at her. He didn't want to slap her after what he had put her through. He felt a little guilty. Instead, he tapped her on the forehead three times hard with his finger. The moaning stopped immediately.

He brought the phone over to the bed and lay back up against the pillows. The directions on the phone's package were hard to read. The type was really small. In prison he had noticed that his eyesight had started to go. He had been getting old. He brought the package over to the table lamp by the bed and turned it on. He was just able to make out the type. Following the directions, he activated it. A few moments after that, he dialed the number he knew by heart from so long ago. He hoped it was still working. It rang once, twice, three times and then someone picked up.

"2799," was the answer. It was the last four digits of the number.

"Rankin," Jack said quietly.

"Not available," was the answer.

"When?" Jack asked.

"Who's calling?"

"The man on the TV."

There was a pause. Then, "One hour."

Jack hung up.

He had an hour to kill. He had been thinking about releasing the girl from her bondage and fucking her, but he didn't want her listening in to the call. He didn't even want her to know he had a phone. So she would have to wait another hour or so. "In the meantime," he thought, "maybe there's something I can do to make up for the whipping I gave her."

After imbibing another swig of sour mash, Jack got up out of the bed. He approached the girl. She must have sensed him near her because her body seemed to cringe and she took a deep breath. He couldn't tell her that he wasn't going to harm her, because she couldn't hear. So, without ado, he went to work.

He took a position between her outstretched knees and crouched down. He ran his hands over her bound thighs, appreciating their warmth and softness. Then they flowed up over her red striped belly to her poor breasts, crisscrossed with the evidence of her lashing. Her body flinched when he took possession of them. He kept his touch gentle. He massaged them slowly, caressing them, lifting them from her chest, holding them in his hands like little creatures. He leaned over and kissed them softly, first the nipples, and then all around, first one and then the other. He brought his hands down to her belly and thighs again, rubbing them firmly, stroking the soft, pale, interior flesh. Her brought his hands up to her crux, slipped a finger between her outer lips, tickled gently at the nubbin at the top, and then started the process once again.

The second time he passed over her breasts, his mouth lingered on them. He suckled her teats while his hands ran up and down her thighs. He pulled at them softly, then hard, then softly again. He tickled them with his tongue and then took them between his teeth and bit at them softly, just enough so that the sensation of pain would rise up over the sensation of pleasure for an instant and then slide back down.

It was then that Carly moaned. She hadn't exactly been fighting it off. She had been grateful when his hands had finally convinced her that they did not intend to bring her pain. It was glorious, in a way, to have contact with a human being again. She had no idea how long she had been confined this way. Her neck was aching from being bent over backwards and her back hurt. She was thirsty and tired too. A few times, she had nodded off, but the rush of sound in her ears always brought her back to consciousness. She had tried not to think about what was happening to her. She thought about her mom, Randy, her job. She recalled high school and the friends she had known there. She thought of her apartment and her cat.

But her mind always returned to where she was and what the man was doing to her. It made her body sour with unhappiness. She imagined him eating, watching TV, his eyes occasionally floating over to her displayed form and smiling, that insidious, fear inducing smile that he had, knowing full well the agonies he had condemned her to.

There was a long time in which there had been no movement around the cabin. That had been the worst. It was like being abandoned in outer space and someone had turned all the lights out. She wanted desperately to scream and beg to be freed from the virtual torture chamber he had concocted for her, but she was terrified that he would whip her again, so dreadfully terrified that it made her heart pound when she thought of it, when the need to release a blood curdling cry of despair became almost overwhelming.

In a way, it reminded her of childhood. There were occasions when time seemed to stand still. Her parents had not believed in spanking. She had been punished by time outs. They would make her sit in a corner facing the wall, sitting in one of her little chairs and wait and wait and wait. If she made any little noise, they added time to her punishment. It had seemed like it never would end, that the rest of her life would be spent in that little chair doing nothing, seeing nothing, saying nothing. She would end up crying desperately for a parole from her sentence. Her parents were relentless though. They never shaved off even a minute.

That was what it seemed like now. She had to serve a sentence. And like then, there was no clock to watch, no way to measure how many agonizingly long minutes had gone by, how many more there were to come. It was a torment of a particularly cruel nature. She wasn't a woman. She was just another object in the room. The chairs didn't get up and demand attention. The stove and the small fridge remained mute and still. The table didn't move even one iota. She had more in common with them than she did with the man, who was free to walk around, entertain himself, watch TV, snack, smoke one of his fucking cigarettes, drink whisky. She was a mere utensil which took on significance only when in use.

Her time was mixed between sorrow and rage. Futility and fury. Harrowing unhappiness and hatred. But also fear. A rabid, soul stealing, mind numbing fear. Somewhere out there he was lurking. He was mulling over how next to make her life hellish. The next blow could come without warning at any time. And if she screamed and yelled and raged and bellowed out her agony, as every ounce of her psyche felt compelled to do, if only to preserve her sanity, she knew that as sure as God made little green apples she would suffer a torrent of pain and abuse far beyond her ability to receive it.

She did muster the courage once to make little whining sounds so that maybe he would hear them and come over and tell her to shut up. Not tell, of course. She couldn't hear a thing. But to indicate it in some way like abusing her breasts or knocking her about the head. She had become so desperate for human interaction that a blow from him was better than nothing. Her noise produced no reaction and she began to cry again. Her whole body went cold and she started to shiver. It took a long, long time to calm herself down.

The saving grace was that she knew sooner or later he would release her and that he would fuck her again. She had actually been looking forward to it both as a termination of her rigid, merciless confinement, and as recompense for the unwarranted beating he had given her and the torturous position in which he had left her.

And so she moaned. Moans of pleasure were permitted. She remembered that. She reveled in the strong hands that were caressing her. The mouth on her teats felt so good, pleasure washing through her as he suckled them. Then his hand dropped down her belly to her sex. A finger slipped inside the moistening gash and began to delicately rub the roof inside, the spot that brought her so much pleasure. She groaned.

Any sound she made reverberated in her ears like a radio with the volume set too high. Her breathing became heavy, adding to the sound of the rush of her blood. She didn't mind the sounds, though. It was so wonderful not to be alone anymore and to have the hot hands caressing her. His soft touches were just the thing that she needed to assuage her suffering. The finger began to tickle her clit and she breathed in deeply through her nose when it began to rub it in earnest.

It took a moment or two for her to realize it. The mouth had left her breasts and the other hand had departed as well. The only contact between her and the man was his finger on her clit. It was running slowly over it back and forth, occasionally dipping down into her moisture and back again. The feeling was mesmerizing. It went on and on. She reached a point where it became almost agonizing, but she held her breath as long as she could and that passed. She could feel her orgasm coming. It was building up all around her pussy and spreading little tendrils all over the inside of her body. The finger just went on and on.

When the moment came, a feeling of remarkable warmth spread through her. It was among the softest, gentlest orgasm she had ever had. Her whole body felt soothed as her pussy pulsed slowly and softly. It felt like it would go on forever. When it began to wane, her body had lost all its tension. It had been a gift amongst all the pain and torment and she was grateful for it.

But the finger continued. After a few minor aftershocks had passed, she wanted the finger to stop. "…ulg," she garbled almost silently, not knowing what word she had intended to form, but needing to make some sound in protest. The man ignored it. She felt his mouth on her teat once more. It subsumed her breast up over the areola, suckling at it hard. His hand had taken hold of the other one and he had begun to squeeze it, massage it, caress it.

Her pussy began to tingle once again. A second finger had joined the first and they were both rubbing over her clit and then descending into her cavern, abrading the walls. "…ulg," she again let out, a word that had some particular meaning in the context of what was happening but she didn't know what. He had abandoned her breasts and was caressing her pussy with determination. She yearned desperately to close her knees, to stop, even for a moment, the fingers that were tormenting her.

It was so strange, otherworldly, to be closed within a cocoon, away from the world's stimuli, except for the singularity of the fingers that were traversing her sensitivity. She was floating in a strange void. Her climax was coming. She could tell it was not going to be like the last one, gentle and soothing. No, this one was going to be big. Too big. Her whole consciousness was focused on the fingers driving her lust.

The wave inside her rose higher and higher. She felt like some lonesome surfer who had been waiting for a ride only to find a tsunami towering over her. The whole sensation of being helpless to prevent it, being forced to the man's will, to being played like a finely tuned instrument, an object or mechanism for which input in meant output out, made something snap inside her, blow away all her reservations, all her caring.

It was here now, towering over her. It was beginning to crest. She could see the townspeople in the little fishing village up ahead scurrying for the hills. It teeter tottered over her. She protested again, louder now, desperately afraid of the consequences, "…ulg! …ulg! …ulg!"

And then her pussy exploded. Her body shook. Violent spasms shook within her. She yanked and pulled at her bonds, bit down on her gag, groaned and sobbed as her pussy delivered shock after shock to her system, sent heavy laden messages of pleasure to her body and brain. The fingers just kept going. Her orgasm slowed, descended into a trough, but refused to die as the agitation of her crevasse continued.

Her need began to climb again. "Please stop! Please!" she thought desperately. The sensations from her sex were so strong, so body pervading that she felt she might shatter into a thousand pieces if he made her come again.

"...ulg! ...ulg!" she cried out as loudly as she could. But the fingers wouldn't stop. She lay on the beach, her body wrecked from the first wave and here came another. It would pound on her as it landed, crushing her bones, snuffing out all consciousness. It hit and it was as she feared. Her mind went delirious. Her pussy ached as it convulsed again and again. Her breasts felt near to burst. Her mind froze over. Pulse after pulse of pleasure poured through her.

He had stopped rubbing her pussy long before she seemed to notice it. Her torso was covered with sweat. He could see a vein pulsing in her bent back, strained neck. Her chest was a deep red. Her thighs still twitched. Her breasts rose and fell delightfully as she tried to recover her breath.

"She is sooooo hot!" he thought. He rubbed her thighs, caressed her breasts gently and then stood up. His cock was stiff and needy, but he knew he had to resist untying her and fucking her for just a little while yet. His rigid pole was jutting out from the slit in the front of his boxers. He gave it a couple of friendly tugs and restored it. He poured himself some more coffee. There was still almost 40 minutes before he could call again. He flicked on the TV and settled on the bed, ignoring, for now, the girl's soft moans.

He watched the end of an old episode of Magnum, PI. He knew that the bad guys always got caught, but he rooted for them anyway. After, he watched a little bit of a movie and then surfed the channels again. The girl's moaning stopped. She remained mostly quiet. Once in a while, she would get antsy and struggle a bit in her bonds, making a barely audible, piteous whining sound. It was enough to catch his attention, but not enough to make him get up and cross the room to silence her.

When the hour was up, he made the call again. A voice answered again, the same one, "2799."

"Rankin," Jack repeated.

The man on the other end didn't respond. He must have initiated some kind of transfer or forwarding thing because Jack heard a few science fiction sounding bleeps in the phone and then a single ring. "Yes?" a new voice answered.

It was Rankin. That wasn't his real name, or even the name he always used. He was different names to different people. His talent was putting people together. Jack had done him a number of favors back in the day and was counting on him to remember him.

"It's me," Jack answered.

"Well, isn't this a surprise," Rankin stated. "I take it you're not a little pile of ashes back in Wausau, Wisconsin."

"No, I'm not."

"Isn't that nice for you. What can I do for you?"

"I need to get in touch with certain people. In New Mexico."

"Is your phone safe?"

"I bought it yesterday at a convenience store. It says it has 120 minutes."

"Just the same, we'll keep this short. I have your number from my caller i.d. Someone will get in touch with you. How soon will you be there?"

"It's hard to say. Probably tomorrow night or maybe the next morning."

"And you have a package with you. I've seen her picture on the news. She's quite a dish. Having fun with her?"

"My share," Jack replied.

"My advice is dump her. There's plenty of pussy where you're going. You're taking a big risk."

"That's my business."

"As you say. I wouldn't advise you getting your friends in any trouble because of her."

"Don't worry. I won't."

"Okay. Someone will call later. Between 10 and 11 tonight. Make sure the phone is on because they'll only call once."

"Got it."

Jack was about to ring off.

"Hey," the other voice said. "Good luck."

"Thanks," Jack answered.

It was a little after 2 in the afternoon. Jack went over to the picture window again and opened the blinds slightly so he could see out. The snow was still coming, but it had lightened considerably. Frost had formed on the corners of the window. It remained nice and warm inside though. The gas heater kept the small room nice and toasty. The cabin's insulation wasn't perfect, but it was tolerable. Their car could hardly be seen. He tried to remember whether there was any ice scrapers or tire chains in the trunk. He didn't remember seeing them.

For a moment he thought he saw someone moving out there. It was a flash of red. A second later he was certain. The reddish white form of a person emerged heading for their cabin. He seemed to be carrying something.

He quickly closed the blinds. If it was the motel manager, he might want to come in. He had to make the place look normal. First was the girl. That was easy. He got behind her chair and lifted it up. She issued a moan of surprise. He carried the chair into the bathroom and closed the door. Then he quickly went about the room gathering clothes and rope and everything else and putting them in bags. He was glad that he had already done the dishes.

He was pulling on his pants when he heard the heavy knock on the door. After slipping on his shirt, and making sure that his pistol was in the pocket of his pants, he slipped on his boots and stepped to the door. When he opened it, a snow brushed creature stood at the threshold. It had a heavy woolen hat on and a muffler across its face. It wasn't too tall but was a little broad shouldered. Jack stood aside and let the person in.

He knew that if he killed whoever this was he would have to go to the motel office and kill everybody he found there. The office was connected to a house and the motel owner, his wife and his kids probably lived there. It would be messy. He'd never killed any kids before. He wasn't sure he could do it. But he would have to. So he determined to make as good a show of it in front of whoever this was as he could.

The creature stamped its boots and then removed the reddish scarf. It was a woman, the woman from the motel office. She was carrying a large Corningware casserole dish. It was covered with a glass top.

"How are you and your wife making out?" the woman asked. She was dripping all over the floor.

"We're doing fine," Jack answered.

"Some storm, eh?" the woman stated more than asked.

"Yeah," Jack replied. "Kind of took us by surprise."

"I know you and your wife are all snowed in here. I wasn't sure what you had by way of food so I brought you a little something."

The lady had long grayish black hair and a weathered face. Jack hadn't seen a man inside the motel office when he registered. Maybe the lady was all alone in the house. His speculations were answered right away.

"My grandkids are all happy that they don't have to go to school, but my son is a little put out about all the shoveling he'll have to do." the woman said. "Since the old man passed away I'm afraid I rely on him a lot. He and his wife live with me, and their kids. It's nice to have kids around again after all these years. Funny how's your certain your all done with 'em and they come popping back like that."

"Yeah," Jack answered. Kids, what a strange concept, he thought. He hadn't seen a real kid for 12 years except on TV. This was a strange little interaction he was having with the normal world.

"Where's your wife?" the woman asked, looking around. There weren't many places she could go.

"She's in the bathroom."

"Oh, yeah, a nice hot bath's great on a day like this. I don't blame her." There was a moment's silence. Then the woman spoke again. "This here's venison stew. My son likes to hunt, like his dad did, and when he brings home the meat I usually make stew and freeze some of it. I defrosted this last night." She handed the casserole dish to Jack. He took it in his left hand, wanting to keep his right hand free in case he had to shoot her.

"Well, give my best to your wife and all. Sorry I couldn't meet her. And don't worry about the extra day stayover. It's no charge there being such a storm and all. And don't worry, if'n the electricity goes out we got plenty of room up at the house and a generator the old man bought a number of years ago. Or if you just get lonely. I wouldn't be in this business if I didn't enjoy company."

Jack just stood there, not wanting to encourage any more conversation. Then he decided he had to answer.

"Thanks for the venison. It's one of my favorites. And thanks for the consideration. My wife and I are much obliged."

"Don't think nothin' of it," the woman replied. "The main road'll probably be open tomorrow morning. They always get to that first. Where you headin'?"

"Houston," Jack replied quickly. "My wife's got some family there. Sister. She's been sick and all and we just want to get there and help out."

"Sure. Sure," the old lady said. "Family's the most important thing." There was silence again. The woman leaned over slightly as if she was waiting to hear something from the bathroom. Jack hoped that she would hear nothing.

"Well," she finally said, "I'll be gettin' goin'. I'll knock the snow of'n your heater before I go. Don't want to get it all froze up. No heat then," she said. She wrapped the scarf back around her head. She looked down at the puddle of water around her boots. "Sorry about the mess," came her muffled voice.

"Don't worry about it," Jack told her. "And thanks again for the venison."

"Sure," the old lady said. She opened the door and a blast of cold air came in. She stepped out quickly. Jack slammed the door shut. A few moments later he heard the woman banging on the heater from outside. Then it was quiet again. Jack opened the blind to make sure she left. He could see the flash of red from her coat and hat moving off back to the house. He closed the blinds.

That had been a close one. He looked around quickly to see if there was anything that the woman might have seen that might have made her suspicious. Other than the fact that one of the chairs that had been around the small table was missing, he couldn't see anything. The bags that had their stuff in it were all neatly arranged and he had untied the ropes from the bed frame. Everything seemed ok. He hoped it was. He decided that he would keep the pistol near him at all times from now on. If the cops came in suddenly busting down the door, he didn't want to be caught with just his dick in his hand. There was no way he was going back to prison.

Back in the bathroom, Carly was wondering, unhappily, what new fantasy of her captor was at work. She was startled when her chair had been, without warning, lifted into the air and she had been carried here and plopped down. She could not hear the door shut, but she somehow sensed it. She was in the bathroom, she knew it. Was it merely just another act of isolating her or was there more to it? The man had seemed rushed as if he needed to get her out of sight. That meant only one thing, someone was coming into the cabin, someone who, if they saw her all tied up like this, would be likely to raise an alarm.

Should she scream at the top of her lungs? Make the chair bang against the floor by rocking her body on it? Do something, anything, to signal to the visitor that she was in distress? That was her first impulse. But when she took a second to think about it, she realized that she would just be sealing her doom. He would kill the visitor and then he would kill her. She didn't want to die just yet. Or ever, when you came down to it, but she was determined to string out her captivity as long as she could so she could enjoy the beating of her heart, the taste of air, the exciting feeling of being alive.

It seemed a long time before she felt movement of her chair again, time she had spent bemoaning her fate, trying to remember the faces of her friends and loved ones, reliving the experiences of the last 48 hours or so. He was carrying her back into the main room. He placed her chair down and she could sense him standing there looking at her for a while. When she felt him begin to untie the rope that held the pillowcase firm against her face, she felt a twinge of hope that this phase of her torment was over but also a twinge of fear that a new one was about to begin.

Once the man removed the pillowcase from her head, she was able to raise it up for the first time since the late morning. Her neck was sore and stiff. He removed, then, the blindfold and the plugs from her ears. She cringed at the brightness of the day, and then looked at him forlornly. She was able to see the clock on the wall over the stove. It said 2:20. She had been tied to the chair for almost 3 hours. The man was dressed in his white t-shirt and camouflaged, green cargo pants. She could see the lump that was his gun in one of the pockets.

Someone had been here, she thought. That someone had been so near that could end her captivity was disheartening. A regular, normal human being had been no more than 10-15 feet away from her and she had been helpless to convey to him or her her plight.

She looked about the room furtively to see if the person might have seen something that would have alerted them that she was being held against her will, but there was nothing except a little end of rope that was peeking out of one of their bags. But what would happen if the police were called? They would surround the cabin and call out to her captor to surrender. He would probably answer with a fusillade of bullets. They would maybe try and wait him out. Either, eventually, he would become tired of being trapped and kill himself, and probably her too, or the police would tire of the standoff first and they would rush the place. No doubt she would be killed either by him or by a police bullet meant for him.

Either way, she was doomed. No, the only way to live is to somehow convince him to release her. But how was she going to be able to do that when he had forbidden her speech and had done everything he could think of to dehumanize her? Looking up at him now, she feared what new travail for her was working in his head. It was still daylight. They had the rest of the day and the night together. That he would fuck her again went without saying. But she had the sense, looking at him now, that he had not removed her blindfold merely to get another look at her.

Carly, of course, had got it right. Jack had something in mind. For the moment, though, he was staring down at her, looking back at him, and wondering, idly, what was going on in her head. Fear, he could see that. Did she know that she was doomed? Did she still harbor hope that she would be free to return to her 'normal' life? She had to know that there was no way he could just let her go. She was smart, so she would have to know that. She was, undoubtedly, biding her time for a moment of neglect by him, a moment of inattentiveness, when she could make an escape. She would also know that, since she had tried it once, he would be ever vigilant against it.

Her blond hair was all mussed and her face looked gaunt and tired. Well, that didn't matter. She was on borrowed time. As far as he was concerned, she should be lying in a hole somewhere in Missouri right now. The only way she could justify her continued existence was to give pleasure to him. It wasn't his fault that fate had made her a vulnerable woman. It wasn't his fault that she had shown up right at the right time for him to make his escape. It wasn't his fault that she was so beautiful and desirable and hot and that his cock was so needy. That's just the way things went.

In his next life, if there was one, God or Fate or whatever force controlled these things might make him a cockroach. And then, if those same forces made her a human again, she could squish him without thought or remorse.

Leaving her in place, Jack retrieved the bottle of Jim Beam that was still sitting beside the bed. He poured a glass about 1/3 full with it and then filled the rest with water. Then he rummaged around in their bags, found the girl's pretty, yellow pocketbook, and took out the little canister that held her joints. There were three left. He took one out and replaced the canister in the purse, putting that away in the bag. He returned to the girl. She was looking at him warily. He took the other chair and dragged it in front of her. The glass of booze was at his feet. After unbuckling the gag from behind her head, he slowly slid the penis like prong from her mouth. When it was removed he tossed it onto the nearby table. The girl stretched her lips and exercised her mouth.

He couldn't resist caressing and squeezing her breasts a little. Her expression was dour, as if expecting the worse. It made him laugh.

Lighting the joint, he brought it to her lips. She hesitated for a moment, and then, resignedly took possession of it and took a deep drag.

The man had her alternate between taking deep drags of the joint, holding it in as long as she could, and drinking the Jim Beam. She wasn't sure why he was getting her wacked, but it certainly had something to do with bed that was behind him. From time to time, he took a little toke of the pot and a sip of the bourbon. It frightened her to see that. She didn't want him to get all drunk and mean on her. He was mean enough sober.

Once she had consumed the contents of the glass and all, including the bitter end of the joint, which he popped into her mouth after he had extinguished it and made her swallow, washed down by the last teaspoonful of the bourbon, he reinstalled her gag. Her mind was really spinning. The joint had gone right to her head. The room seemed to be flowing as if she was perceiving it from behind a glass of water. Her body was tingling and it made her enforced posture, her hands locked behind her chair, her thighs raised and spread as if she was sitting in a jockey's saddle, all the stranger. The faux cock in her mouth had never felt so cock-like. She couldn't help suckling on it.

It took longer for the booze to hit her, maybe about 20 minutes. The man just sat in his chair, which he had pulled back to the table, watching her and smoking cigarettes. She tried, in her confused mind, to think of why he might be doing this. The time was long past when she would think of resisting his use of her, and if he wanted her passionate and wet, all he needed to do was put his hands on her, as he surely knew by now.

It was so strange to be just sitting there together, no words passing between them, as if they were strangers waiting for a train. Carly knew better than to make any noise, but the tension of waiting for the man to take action made her belly sour. "Why am I here?" she thought desperately. She started to cry silently from fear and loneliness. No one knew where she was. No one could help her. No one knew what she was going through. All these things she thought. They made her desperately unhappy and led inexorably to the conclusion that no one cared.

When the man finally rose, after crushing his third cigarette out in the ashtray, her heart skipped a beat and began racing in her chest. She felt woozy and sluggish. She closed her eyes, bent her head and prayed for deliverance as he untied her hands from behind her. He came before her and fastened her wrists to the front of her collar with the small chain, letting her arms rest upon her breasts. He untied the rope from around her torso and then unloosened her legs from the chair and let them fall down to the floor. He then took hold of her hair for the umpteenth cruel and crude time and led her to the bed.

The upper sheet and blankets were all pulled down to the foot of the bed. He made her lie down on it crosswise, with her head to the room, on her back. He pulled her hair until she had shifted herself enough so that her head overhung the edge. She watched him, upside down, as he stepped away, stripped off his t-shirt and removed his pants. His cock was already half filled with blood, long and thickening. He gave it a couple of pulls. Then he stopped by the table, opened the bottle of Jim Beam and took a long swig. He put the bottle back down and turned back to her.

She knew what he was going to do. He was going to fuck her mouth. He must have been thinking about this for a long time. Maybe all the time she spent tied up, blind and silenced in her chair. And she knew why he had gotten her high. It was so she would be relaxed and compliant as he drove his cock deep into her throat. He had breeched her throat before, when she had sucked him off on her knees. It had been a strange, uncomfortable feeling, like he was entering her body proper, going down inside her. And she had been unable to refrain from choking and gagging. She knew what he was going to do now would be worse. He was going to put his whole cock, or as much of it as he could, deep into her, oblivious of her discomfort or panic as she strained to draw breath. A pang of fear sliced through her.

Jack heard her whine as he approached her. "See how smart she is," he thought. "She knows exactly what is going to happen now." He stepped close to her, close enough so that she could feel the heat of his loins on her face. His cock was long and still slightly pliant and he rubbed it over her cheeks, her eyes, slapping her playfully with it on the side of her head. She closed her eyes and grimaced. He smiled.

Leaning down, he unlocked the penis gag from behind her head. He drew the instrument out slowly, emphasizing its peculiar design. He told her to force her lips around it, and when she had tearfully complied, he drew it in and out several times, enjoying the sight of her pursed lips moving in and out as the leather prick slipped between them. He cupped her chin with his hand, holding her face still and in position as he traversed her lips with the faux cock. She suckled it obediently as if it was real. Tears were flowing from the corners of her upside down eyes.

Finally, he pulled the gag free. He centered himself over her. His cock was fat and rigid. His hand was still over her chin and he squeezed her cheeks firmly, making sure that her lips were still pursed and open. He presented the head of his cock to the trembling opening. She whimpered, and then slowly, steadily, he slid it in.

He pushed himself to the back of her mouth, brushing against the entrance to her throat and then pulled back until just the head was between her lips. He did this several times, getting the feel of her mouth, priming her for what was to come. Then he retreated until he was just inside her mouth and he ordered her to suckle it.

She obeyed instantly. She slithered her tongue over and around his sensitive glans and pulled gently at his meat, sucking steadily. She ran her tongue over the bulbous head and over the tiny, little slit, sending him a tingle of pleasure.

Placing one hand on the bed, he leaned over. Her legs were jammed together. He told her to spread them and to lift her knees. When she had obeyed, he took his free hand, ran it across her belly, up and down her tender, pale thighs, and then took possession of her mons.

He began a slow motion of his hips while his fingers worried the girl's slit until it moistened. He dragged his fingers up and down just inside her labia and then centered his attentions on the crux above. Sliding his fingers up and down her crevasse until covered with her ooze, he made her clit slippery and rotated his fingers all around and over it. It stiffened and her pussy dilated. Her thighs trembled and she spread them wider apart. When she moaned, he could feel the vibrations on his prick.

Carly hated her moan, but she couldn't stop it. The booze and pot were swirling around in her head. Her pussy had welcomed his attentions despite her fear for what was to come. When he rotated his fingers around and over her clit, she had lost it, forgotten why she was postured like this, forgotten that she was his prisoner. It just felt so good and so right that the moan built up inside her and escaped.

She was suckling his cock as best she could. It was difficult, upside down, to put the same effort into it. His lusty odors emanated from his loins and, although her eyes were closed, she could feel his testicles sliding up against her nose when he thrust himself inwards. His strokes were long and slow and, each time he thrust inwards, his cock butted up against the entrance to her esophagus. Then, to her dismay, when his cock pressed up against the rear of her mouth, it stayed there.

She felt him shift his balance. His fingers had hold of her clit, prepared to inflict agonizing pain should she falter in her duties. She issued a, "gaaaaa!" in protest, in the hopes that he would, perhaps, wait just one more second or two, to spare her if only momentarily from her upcoming ordeal. He ignored it.

The massive member in her mouth began to press inexorably forward. Her throat resisted his entry for a single moment, and then seemed to 'pop' open, granting him admission. Her eyes widened, her hands clenched. She gagged and choked and she felt her stomach revolt. "Ouuuuurg! Ouuuuuuuuuuuurg!" she protested. She closed her legs and dug her heels into the bed. She tried to squirm away, but his hand held her face firmly in place.

Her throat was expanded as he sank deeper and deeper into it. "Ooouuuuuuuuuuurg!" she protested again. "Ouurrrrrrrrrg!"

He reached the pinnacle of his penetration. Her lips were up against the base of his cock. He held himself there momentarily and then, just as slowly, just as deliberately, withdrew. When his manhood eased out of her channel, the bulbous head on her tongue, Carly took a deep breath through her nose and whined in misery.

Suddenly, there was a fierce burning on her clit. "Mmmmmmmmmmmmm!" she called out. His cock was still in her mouth and her voice was muffled. He was squeezing her pleasure bud hard and the pain became a sickening sensation all over her body.

"Mmmmmmmmmm! Mmmmmmmmmmmm!" she called out. He released her, withdrew his cock from her mouth and crouched down. His lips were inches from her ear. Tears were flowing down her face, tears of pain, fear and hatred.

"I'm going to tell you this just once," he uttered sternly and forcefully, his voice heavy, grating and thick. "I don't want to hear any sounds coming from you except the gurgling of your throat. Got it?"

She nodded her head miserably.

"And keep your legs spread. If you disobey me now, you'll dance to the whip later. Understand?"

Cary pressed her lips together in fear and unhappiness. Her face cringed. She nodded her head again dolefully. The man stood. He presented his cock to her lips. She spread them obediently, widely.

He entered her slowly. She suckled him down his length. She had spread her legs again and she felt his hand there as it began to worry her clit once more. She tried to let the beneficent sensations course through her, but she was too nervous.

As before, he drew himself back and forth several times. Carly accustomed herself to the rhythms of his thrusts. The soporific effect of the drug and alcohol turned her acquiescent and she became mesmerized by the motions of his cock and excited by the ministrations of his fingers. Then, like before, on the sixth inward stroke, he paused momentarily at the edge of her throat and then began to press himself forward slowly.

Carly whined and gurgled. She fought off the urge to draw her legs together. She wanted to shout out a protest, but knew better. The thick meat filled her passage. It went deeper and deeper until it could go no more. She heard him moan with pleasure. She was gagging and the fluids of her belly were churning. She couldn't believe that this horrible thing was happening to her. The cock seemed paused at its extremity for an eternity. And then, mercifully, albeit slowly, it began to withdraw.

When her throat was free, Carly took a deep gasp of breath. She had only a moment's respite though, because immediately, the rigid pole recommenced its relentless, merciless drive. This time, the iron hard member slipped more easily into the narrow passage. A wave of dizziness swept through her. The booze and the weed were having their effect, relaxing her muscles, making her more passive, more accepting of the rude invasion. Still, when the prick reached its apogee, she felt her thighs trembling, her knees shaking as her body recorded the insult. The man's hand was worrying her clit, stroking the length of her gash. Her lower half was responding to the man's excitations, while her upper half concentrated wholly on the massive intruder in her throat.

Once again, the feeling of powerlessness returned to her with a vengeance. She clenched her bound hands at hr breasts. She had no control over what was happening to her, not at one end of her body or at the other. It was more than just being the victim of the man's cruel assault. It was the utter callousness with which he used her, with nary a sop to her wants or desires. He had hardly a need to even talk to her, and then only to tell her to open her mouth or spread her legs, or to convey curtly his unveiled threats.

He continued his rhythm for a few more moments, running his cock back and forth in her mouth, and, after a few strokes, pausing at the entrance to her throat, giving her a moment of warning, and then plunging in. But then he altered his pattern. Instead of short thrusts in her mouth, all of his strokes became long and slow. Each one now penetrated her throat, slipping in without a pause in a smooth motion. Between each one he paused to let her exchange her air, and then proceeded inwards until he was buried to the hilt. At this end too he would pause, letting her need for sustenance build up, seemingly holding it longer and longer each time.

Carly's mind glazed over. It was no use wondering when her ordeal would end. She had no control over that. She tried to let the sensation of the hand in her quim dominate her psyche. She had just started to accommodate herself to strokes of the man's prick when he changed them again. He had achieved his goal. He could pass in and out of her throat without problem, without complaint or struggle. He had trained her to take it. Now the real face fucking would start.

His thrusts became quick and hard, repeated in series of four or five powerful strokes, then withdrawing the head back into her oral cavity, letting her gasp for air, and then repeating the exercise. It was as if his lust had been suddenly ratcheted up to high. She was still whining and crying as the thick meat plunged again and again deep inside her. His passion, though, was contagious, and his manipulations of her slit were having their effect. Suddenly, he leaned his torso forward. His hand left her pussy to be replaced by his hungry lips. He started to suckle on her rigid love button. She would have gasped had not her mouth been full of cock.

His tongue fluttered over her stiff nubbin. She groaned. The cock kept passing in and out. The gaps between each series of thrusts became shorter and shorter and she started to become oxygen starved. Her mind was a swirl of lust, intoxication and oxygen deprivation. He was grunting now and his hands were pressing her thighs further apart. Everything seemed to be building to an immense crescendo.

"Arrrrrrrrgh! Arrrrrrrrrrgh! Arrrrrrrrrrrrrrgh!" he cried as his cock began to pulse in her throat. He held it there, firmly encased, as he groaned and, at the same time, suckled at her crux. Carly's orgasm quickly followed. She felt like she was passing away into another plane as her pussy pulsed and throbbed while her mind fogged over. It was almost as if she were miles away and all of these feelings were being telegraphed to her, intensifying on their journey, to be delivered to her waning consciousness. She was past struggling, past resisting, past worrying. She just let it all flow through her like waves of dreamed ecstasy.

When he pulled out, she was brought back swiftly from her distant shore and she took in a deep, panicked breath of air. Three times her chest heaved as she acted to restore the needed balance of oxygen to her blood. The man was huddled over her, breathing deeply too, his head down, relishing the lingering sensations of his experience. Then she coughed and choked and began to cry.

CHAPTER FIVE

"Ohhhhhhhhhhh!" Jack thought. "That was fine!" He had trained most of the whores they had put on the street in the old days to take a cock down their throats. He had continued his instructions in the joint, teaching fearful little college boys sent up for a little stretch on drug charges. They were supposed to be kept in administrative segregation, but a little juice usually was enough to have them released into general population. And then there were the young street punks who were doing life stretches for capping some kid or 15 to 20 for armed robbery. They learned quickly that they weren't so tough after all.

But there was nothing like having a pussy on the other end rather than a cock. The smell of a woman's juices was so exotic and stimulating that it made the experience much, much better. When he got to Mexico, he would have to get his own little senorita and train her well. It was too bad it couldn't be this one though.

He stood up from the girl. She was still taking in deep breaths and crying from her ordeal. He leaned over and released her bound wrists from the front of her collar. Then he took hold of her hair and pulled her back up fully on the bed and guided her to her belly. He joined her wrists again behind her back and fastened her ankles together.

She had calmed some so he brought her gag back to her lips. She was still upset about what he had done and he had to slap her twice fiercely on her ass to get her to open. Sobbing now and moaning in pain, she complied.

He fastened the gag behind her head. When he was done, he retrieved the switch he had been using on her and gave her five strokes on her ass and the backs of her thighs for disobedience. She squealed and screamed while he did it. He felt a little guilty since she had been so compliant about the face fucking, but he couldn't have her refusing her gag.

Afterwards, he put the blindfold back on.

He stood up and stretched. The casserole dish was sitting on the table. He was ravenous. He turned on the stove and placed the dish in the oven. He would heat it for a half hour at 200. While waiting for the venison to warm, he decided to take a shower. Before he went into the bathroom, just to make sure that the girl didn't get into mischief, her locked her bound ankles to her hands and drew ropes around her knees and elbows.

He went into the bathroom, took a piss and then turned on the shower. He let it run a little until it got hot enough and then stepped in. It was great to be under the hot water. He soaped up his strong, scarred body, relishing the luxury. It was great to be alive and free. As far as he was concerned, it could keep snowing for another week. His setup, the food, the pussy, the shower, everything, was just about as good as it could be.

Carly had heard him go into the bathroom. She heard him piss and then flush the toilet. Being in the dark made every sound reverberate through her mind. Then the water to the shower came on. "Good," she thought. For a while at least she would be free of any new torments from him.

Her thighs and rear were still stinging from the punishment she had just received. It wasn't that she had been actually refusing to let him put the gag in, it was just that she wanted desperately some time to have her mouth free after her ordeal with his cock. She had known he would probably spank her to force her to comply, but those vital seconds, seconds in which she was in rebellion, although in just a small way, restored, momentarily, her self respect. It was just a little space of time in which she was free again, doing what she wanted, not what he commanded. She had complied immediately though when he slapped her buttocks two times hard with his powerful, heavy hand. It stung fiercely and she wanted no more of that. Her bravery didn't extend so far.

That he had actually whipped her for it had startled and surprised her. It had sparked another round of uncontrollable tears. She couldn't help it. His control of her was absolute and merciless. His commands were more like commandments, by-laws of her existence. Deviance was met with immediate, overwhelming violence. Her stomach turned and twisted with unhappiness. Her life had become so horrid. She was constantly on edge, like someone trying to cross a lake on thin ice. Any moment you could plunge into the unforgiving waters and drown.

The throat fucking had been a harrowing experience even though she knew deep down that he wasn't about to let her suffocate. He had too much fun to look forward to with her to let that happen, at least yet. But it sure felt that way at the end when he just kept pumping away. When he started to come, he just stayed there and stayed there while his jism was jetted down her throat. That her pussy was throbbing and pulsing rabidly at the time did not vitiate the horrid feeling of oxygen denial. The worst part was now that he had taught her to take his cock down her throat, he would expect it every time.

Her heart fell into her stomach when he hogtied her. She knew it meant that she would be cruelly bound for a long time. The rope connecting her elbows made it even worse. Her shoulders and back began to ache almost immediately. She couldn't move an inch. All she could do was think about the terrible things the man was going to do to her, bite down on the penis like gag in her mouth, or raise her head and twist it back and forth. Having the penis gag in her mouth was like reliving her recent experience. She half expected it to come to life and ram down her throat at any second.

She lay there helpless while she listened to him in the shower. Now she knew why he had tied her so thoroughly. He needed to make sure she was secure while his focus was elsewhere. She imagined the pleasure of having the hot water flowing over her own body, the ability to feel with her free hands her own skin, to move about, letting the water flow over her head, splash into her face. She quickly put those thoughts away. Her heart started to pound and she felt a deep despair that she was powerless to take advantage of his inattention. She pulled at her bindings uselessly. She couldn't help it, but she started to cry again.

She felt like she had felt when she was tied up and placed in that hole the other day, like he had cast some evil spell over her that kept her cruelly confined whenever he wanted it. It was like he snapped his fingers and, presto chango, she was bound like this, a helpless prisoner. And the darkness she was in, the blindfold taking away all light, made it seem that she had been sent into another dimension, some dimension parallel to our own, where you could store helpless young women until you wanted to fuck them again.

Suddenly, her whole mind and body rose in revolt. She began to struggle desperately to get loose. The bracelets she wore were clipped together and she knew that she couldn't break them apart. But if she could just slip her wrists free of them and get her hands loose that way, she might then be able to undo the rest of her bonds and run out the door, snow or no snow. If she couldn't free her ankle bracelets, she would hop out the door if she had to. She knew that she had to get free or she would die. She would do anything to get away and this was the best chance she had had in a while.

She pulled and pulled on her hands. Her feet were serving as a kind of anchor for the bracelets, holding them still while she tried to slip her hands out. She strained and strained. She could feel the leather digging deep into her skin. She groaned. She was pulling her legs away from her hands as hard as she could. Her shoulders were straining. Her elbow joints were distended and felt like they were going to pop apart. She was holding her breath and she felt all the blood running into her brain, making her dizzy.

Suddenly, she felt one of the bracelets moving, shifting just a smidgeon. She paused for a moment, releasing her breath and relaxing her muscles in preparation for another assault. Her heart was pounding madly in her chest and perspiration had broken out all over her body.

Just as she was about to take a deep breath and start again, she heard the shower go off. "Oh my god! Oh my god!" she cried to herself. She knew that her window of opportunity was just about up. "One, two, three," she called in her mind. She took a deep breath and pulled, pulled, pulled, with all her might. It felt like her hands were about to fly off of her wrists. The leather was tight to her skin. It moved again, just a teensy, weensy bit. She knew that all she needed to do was get the bracelets over the heels of her hands, or just one of them, and she could be free. "Please! Please! Please!" she thought desperately. "Please!"

She ran out of breath and had to try again. Her muscles were aching from the strain. Her wrists were burning. "One, two, three!" she thought again. She pulled as much air into her lungs as she could and gave it another try. After about a minute, the bracelets started to move some more. "Please! Please! Please!" she cried out in her mind again. "Just a few minutes more! Pleeeeeeeeeee-eease!"

A moment later, she heard him emerge from the bathroom. All of her efforts immediately stopped. It was too late to do anything now. If he saw her trying to escape he would beat her and then make sure she was even more secure the next time he left her alone. Or he would just kill her. She sank into a deep funk. The futility of struggling had been made clear to her so many times. But the bracelets had moved! They had definitely moved! Maybe there was a chance she could escape after all!

When he came back into the main room, Jack took out a fresh, new pair of boxers and a t-shirt and put them on. Looking over at the girl, he saw that she was breathing hard but otherwise everything seemed normal. He opened the oven to see if the venison was done. He could see the sauce bubbling around it. He took it out and turned off the stove. He put a plate and silverware on the table together with a glass of cold milk. Then, using a dirty t-shirt as a potholder, he brought the casserole dish to the table and spooned some out. He sat down and dug in. It was delicious.

The meat was smoky. It was in a dark, brown gravy. There were some peas, carrots and cut up potatoes. He ate it slowly, savoring every bite. He had bought some bread when he bought the peanut butter the night he had kidnapped the girl and he buttered up a couple of slices to soak up the gravy. Yet again his mind and body celebrated the joys of his liberation. It was hard to believe that a mere few days ago he was locked up, an abysmal prisoner.

He thought of his little cell. He had decorated the walls with posters of famous motorcyclists, James Dean, Evel Knieval, Marlon Brando. He had had his own little TV, although the reception was shitty. He had a shelf for his books. The cell was a little smaller than 15 by 10. And his little bed with the worn out lumpy mattress. It was nothing like the beds he had been sleeping in since his escape. He looked over at it now. And there had never been anything as sweet in it as the naked, bound girl who waited at his pleasure now.

He ate to his fill. There was almost a third of the dish left. He looked over at the girl, still hogtied on the bed. He was sure she was hungry, but he didn't know if he should waste the venison on her. He lit a smoke and gave the issue some thought. He might want to eat some more of it later. In fact, he knew that he would want to eat more of it later.

And that should have been the end of the discussion. But something was bugging him. He had been treating her rather badly. And she had been obedient mostly, except for that little thing with the gag before, which was, when you got down to it, really nothing. He was sorry that he had whipped her, but just a little. The image of her squirming and wailing under his whip was a delight in and of itself. And while she really hadn't deserved it, it would guarantee continued compliance.

He took a deep drag of his Marlboro and spread a wide swath of grayish smoke throughout the room. The girl issued a little whimper and twisted her head. She had been bound up for a little over an hour and it was undoubtedly getting to her.

And then what was really bothering him kind of floated to the surface. He was either going to have to kill her or hand her over to those who would. He didn't really like killing and especially didn't like killing women. And he especially didn't like the idea of killing one he had been fucking for the last couple of days. He knew that he would have a hard time of it later, just like he did about that whore that Drummer had made him kill. Maybe it would go just a little bit better if he didn't treat her so bad. Maybe if he went easier on the things that he could, like letting her have some of the stew, later on he would be able to handle it better.

But she had to go. In a way it would be just like killing that whore. He hadn't had a choice about that. Drummer was the club president and his word was law. And he really didn't have any choice with this one either, not since he stepped into her car. If he wanted to get away he couldn't very well leave her somewhere where she could blab about where he was or had just been. And once they got to New Mexico and he caught some help from his club brothers, they couldn't very well let her live to tell the tale. So maybe, just maybe, if he treated her a little better, he would be able to put her out of his mind. He hoped so.

She had heard him fiddling with the oven and then setting the table so he could eat. She was doing everything to prevent herself from starting to cry again. She hated him so much that she prayed that somehow he choked on his food. But she knew that she wouldn't be so lucky. So far, all the luck had been on his side.

Whatever he was eating smelled delicious. She knew that it was not for her. He would feed her a can of beans or a can of watery soup and then probably make her blow him. But even that would be better than nothing. And she had to pee too. She was frightened of what he would do to her if she peed on the bed. She had gotten five strokes of the whip for just delaying his gagging of her. For peeing on the bed she would get a whirlwind of blows.

When he lit the smoke, she knew that she would have to wait to eat. The smell of the tobacco surrounded her. She had disliked the smell of cigarette smoke before. If she ever was freed, she would detest it with a vengeance. It would always remind her of him and his cruelty to her. Now, the smell reminded her that she was living in his world, one that he completely and utterly dominated.

She had a pang of hunger. He would eventually feed her, she knew, just like he would eventually release her from her cruel tie. But in the meantime, she suffered and languished. Every once in a while, her mind exploded with unhappiness and she thought of the thin walls of the cabin that separated her from the real world. Just outside was freedom. Just outside was rescue. It was so horrible to think of it as so close and yet to have no hope of deliverance. There had been somebody inside the cabin today, she knew it, even though she had not been able to hear a thing. It was the only thing that made sense of him putting her in the bathroom. Freedom had been a mere 10 or 15 feet away! But it might as well have been a hundred miles. She whined in unhappiness.

Jack crushed the smoke out in the ash tray. He had heard the whine. He got up and walked over to the bed. The shudder she gave showed that she had taken note of it. He released her ankles from her wrists and let them fall on the bed. Then he undid the ropes tying together her knees and elbows. She issued a sigh of relief. After unbuckling her ankles from each other, he took hold of her hair and pulled her to her knees and then off of the bed.

He took her to the bathroom and let her pee first. She went a long, long time, like she had been saving it up, which she had since he hadn't given her the opportunity since that morning. "See, that's what I'm talking about," he said to himself. He resolved to be a little more aware of her needs.

When she was done, he wiped her pussy carefully and brought her back to her feet. He took her into the living area and coaxed her to her knees. Leaving her in place, he got the rest of the venison stew and put it in a bowl. Then he filled another bowl with milk. He brought them to where she was kneeling and put them on the floor in front of her. He removed her blindfold and then her gag, snapped his fingers and pointed to the floor. She looked at him unhappily, then spread her knees apart, leaned over and started to eat.

When the man removed her blindfold and she looked down, Carly was surprised that he had given her some real food. She had smelled it while he was cooking and eating it. It made her stomach growl. She had resisted the urge to whine and moan to communicate her hunger to the man; she knew much, much better.

After waiting for his permission, she started munching on the stew. She realized that whoever had come into the cabin had brought it. It was a neighborly thing to do. She was glad that she had not made a ruckus in the bathroom. It would have been a fine payback for such a friendly gesture to have the man blow off his or her head. And then he would have come back and blown off hers. No, if she escaped, she promised that she would do it in a way that didn't involve another person's possible death.

The meat was strange tasting. It was definitely not beef. It wasn't pork either. It was pretty good whatever it was. It was her first real meal since she had been kidnapped. The man had gone back to sit in his chair and he was watching her carefully. She didn't care. After she captured a piece with her teeth, she knelt up and chewed it slowly, savoring it. The sauce was tart and heavy and had a hint of rosemary in it she thought. It was just a little spicy.

The milk was cold and refreshing. She alternated between mouthing up the stew and lapping up the milk. She was getting sauce all over her face, but she didn't care. When she had all the meat and vegetables scooped up, she started to lick the bowl to get the rest of the sauce. She was so enthusiastic about it that the bowl kept moving and she found herself wishing that she could free her bound hands just so she could hold it still.

Once all the sauce was gone, she shifted over and finished off the milk. She had never really been big on milk but now it tasted wonderful. It was much, much better than having the taste of the gag in her mouth. When the last drop of the milk was lapped up, she raised her torso and sat back on her heels. Her stomach felt warm and comfortable, sated. It was a good feeling to have. She realized though that she should have taken more time finishing off her food because now the man would do something to her. Nothing could be done about that. She licked her lips and eyed the man warily, waiting for instructions.

Jack had enjoyed the show, like he always did. Watching her breasts jiggle and dance like that while she ate was amusing and pleasing. They had such wonderful shapes and seemed almost to have lives of their own as they moved about. And to watch the girl bury her face in the bowl, her arms bound behind her, her knees spread, reminded him so much of the old days that it seemed just a little that he was still there. Then afterwards, he would fuck the girl and then have her put into one of the cages they kept in the clubhouse basement. He would then roar into the countryside on his hog, certain that she would still be there when he came back.

He would like to do that with this girl. They had said her name on the news, but he couldn't remember whether it was Carol or Charlene. Not that it mattered much. But he knew he would remember her for a long time and it would be nice to have a name to remember her by other than the blond cunt he had kidnapped during his breakout.

She was kneeling there watching him warily. There were brown smudges of sauce on her face. Her hair was messy and unkempt. There were rings under her eyes. The strain of being a captive was showing on her. Well, it wouldn't be for too much longer.

He got up from his chair and wetted a paper towel in the sink. Then he sat back down in his chair and beckoned to the girl with his finger. She grimaced and then obediently shuffled over the ten or so feet on her knees until she was inches away from his legs. He spread them and used the paper towel to clean her face.

She was pretty. He had to give her that. He put the towel down on the table and turned back to her. He ran his hand over her cheek and under her chin, touching her softly, but proprietarily. There was just something about her that drew him to her. He leaned over and took her face between his hands. He looked deep into her troubled eyes. He could see that she was trying to hold off from crying. She was such a good girl. He rubbed his thumbs gently over her eyebrows and then his hands over her hair. He circled them back so that they were under her chin and he raised her face. He leaned forward. Her lips were trembling. He placed his own lips upon them, guided her compliant mouth open and then entered her mouth with his tongue.

Carly's body melted when the tongue entered her mouth. His hands still held her head in place in a firm yet gentle vice. She couldn't understand how the man could be so tender and gentle with her one moment and then so harsh and cruel to her the next. "That's because I'm not a sociopath," she thought briefly, just before the hot, passion inducing tongue entered her mouth.

At the same time as her lusts were growing, her mind, confused, lonely, afraid, yearning for comfort, sent a surge of unhappiness through her. She wanted to give herself over to the all encompassing lust that he created in her, but she couldn't. He withdrew his tongue from her mouth and leaned back. He was gazing into her troubled eyes once more. He stroked her head again, like he would an unhappy child or a pet. It was too much. She burst into tears.

He knew that she needed to cry. He rubbed his hands in her hair again, stroking it front to back, patting it down. She started to sob. She was sitting back on her heels and he placed his hands under her chin and made her rise. Once up, he placed her head on his lap and began to give it soft caresses.

She went on and on. He knew that she wouldn't go on forever, that she would stop sooner or later and so he just continued to stroke her patiently. When her sobs reduced in volume and tempo, he lifted her face once more. He placed his lips on hers, kissing them softly. Then he gave her a series of kisses, over her cheeks and chin, up over her eyes and forehead, all the time caressing her head, petting it, actually, bringing her the tenderness he knew that she needed now. Then he held her head still with his hands and pressed his lips on hers. He ran his tongue lightly over the gap between them. They parted obediently. He slipped himself in.

While her kissing a few moments ago had been accepting, dutiful, obedient, it was now was full of passion. She pressed her lips hard against his and her tongue joined his in a lustful dance. She moaned lowly and he knew that he had her.

Carly was beside herself. She was so confused. He had done it to her again. He had shifted gears and capitalized on her vulnerability. She knew what he had done and yet she needed the illusion of his affection, needed a gesture of kindness more than she ever needed anything. Maybe, maybe he was beginning to see her as a person, an individual. Maybe he saw her as something special. She needed to be something special for him, wanted it now with all of her heart. She wanted to please him, to worship him, to obey him. "Oh, God," she prayed, "please let him see me as real! Please! Please!"

Her hands writhed behind her as they kissed. Her lust was rising. His hand slipped down from her head and softly caressed a breast. His hand was hot and strong. Heavy. Manly. Masterful. It was the hand of a god! She moaned as the hand massaged her feminine mound. His hand slid off and his fingers captured a nipple, squeezing it sharply, just sharp enough to make her pussy tingle.

He broke their kiss. He reached into the slit of his boxers and withdrew his cock. Carly needed no instruction. She leaned over and took it in her mouth.

It was already rock hard. Its largeness, its irrefutable presence in her mouth, its solidity, all brought Carly rushes of passion. She promised herself that she would give the man the best blowjob he had ever had. He would see that she was someone special. He would see it and be good to her, free her when the time came, let her live. It was her only hope. She couldn't talk to him. She couldn't make him see her humanity that way. But if he could see that she had human feelings, gratitude, even for his touch of kindness to her, maybe then he would see it, her humanity, her worth.

Jack leaned back and let the girl work on his prick. He knew that she was engaged in a desperate effort to save her life. All the better for him. She was suckling his cock with a wild devotion. She nibbled at the bulbous helmet, subsumed the pole between her lips, clamping them down firmly, pushing her head down until it was as far as it would go in her mouth. She did that several times and then, capitalizing on the lessons he had taught her, pushed his prick past the opening to her throat and took him in. She did it once, twice, three times and then came back up for air. Then she did it again, three times in rapid succession. And then again.

He pushed her head away for a moment while he lowered his boxers and cast them off. Then he spread his legs and lifted his cock towards his belly. The girl took his cue and began to lick at and suckle his bulging sack, taking first one, then another of his balls in her mouth, suckling them gently. He let her work at his stones a long time, relishing her efforts. Then pushed her head back again and lowered his cock. She took in back in her mouth, sighing deeply as if in gratitude.

His blood was way up. He groaned as she suckled his pole, washing it with her tongue. He reached behind her head and took hold of her hair. He began to guide her mouth's thrusts, slowing it when his passion threatened to erupt and over boil, speeding it up again once he had regained control of his lust. She followed his hand's instructions dutifully. When he guided her head down all the way, she accepted him in her throat's tight passage without struggle or objection. When he brought her head up, she took a deep breath and then went immediately back to her chores.

She was moaning and groaning as she worked him with her lips and tongue. He gave out a groan of his own. His need was becoming irresistible. His balls ached with longing to erupt. His brain coveted a release, his whole body yearned to climb over the edge of desire.

When his cock began to jerk and pulse within her mouth, Carly needed no guidance or instruction. She suckled the length of the throbbing instrument rapidly up and down, plunging it deeply within her on each stroke. His hand, which had been laying lightly in her hair, gripped it tightly now as if he needed something to hold on to to prevent himself from cascading about the room. He grunted and groaned and thrust his prick up towards her. It throbbed and pulsed within her. She absorbed his discharge dutifully.

Jack gave out a great sigh when his cock finally came to rest. The girl continued to suckle it gently and the warm tightness around his member sent him several post orgasmic shudders. Leaning back, he loosened his grip on her hair. He kept her there, his softening cock in her mouth, for several minutes, enjoying the rapture and then eased her head up. She kept her lips sealed around his softening manhood until it popped from her mouth.

She looked up at him expectantly, seeking a sign that her energized, desperate ministrations had had the desired effect. His face, as usual, betrayed little of what was pending in his antisocial mind. Her bound hands were clasped tightly into little fists behind her back. Her chin was trembling. She felt the nausea, shame and hopelessness welling up inside her. Had her efforts gone for naught? Wasn't there a single shred of humanity in him? She wanted desperately to speak, to talk to him, to beg him, not to desist from his abuse of her. No, she knew that that would be asking the impossible. But to treat her humanely, as a fellow human creature, not as some fuckable being way short of personhood, to speak back to her, to exchange the basic niceties of fellow creatures.

The tears were coming again. She could feel them. She tried to staunch them, really she did. But it was the only way she had of expressing herself, the only outlet for all her unhappiness, the only way to mourn what she had lost and what she had yet to lose. She bent her head, let it lay upon his thighs, and began to softly cry.

Jack stroked her head. He knew that she had reached the breaking point. If he didn't do something, she would become useless. He would have to beat her to get her to do anything and even then her obedience would be lackluster and perfunctory, if that. He took hold of a large tuft of her wispy blond hair and eased her head up. Tears were streaming down her face.

Cradling her head in both of his hands, he used his thumbs to wipe away the tears from the corners of her eyes. Then he leaned over and kissed her. It wasn't a passion inducing kiss, but a kiss meant to provide comfort and tenderness. Not that tenderness was anywhere part of his being. But he understood other creatures and he knew when one needed a whip and when one needed a caress or, as here, a kiss. She would get the whip later, crying was against the rules, after all, but for now, it would be kisses and caresses.

Her tongue danced energetically with his. She issued a moan. It lasted several minutes. His hand reached down and cupped her breasts, each in its turn. Its purpose was not to induce passion, but to convey a warmth and approving, if not caring, message to the girl. She had been obedient and deserved praise, even gentleness.

He broke their kiss and pulled back his head so that she could look into his eyes. He gave her a warm look, almost a smile. This seemed to be the message she was seeking, because a wave of relief flashed across her face. "She's pretty," he thought, looking at her. He had noted this before, of course, but looking at her now reminded him of it again. And her face looked prettier when she was pleased than when she was in fear, although that look had a piquancy all of its own.

Admiring her natural, uncomplex beauty was as close as he could get to appreciating her humanity. For even the concept of humanity was beyond him. It was as foreign to his conception as global warming would be to an ant. He would never understand the reason for it. People did what they wanted, what they could get away with. And the stronger, braver, more audacious people got to rule the others. Everybody was in it for themselves. Even the girl. And if she had beauty and charm, they needed to be understood and perceived as nothing more than her particular weapons, female weapons, to get what she wanted. Now she was using them to mollify his treatment of her. To some extent it was working and he would allow it to as long as doing so satisfied his needs: to keep her cooperative, obedient, docile and available to fuck.

He remembered something he had bought that might be useful now. Reaching behind his chair, he rooted around in one of the brown paper bags he had gotten at the supermarket. When he found what he was looking for, he pulled it out. It was a large bar of Hershey's chocolate. He tore open the wrapping and broke off a small block. The girl was watching him with intense interest. He proffered the chocolate to her mouth. She opened her lips and he placed it on her tongue. She pulled it in and, after sucking on it briefly, began to chew it slowly, a hint of satisfaction and enjoyment breaking out onto her face.

"Ohhhhhhhhh," Carly moaned inside. The chocolate was delicious. She chided herself mildly for finding joy in such a minor beneficence, but since almost every aspect of her captivity had been to date cruel and impersonal, this tiny concession to her need to feel human felt blessed. She chewed the chocolate down and then swallowed it, delight passing through her body.

She watched as he broke off another piece. He held it out to her and she plucked it from his grasp with her lips. She felt herself smiling at him. It was not a voluntary reaction. She knew that she had little or no reason to smile. But the gesture of kindness and the delicious taste, a taste that brought her back to the simplicity and happiness of childhood engendered the Pavlovian reaction. He stroked her head again with his right hand while tweaking and tugging gently at her nipples with the other. When that piece was done, he gave her another. She chewed it gratefully.

For some reason, she understood that this was to be her quota. She didn't mind. The gesture had been more than enough to signal to her that her proffer of her humanity to him had been, to some small extent, a success. It was at least a beginning. She would work on it some more. For now though a feeling of relief and satisfaction passed through her. She felt more tears, this time tears of relief, bubbling to the surface. She didn't want him to see her cry, she knew she was skirting if not outright breaking his rules, so she bent her head down and laid it in his lap, a small gesture of her gratitude to him.

CHAPTER SIX

He let her head lie there for a while, stroking her occasionally. He sensed a certain relaxation and return to resignation in her. That was good. He looked up at the clock. It was almost 4:00. The day was passing slowly but surely. In 14 hours or so from now he wanted to back on the road. Their little idyll here couldn't last forever. There were preparations that needed to be made, ones that the girl might not react to very well. She was undoubtedly in a better mood to accept them than she was before. And, he might as well get it over with now.

He wrapped up the chocolate, after taking a small piece for himself, and put it away. He urged her head up off of his lap. She stared at him expectantly with her big, blue eyes. He gave her a slight smile and patted her cheek. Then he reached back down into one the bags behind him and produced the small, blue ball the girl had worn in her mouth the first day. Her face winced when she saw it and she sadly opened her mouth to receive it. He popped it in past her teeth, patted her on her cheek one more time, rewarding her obedience, and then, taking hold of her hair, brought her to her feet.

She followed his lead into the bathroom. He seated her on the toilet so she could pee and began to run the bathtub. He poured in some bath oil. She looked at him expectantly. She looked so cute with that little bit of blue emanating from between her lips and her cheeks all puffed out. After wiping her and locking her ankles together, he left the bathroom for a moment. He came back with the long chain in his hand. Releasing her ankles, he affixed the chain to the ring in the back of her collar and then locked the other end around one of the bathtub's claw like feet. They stood together at the edge of the tub, watching the water rise. He was at least a head taller than her and one third again as wide.

Leaning over to test the water, he became satisfied and turned it off. He loosened and removed the belt that she had been wearing around her waist that was accessory to the anal plug. The loose chains had been dangling down her thighs. To Carly's surprise, he crouched down and unfastened the leather bracelets from around her ankles. A sense of doom came over her. If he released her wrist bracelets as well, he would undoubtedly find evidence of her trying to remove them. She had felt the burning of her skin at the time and feared there would be red marks left behind. She began to tremble as he disconnected her wrist confinements from each other.

When she felt him begin to unlock the bracelet on her right wrist, she had to suppress the urge to run out of the bathroom. Of course, the chain was still connected to the ring in the back of her collar and she wouldn't have gotten far. Yet the urge to do something to avoid the man's almost certain, immediate, infliction of punishment on her was almost overwhelming.

A lump formed in her throat. Although she knew that she was entirely within her rights to try and escape, after his few moments of tenderness towards her it seemed like the worst kind of betrayal. He would see it like that too. She knew it. "Oh god! Oh, god! Oh, god," she thought desperately, hoping that there would be no reddened mark there.

But her frantic attempts at freedom had been too intense not to leave some evidence behind. As soon as the cuff had been removed from her right wrist, she felt his hand tighten suddenly on her wrist and her arm pulled straight. He rose to his feet and pulled her wrist in front of her face. There was anger in his eyes. Carly sobbed and tried to pull her wrist away from him, but he held it too tight. Then he released it and grabbed her other arm. He raised her wrist and removed the bracelet that adorned it. There, accusingly, was a deep red arc under the heel of her hand. There could be only one explanation for it.

It didn't seem fair to Carly that she should be punished for trying to escape. What did he expect, after all? Did he think she should enjoy being his prisoner? Didn't she have at least the right to try and save her life? Wouldn't he do the same?

Her whole body cringed as she watched the man for a sign of impending retaliation. The pause between his discovery of her perfidiousness and his reaction was too much to take. She moaned and tried to pull her hand away from him again. He gripped it ever more tightly. Then, to her surprise, he released her wrist and took hold of her upper arm. He nodded to the tub. "Get in," he said gruffly.

Shaking with terror, Carly climbed into the tub. The water was hot and it took her a few seconds to gain the courage to sit down in it. The chain which held her neck in bondage rattled against the side. She looked unhappily at her lord and ruler.

Jack didn't want to create a fuss about the marks on her wrists just yet. It was his fault, really, for not keeping a better eye on her. He would make sure she was double tied the next time he let her leave his sight. It was yet another sign of the risk he was taking by letting the girl live. For a second he reconsidered what he had planned to do. He could just drown her now and get it over with. But he looked at her naked form, the water glistening on her soft flesh, her anguished face, her soft breasts, and he decided against it. He would just have to be more careful, that's all. And he would have to reinstill the fear of god into her.

Patting her on the head to reassure her, he let her settle into her bath. Gradually, her look of uncertain fear diminished. Except for her collar, her entire body was nude for the first time in a while. She could almost look like a normal girl taking her Saturday night bath, getting ready for a date with her sugar plum. He thought of the boy's picture he had seen in her wallet. "Yeah," he thought, "she could be getting ready to fuck him." His cock stirred.

He decided to let the girl wash herself. It would be fun to watch. He handed her the bar of soap and sat back on the toilet seat a few feet away from her. He had brought in his smokes and lit one. He released a large, bluish gray cloud and then nodded at her to get her started.

Carly cringed at what the man was demanding. It was bad enough to have him manhandle her against her will. He had not had her caress herself for his pleasure yet. If he enjoyed the show she gave him now, that would be only one step away. She hesitated only briefly. She knew that refusal or untimely delay would result in punishment. She had already earned one, she was sure of that. Maybe two if he decided to punish her for crying. She didn't want to earn another.

Taking the soap in her hands, she worked up a nice lather and then spread it all over her chest and breasts. It felt funny to be able to place her hands on her body. She hadn't had that right for days now. Whether it was still her body or not was open to question. He seemed to have staked a firm claim to ownership of it. He was staring at her intently, awaiting his show. She wanted to speak to him, to say something, anything. Her mouth was bloated by the blue rubber ball he had thrust into it. She pressed down on it unconsciously with her teeth. She suppressed a moan and then raised herself first to her knees and then her feet in the tub.

The chain was long enough to let her stand. She spread the soap over her belly, upper and lower, over her thighs. Placing her hand on the side of the tub, she lifted first one foot and then the other, washing in between the toes. She saw that her toenail polish was fading. She had put it on for Randy. She hadn't thought about him for a while. Where was he now? Was he fraught with worry over her or had he already written her off as dead? Where were the police? The man seemed much too clever for them to ever catch him. And if they did, he would shoot it out to the death. His and hers.

It was unavoidable, so she just went ahead and did it. She gathered some soap lather on her hand and wiped it over her hairless pussy. He was watching her hand intently. She took her time, laboring over her outer and inner labia, washing all around it. She saw how much he desired her. It was because of that desire that she was still alive. She knew that she needed to do everything that she could to maintain his lustful interests. She spread her love lips and drew her slick, soapy finger up its length. Lingering over her button of pleasure, she gave a slight rotation to her hips, just enough to create the illusion that she was deriving pleasure from her lascivious show.

And strangely enough, she was. She felt a tingle pass through her pussy as her finger continued to excite her. She felt her nipples tightening. Her eyes had been diverted from his, the only way she could bring herself to do this in front of him, but she lifted them now. His eyes, deadly, black eyes, were peering at her sex, hungering for it. He lifted his eyes to meet hers, catching them just for a second until she moved them away, looking down at the water that rose up just under her knees. She closed them and ran her finger deeper inside her. Her interior was slick with her fluids. She slid her finger in and out a few times, gathering moisture, and brought it back up to her stiffened clit, rolling it back and forth until the sensations made her shudder.

She quickly drew her hand away. She looked up. The man's hunger was in his eyes. She felt a wave of shame go through her. Somehow, standing here in the tub, her skin glistening from water and soap, she felt more naked than she had before. She looked back down at her hands as she lathered them up again. She moved her hands to her backside in order to soap up and clean the crevice there and the little hole that the man liked to pierce. She heard the man snap his fingers and she looked up at him. He made a motion with his hand that she understood to mean that she should turn around.

Obediently, she turned so that her ass was facing him. Slowly, as if in a daze, she placed her arms behind her and began to soap up her porcelain white, soft rear orbs. She delved into the crack between them and spread soap over her little bung hole. She felt the man's eyes piercing her from behind. The chain from her collar clinked on the side of the tub. She knew what he wanted to see. She would give it to him, although every ounce of her psyche revolted at it. She needed him to want her. Tomorrow they would be leaving. Whether she was dumped in a ditch somewhere or whether she would continue to live until the end of the day depended on the level of his lust for her. She wanted it as high as she could make it.

Overcoming her revulsion, she spread her legs as wide as they could go and bent over, as low as she could without falling over. She slid her left hand between her legs while she spread her rear cheeks with the other. Slowly, deliberately, she soaped her rear entrance, delving the tip of her longest finger into the flexible hole. The sensation of crossing her sensitive anal ring had been made familiar by the man's earlier depredations. Her body recalled those prior invasions and the explosive orgasms that had been generated while he possessed her there. She pressed the finger in deeper and began to run it back and forth. She had to be careful. Her fingernails, while not prima donna long, were just long enough to cut and slice and the last thing she wanted was a laceration on that delicate tissue. She moaned through her ball gagged lips.

A wave of wantonness passed through her and she had to move her left hand in front of her to rest on the rim of the tub to avoid falling over. Her pussy was yawning with need. She dropped her soap covered finger from her rear entrance to her gash and slid it up between the folds of her outer labia. She toyed momentarily with the button at their apex and then slipped her finger in her aching hole. It felt so good. And knowing that the man was watching made her pussy burn all the more.

She hadn't planned on making herself come when she had started her little routine, but now her pussy craved completion. Her fingering of her rabidly hot channel became quicker and quicker. Her body felt electrified. She pulled her finger back and, coupling her two longest fingers, began to stroke her pleasure button with earnest. She imagined what the man could see, her hairless sex, her brightly polished nails and her long, thin fingers pressing on her nubbin of delight, all framed by her lean, delectable, alabaster thighs and topped by her roundish, glistening rear orbs.

Her clit was hard now and it slipped and slid against her fingers. She could feel her orgasm rising. Her groans of pleasure echoed through the small room. She prayed and prayed that the man would not order her to stop. "Please! Please! Let me do it! Let me do it!" she thought madly. In the background of her sighs and moans, she heard the sound of him lighting another cigarette and shortly after, sensed a large cloud of gray, acrid smoke fill the room. The thought of his cold, controlled passion while he eyed her self ministrations made her blood steam. She didn't know why, had never experienced the need or compulsion to do this before any of her other lovers, small as their number might be.

The first contraction of her pussy's walls hit her like a hammer. She groaned loudly and her hand's motions accelerated. Her pussy spasmed again and again, drawing repeated exclamations of pleasure from her. "I'm such a whore!" she berated herself as the jolts of pleasure from deep in her chasm made her heart pound and her brain go numb. She was out of breath when her pussy's contractions crested. Her hand slowed and she began to slip her fingers again in and out of her still throbbing portal. Her reason began to return to her. She had forgotten for a moment where she was, what she was.

The man's presence as an ominous, undifferentiated threat returned. The chain that affixed her to the tub became again a heavy weight upon her collar. Her passion spent, the obscenity of the act she had just performed came home to her. She kept telling herself that she had done it to garner additional value in her captor's eyes so that she might live all that much longer, but she knew that she was fooling herself. Something had taken a hold of her, something not unrelated to being an abject prisoner, to being a mere jumble of soft tissue and lubricating excretions, a creature with no will, subject to the never ceasing demands of her cold, cruel master. She had done it to help save her life. She had enjoyed it due to satisfaction of some deep, dark need.

She kept waiting for the man to say something, but he remained silent. Eventually, she withdrew her hand from her crevasse and raised her torso up so that she was standing straight again. She turned to him, shame faced and then crouched down until she was sitting again in the water, rinsing off the soapy residue on her skin. The water had cooled. She closed her eyes to avoid the man's piercing gaze. She was so ashamed of what she had done that she wished she could be sucked down the drain.

The water smelled good from the bath oil the man had put in and she knew that she would emerge from the tub with a tantalizing scent on her. She used the soap to wash her face even though she knew it would make her skin dry. He hadn't allowed her to put on any makeup when they left the motel the other day and she wondered what she looked like. She always liked to put on some moisturizer and a little blush. She did her eyes regularly too. She knew that her eyes must be dark with bags under them from so much stress. Well, it was his fault if she looked this way. He had done it to her.

There was a bottle of shampoo on the shelf next to the tub. She drew herself down so that her head was covered with water and then rose. He watched her as she dropped a dollop of the shampoo in her hand and then soaped up her head. She massaged it in well, covering every strand with shampoo. Then she closed her eyes and lowered herself again, wetting her hair and rinsing out the suds.

When she opened her eyes, the man was still looking at her. He was as naked as she was. It was odd how she just accepted it. She didn't know what he wanted her to do, but if he expected her to lie still in the water, she needed to heat it up a bit. She didn't know whether such voluntary activity would be allowed, but she chanced it.

She leaned forward and turned on the hot water. The water level was just below the overflow drain. She pulled the plug to the tub to let some of the cold water out. She looked at him. He was looking back at her in that disconcerting crooked eye way that he had. It was like there was a jumble of ragged edged things going on in his head and it made him cockeyed. She quickly tore her gaze away. She didn't want him to have any inclination that she thought he was crazy. For all she knew it might enrage him. And he was nasty enough even when he wasn't mad.

After reinstalling the plug, she let the hot water run until the level was up to where it was. She turned it off and leaned back. The chain that was connected to the back of her collar rattled against the porcelain. It reminded her that she wasn't sitting at home wiling away the end of a day. She closed her eyes. She heard the man

light another cigarette. The water felt soothing. She
didn't know why he was giving her this peaceful respite
from his torments, but she intended to take the fullest
advantage of it. After a few moments, the hot water
coaxed her into an almost blissful state. She took a deep
breath and let all of her muscles relax.

Jack was enjoying just watching the girl. He had been
pleased at the little show she gave him. It demonstrated
just how well her training was going. It was too bad it was
all to go to waste. He intended to enjoy every moment of
he could until the end.

She looked so peaceful lying there with her eyes closed.
Her breasts were just breaking through the surface of the
soapy water like little, soft islands wearing reddish top
hats. Her chest gleamed where it had been wet. The blue
ball was just visible between her slightly spread lips. The
chain from her collar ran over the back of the tub behind
her, a stark reminder of her status. Her blond hair was all
wet and matted against her head. It needed to be brushed.
That would be taken care of in a little while.

She lifted her hand and, with her eyes still closed,
brushed a tuft of it off of her forehead. He saw the ring of
red on her wrist from her escape attempt. He had to give
her credit. She was resourceful. If he could figure out a
way to keep her, he would have to maintain a close watch
on her. He would have to keep her away from all sharp
objects and fastened down all the time.

It would be a challenge. He enjoyed a challenge. His
cock was getting hard at the thought of the two of them
in some hacienda somewhere down in the Baja, her naked
and chained, kneeling on the floor, him sitting back in a
big comfy chair smoking a large, hand rolled doobie. He
would have to bar all the windows and keep a little cage

for her for when he had to go out. He would put it on wheels so that he could roll her into a closet when she was bad or when he just got tired of her. And he would want to keep a good stock of whips. Different ones for different occasions.

He looked at her body, partially obscured by the suds and the translucence of the water. It still bore the evidence of his assaults. It would bear more later when he punished her. The thought of her flesh, vulnerable, pale, inviting the lash by its mere existence, almost made him tremble. She was getting to him all right. Getting rid of her was going to be hard to do. But if he played his cards right, they would have at least one or two more 24's to spend together.

Enough was enough. He tossed his smoke in the toilet beneath him and then snapped his fingers. The girl's eyes came immediately open, alert to danger. He motioned her to stand. She rose slowly, the water sluicing off of her fine flesh. When she was standing, the chain to her collar descending down her back, he reached into the tub and drew out the plug. The water began to empty in a rush. He waited until he heard the sucking sound of the drain, indicating that it had all gone down, to order the girl to get out.

He toweled her off, enjoying the sensation of her nearby body. It still radiated the heat of the water and it smelled sweet. She docilely allowed him to move the towel over her breasts and belly. He made her spread her legs so that he could dry her coosh, and then he made her turn around so that he could do her back and her ass.

When he was done drying her, he released her chain from the base of the tub and made her sit on the toilet seat, lean back and spread her legs in the air. She took hold of her ankles to steady herself. He ran his hand over her pudenda. There were a few bristles. Signaling her to remain as she was, he got the soap and razor and turned on the hot water in the sink. He lathered up the soap and covered her loins with it and carefully scraped all the tiny little rebellious bristles away.

After putting the soap and razor back, he ran his hand over the soft skin. It needed lotion and so he got that out and spread some first in his hand to warm it up, and then spread it over the areas where he had shaved. He took his time doing it. Within a few moments, the girl began to shift herself and her breathing became a little labored. He looked her in the face and smiled.

She was hot all right. Placing his thumb just inside the gap between her smooth love lips, he slid it up and down gently, slowly, until the gap began to moisten. He slid some of her pussy's aromatic excretion over her love bud and caressed it with his thumb until she had to draw in a deep breath and suppress a moan. Smiling again, he let her lower her legs and made her stand.

Her hands had been free since he had taken her bracelets off before her bath and he needed to rectify that before he did anything else. The bracelets were lying on the floor. He picked them up and administered them to her wrists, buckling them just a little bit tighter than they had been before and then locking them closed. The girl looked at him dully and forlornly as he did it, knowing what came next. She was right. He spun her around, grabbed her wrists and pulled them behind her back where he locked them in place. She was now as she should be, utterly helpless.

He brought her over to the sink and made her lean over it. He took the chain that led to her collar, passed it between her legs and fastened it to the pipe under the sink. Then he reapplied her ankle bracelets and connected them.

Satisfied that the girl would not go anywhere, he left the bathroom to go back out into the main room. He went over to the bags that held the stuff he had bought at the store the day before and searched around for a box. When he found it, he pulled it out along with a package holding a bright pair of scissors. The last thing was a pair of black rubber gloves.

He brought the items with him into the bathroom. The girl was where he had left her, bent over the sink. She turned her head sideways nervously to see what he was up to. He placed his items on the toilet seat and then turned her head so that she was looking straight down again. He opened the box, pulled out the plastic bottle and the other, smaller containers. There was a sheet of instructions.

He had never dyed hair before, so he was a little nervous about it. But after all, it didn't have to look really good. It just had to be some other color than blond.

The instructions seemed simple enough. He poured the dying agent into the bottle and shook it slightly so that it would mix evenly. He placed that down and then made the girl stand up. He took the brush he had used on his hair earlier and brushed her sun colored hair until all the knots were out.

Carly saw the hair dying kit. She couldn't see what color he had chosen. Her first reaction was outrage. How dare he do that to her! It was her hair after all! But then, she thought about it. She had been worried that he would dispose of her once they got free of the motel room in the morning. She had a vision of him driving down some lonely road and putting a bullet in her brain.

But if he was dying her hair, didn't that mean that he meant to travel with her a while? Of course it did! She was going to live at least another 24 hours. Maybe more. Her heart leapt. She even managed a smile, a difficult thing to do with the blue ball pushing her lips apart. She just hoped that he hadn't picked out a god awful color.

About ten minutes later, he had finished working the foam into her hair. The instructions said that it had to dry for a half hour. He released her ankles from each other, led her back into the main area and tapped the floor with his toe. The girl obediently sunk to her knees, spread her legs and placed her forehead where he had indicated. He drew off the rubber gloves and tossed them into the garbage, lit a smoke and sat down in his chair at the table.

The bottle of Jim Beam was there. He looked at it for a few moments, and then decided that he deserved a drink. The glass he had used earlier to feed some to the girl was still out and he poured himself a few inches. He brought the glass to his nose, taking in the sharp smell, not unpleasant, and then downed a large gulp. It made him shiver going down. It tasted good and he enjoyed the sudden rush of relaxation it brought him. He had not much liked drinking before he had been sent to the joint, but it seemed that 12 years of hard living had changed his tastes. He sipped the remainder of the liquor in his glass while smoking and watching the clock.

When the half hour was up, he rose to his feet and nudged the girl with his toe. She gave a great sigh as she rose from her supplicative position, straightening her back. He took her arm and helped her regain her feet and then led her back into the bathroom. Once there, he had her lean over the sink again and refastened her ankles. He knew that it was strictly not necessary, but he was taking no chances with her. She was liable to take advantage of the least moment of his inattention.

Back in the kitchen he retrieved one of the small bowls in the cabinet. Returning to the bathroom, he started the water from the tub. When it was warm, he filled the bowl and turned to the sink. He poured the water over the girl's head, washing away the remnants of the foam.

He continued to rinse the girl's hair until the water ran clear. Then he lifted her up from the sink. He tested her hair with his fingers to see if all the dye was out of it. His fingers came away clean. She looked up at him concernedly as he toweled her hair dry. Once dry, he brushed it out. Then, he took a look at her. "Not bad," he thought. He had done a good job. No one who looked at her would ever guess that her hair had been blond. In fact, she looked like a totally different woman.

He saw the girl dart her eyes to the mirror several times. She was probably too afraid of him to ask directly if she could see what she looked like. He smiled. "That's right," he thought. "No talking."

He was interested in her reaction to her new appearance and so he turned her around so that she could take a look at herself. When she had been turned, her eyes widened in surprise.

Her hair was now a bright auburn. It almost had a punkish look. It made her seem older. The colors of her face seemed all different. Her eyes seemed darker. Carly suppressed tears. There was hardly a better way for the man to demonstrate his ultimate and complete control over her than this. He had essentially changed who she was. She wondered if she would start to think and act differently to match her new appearance. She would no longer be able to project that light, airy innocence that had been her personality up to the moment of her kidnapping. Who was she now? What would she become?

And then she really had to swallow her grief. Whatever she would become, she probably had no more than 2 days or so to become it. It made her unhappy to think that, if her body was ever recovered, her friends and family would not see the girl they had known, but this new girl with fiery hair. She saw the tears begin to swell up in her eyes and she fought mightily to suppress them.

She sat there docilely on the closed toilet lid while the man snipped away at her newly colored locks. She knew that he was completing her conversion from the girl she once had been to the girl owned and possessed by him. He had draped a towel over her shoulders and chest to catch the snipped of hair. Her hair had been fairly short to begin with. She dreaded to see what it would look like when he was done.

Jack had taken his turn being the cell block barber in stir. He wasn't Vidal Sassoon, but he did a fairly good job. The trick was making it even all around. He was careful to do that on top and on the sides, but he left it long in the back, kind of like a rat's tail. When he was done, he shook the towel out in the sink and brought the girl back to her feet. He took her by the chin and moved her face back and forth, making sure he got it right. He snipped off a bit here and there until it looked perfect.

He smiled and ran his hand over her head. He had cut it down to a little over an inch in length. It bristled nicely when he rubbed it. Now her appearance was really different. In fact, if you looked at her face quickly, she looked a little like a teenaged boy. The tits, of course, gave that away, but tomorrow she would be all wrapped up in her winter jacket. If only he had gotten her some blue jeans at the army navy store the other day, he could complete the picture. But she wouldn't be getting out of the car much, so it really didn't matter.

He saw the troubled look in her face and knew that she was dying to see what she looked like. He reached behind her head and took hold of the length of reddish hair that he had left in place and dragged her over to the mirror. Her face cringed when she saw. That was too bad, he thought. He liked it fine. It was a little like being back at prison when he had been able to get his hands on one of the young kids who had been sent up. There was one he remembered. His name was Raymond, but Jack had changed his name to Ramona. He had sold 5 ounces of cocaine to the wrong man at the wrong time. His was soft and white and slender like this girl. His body had been practically hairless. His hair had even been a little reddish. It had been just like fucking a woman. He had kept her, he had always thought of the kid as a her, for about two years and then, when her time got short, sold her to one of the black gangs for an ounce of dope.

Enough was enough. He pulled the girl back to the toilet and made her pee. He didn't want her making a mess when he whipped her. He had not forgotten her crimes. When she was done peeing, he wiped her and, taking a hold of her hair at the back of her head, dragged her back into the main room.

There was a pipe that went up to wall near the sink. At about 8 feet up, just below the ceiling, it branched off, creating a nice tying off place. He brought the girl there, released her arms from behind her back and then retied them over her head to the pipe. It stretched her arms out over her head, but the front of her feet were still solidly on the floor, her heels lifted slightly. He joined her ankles together. She was turned, facing him, and she had a troubled look on her face. She was smart. She knew that he wasn't doing this merely for amusement, that he certainly had some special purpose in mind. She just didn't know exactly what it was yet.

Carly began to tremble when he had finished tying her off. She remembered the way he had looked at her wrists when he had taken off her bracelets earlier. She had expected a punishment then, but he had skipped it. Now she knew he had not forgotten it. She whined softly and began a little nervous dance, lifting and dropping her feet to the extent that her confines allowed, shifting her weight from foot to foot. Her body had begun to sweat. When she saw him take out the long switch he had used on her before, a sour coldness swept through her.

To Jack, it was like having an entirely new victim. Somehow the girl he had kidnapped had transmorphed into this new, boyish looking, red headed girl. But she was all woman, all right, as her invitingly hairless quim and pleasantly shivering breasts advertised. Beating her with the blue ball in her mouth was going to be eminently better than using the gag since he could see her whole face. It looked so satisfyingly unhappy and distraught. He jostled the handle of the switch, getting his hand used to its weight before using it. Her body was just far enough out from the corner that he would be able to get clean shots at her.

Tears were already streaming down her face. It was a terrible, poignant moment. He knew that most folks would call him an animal for what he had done to the girl, but he didn't give a fuck what other people thought. They were just all hypocrites anyway. Why do you think that all those horror movies sell so well? People like to see horrible things happening to pretty girls, they just don't have the balls to do it, he thought.

Besides, he was doing this for much more important reasons than his enjoyment of it. Though, he did enjoy it. Unlike most people, he would not deny it. But the primary purpose was to ensure that the girl would be too terrified of him to try anything like that to escape again. Even if it only gave her a few moments of hesitation, those moments might be all that he needed to foil her. And about the crying. He didn't need a sniveling, bawling female around. She needed to buck herself up or he would have to get rid of her. He had let her cry before because he knew that she really needed it. But that was a one off. No more bawling after this.

She was staring at him with widened, terrified, starry blue eyes. They matched the color of the rubber ball he could see peeling from her mouth. It made him hard. It was all too good.

His experiences of the last few days were beyond his wildest dreams when he had made his escape. Essentially, he had thought he would be dead by now. Every minute of life now was a gift. Why did he deserve it? He knew that he didn't. He deserved hell for the things that he had done. But here he was, a beautiful, naked and bound woman awaiting his whip. And later he would fuck her. She would suck his cock. He looked at the clock. It was a little before 6 o'clock now. He had at least 6 more hours to play with her before bedding down for the night. He could come three, maybe four more times. He had done a lot of wacking off in prison and he knew just what he was capable of.

No, he didn't deserve this. But didn't that just prove his whole point? There was no justice in this world unless you made it yourself. And, from what he had seen, none in the next. Death was the big sleep, the old dirt nap. Mysterious, unconscious cosmic forces had brought life to this planet. It was all a big accident. A one in ten billion chance. Like the chances of dropping a ball bearing into a cup from the top of the Sears Tower. It could be done, but it was one in ten billion, maybe more. And when it was done, its effects would ripple for a while and then extinguish. In the reckoning of the age and size of the universe, man was just a tiny smudge on the windshield.

She needed to be reminded of her sins before he beat her. He didn't like talking to her. He didn't want her to begin start thinking of herself as a person again. The remoteness between the events and the punishments though made it necessary.

He held the switch up where she could see it well. "Two for crying," he told her. "No more crying. Understand?"

Carly nodded her head frantically. She had forgotten about that. She had known better. He had warned her. She couldn't stop the whine that started in her throat and escaped her gagged mouth. Two was horrible, but she could take it. She had to.

"Ten for trying to escape," he continued. "That was very bad."

The whine that was leaking from her mouth exploded into the level of an air raid siren. "Ten! Oh my god! I won't be able to stand it! Please, please not ten," she thought frantically.

She wanted to beg with him, plead for some lesser punishment, but she knew better than to try and speak. To some extent she had been lulled into complacency about her captivity. The tender way he had caressed her after she had eaten, the wonderful, relaxing bath. Even the dying and cutting of her hair had been done gently.

It had seemed almost like they were on a great adventure together. Maybe they were spies, she had fantasized while she had had her forehead pressed down hard to the floor while the dye had set into her hair and he had sat in his chair smoking and watching her. She had thought about a lot of things, while she had knelt there for so long, naked, bound and silent, fantasies of overcoming him somehow, cutting his throat with a rough blade, maybe watching the police beat the piss out of him and then hang him from the nearest tree. But there had also been the tender ones, the ones in which he recognized her humanity, fantasies of him deciding that he loved her and needed to free her. They had one last, marvelous fuck and then he rode off into the sunset.

Seeing the switch in his hand and the terrible coldness of his eyes dashed all those fantasies apart. She would never escape him. She was doomed. This time with him was all the life she had left. She had to accept it. And she had to accept her punishment for being so stupid to think that somehow she could avoid her fate. He didn't even have to beat her now. She was done trying to escape. But she knew that he would and the idea of having her skin scorched twelve times with that fierce instrument made her knees weak and her throat dry. She closed her eyes and tears ran down her cheeks.

"Turn around," he said.

It was like a voice from the depths of hell. She knew that she had to obey it. But she couldn't move. She was too scared. Then she heard the sound of the whip cutting the air. It landed across her breasts. It felt like a knife had been drawn across them. Her knees weakened. Her body sagged. "Mmmmmmmmmmmm!" she screamed into her gag. Her eyes popped open. He was looking at her coldly.

"That doesn't count," he said sternly. "Now turn around."

Carly moved quickly to comply. All the terror, pain, humiliation and horror of her captivity came down on her all at once. It was so unfair! It was inexplicable! Why was this happening to her? How could it possibly be happening? Her breasts burned like they had been set afire. "Please! Please!" she pleaded to her god. "Make it all go away! Please! Please!"

As soon as she had completed her turn away from the man she heard the whistle of the switch cutting through the air. It landed across the backs of her shins. "Ooooooooooouuuu!" she screamed through her filled mouth. "Oooooouuuuuuuuuu!" Somehow some fierce creature had bitten her. It felt just like that. She had just taken in a deep breath so that she could wail her unhappiness when the second blow fell. It ran across her thighs, just below her buttocks. "Ooooooooouuuuuu! Ouuuuuuuuuuuuu! Ouuuuuuuuuuuuuuu!" she screamed again. She jammed her eyes shut and bit down fiercely on the rubber ball in her mouth.

She waited for the next one, but it didn't come. She whined and cried and pressed her face as hard as she could into the pipe to which she was attached. "Do it now! Do it now! Don't make me wait! Please just get it over!" she prayed desperately.

And then she heard the sound again. She didn't have time to react and brace herself. It tore across her buttocks. She screamed and danced and pulled at her bindings. The next one came directly thereafter just above the last. She didn't have the breath to scream and so her cry of pain just gurgled in her throat.

He waited again. It seemed like he was doing it in groups of two. She was bawling now. She couldn't help it. She tried desperately to stop, frantic that he would double her punishment. She steeled herself for the next pair of blows. She bit down hard on the ball in her mouth. Her eyes were jammed shut. Her hands, confined uselessly above her, were clamped into little useless fists.

She waited and waited and waited. Her crying stopped. She fought off the urge to turn her head and look to see what the man was doing. "Come on! Come on!" she thought. Her mind was overwhelmed by the terror of the moment. She could think of nothing else but the pain she would feel, this time across her back if he was consistent. Her whole body was trembling. Her heart was beating fast and hard and her belly was filled with the ice of fear. Sweat was pouring down her sides. Her joined thighs felt slippery. The backs of her legs and her ass still burned from the wounds he had inflicted.

She was fighting off the urge to break out again into woeful sobs. "Do it! Do it!" she yelled inside. A dismal whine rose up from her belly. She knew it was coming and tried to fight it off. She knew that if it came out, she would fall to pieces. She held it and held it and held it, and then could hold it no more. She released a dismal wail of self pity and sadness and desperation. It was followed by a series of abject sobs. And then, out of nowhere, as if he had been waiting for her to break down from fear, the next two strokes came in rapid succession. They burned and burned and she could not hold back.

"Turn around," she heard from behind her. Later, when she thought about it, she did not know where the strength came to obey this command. She knew that his purpose was to make her belly and breasts subject to his whip. She only realized that she had turned, making little hops on her fastened feet, when she opened her eyes and saw his fearsome, ferocious, naked bulk standing there, the whip at the ready. His cock was hard.

Casting all caution aside, she had begun to form in her mouth forbidden words of supplication when she saw his right arm move forward. She just had time to draw in a deep breath. It landed across her belly. It felt like a line of fire had erupted there. And then the second came across her thighs. She screamed and cried, thankful at least that she would have a moment's respite before the next one, but she was wrong.

A blow fell immediately across her breasts and then on her belly and then on her thighs once again. She screamed and contorted and cried and sobbed as the five vicious strokes consumed her like a devilish whirlwind. There was a pause. She had jammed her eyes shut but she opened them now. It was the last one. She saw the fire in the man's eyes. Her agonies had awoken the demon in him. She saw his hand go back, jammed her eyes shut and stiffened. The last blow came cross her breasts, atop her nipples. She screamed, went limp and resumed her sobs.

Jack took a deep breath. It was a good thing he had told her that he was going to only give her a dozen. The last blows, face to face, had fed the beast that sometimes ruled him. His hand gripped the handle of the switch like it was a lifeline. He watched the girl sobbing and crying. It was spectacular.

Slowly, his blood cooled. The girl's sobs softened to a whimper. Her face was awash with tears. Bright red lines striped her body. He tossed the whip aside. If he held on to it too long, he would begin to use it again and then he might not stop until the girl had been rendered useless. He stepped up to her and raised her chin. "Learned your lesson?" he asked her.

Her red rimmed eyes looked at him imploringly. She nodded her head quickly. He ran his hand over her short, bristly hair. "Obedience or the whip. Understand?" he said.

She nodded her head up and down eagerly again. She would obey him as if he were her god. The old one had not done her any good.

"Turn around," he told her.

Hopping on her bound feet, she obeyed instantly. She was still sniffling from her ordeal, but apparently he didn't really count that as crying. When she had her back turned to him, her wrists bound above her, he stepped away from her for a moment and returned. He slipped the blindfold over her head and deprived her of sight. Then he filled her ears with the rubbery plugs he had used on her earlier in the day. She suppressed a moan of unhappiness at being isolated once again.

She sensed him moving away and then returning. He leaned down and unfastened her legs, pulling them apart. His hands reached around her and she felt him applying around her waist the belt that held the huge plastic prong. A moment later, she felt the head of the instrument probe at her nether entrance. She moaned as he pressed it forward. Her ring had grown taut since its last use and needed to be expanded all over again. It hurt, but she suppressed her whine of complaint, biting down on the ball in her mouth. He had apparently lubricated it. He slid it in slowly as if he wanted her to fully appreciate its girth and length.

When the instrument was fully seated, the man finished up by attaching the chains that ran on either side of her vulva down from the front of belt and the one that led up to the back. Her feet were pushed back together and attached to each other. She felt him connect them in turn to the pipe. Then she felt something pass under her chin. A second later, her collar was also tied off, making her press her body up against the pipe. It ran between her breasts and her knees and belly pressed up against it. She had to turn her face to the side. Then he stepped away.

She was once more reduced to virtually total isolation. She, of course, did not know how long it would last. But while it did last, she knew that she would spend her time contemplating her recent beating and the last words he spoke to her. Obedience or the whip. Nothing could be made more clear.

CHAPTER SEVEN

Jack stepped back and contemplated the figure of the bound girl. He was still all worked up from beating her and he squeezed his tumescent cock just enough to send himself a little message of pleasure. He would fuck her again soon, but he wanted the fire in him to subside first. Otherwise he would fuck her too fast and if he fucked her pretty little, slightly swaying ass all worked up as he was, in remembrance of Ramona, he might damage her. He didn't want to fuck damaged goods. Getting her off was a big part of the fun of the whole thing and it was unlikely she would get off if she was hemorrhaging inside.

He went back to the bathroom to clean up. He swept the floor and the toilet, getting up all the hair. He was careful to put all the stuff related to dying her hair in a small bag with it. He would dispose of the bag somewhere else. If the cops ever discovered he had been here, with any luck they might not discover that he had changed her hair color. Even if it delayed them 24 hours, it could be a big help. In 24 hours, he planned to be in New Mexico getting ready to hide out in a safe house, if not there already.

There were some red smudges on one of the towels and he soaped it up and washed it thoroughly. All that was left were faint traces of pink.

He caught a sight of himself in the mirror. It was time for a shave for him too. He got out the shaving stuff and soaped up his face. Carefully, he scraped away his growth. The razors they had in the joint were little tiny things with shitty blades. He wasn't used to shaving himself with something so sharp. When he had removed the last bristly bit, he washed off the remnants of the soap in the sink. Then, as he was toweling off his face, he gave himself a good look in the mirror.

He tried to recall what he looked like when he went off to prison. He had been younger obviously. But the prison grind had definitely aged him quicker than he would have on the outside. He didn't look exactly ugly, but he was getting pretty close to it. It must freak out the girl, he thought. So much the better. But he realized that it made him somewhat more noticeable, noteworthy. And he realized that a 5 o'clock shadow made it all the worst. He would make sure that he shaved again in the morning.

Carly could hear nothing of what he was doing and had to imagine it. She knew that he would be cleaning up. He was so fastidious when it came to that. And she would be able to smell it if he smoked a cigarette or cooked something to eat. She could also tell when he walked around since she could feel the vibration of the floor in her feet. But she couldn't tell when he was just watching her, plotting some new outrage on her body. He had reinstalled the plug in her ass. It was so very readily available the way he had secured her. She deduced that that was where the next assault would come. Unhappily, she prepared herself for the renewal of that indignity.

She could hear her own breathing and the rush of her blood in her ears, but nothing else. She could have hummed or made some other sound, just to break the monotony of those others, but she was too frightened that he would hear it. She had no way on measuring how loud the sounds might be. For all she knew she might be issuing a reverberating howl into the room, something that she knew she would suffer for. "Obedience or the Whip." That was what he had said. And she knew that he meant it. Her body still remembered the viciousness of her beating. Her mind still remembered the pain and the terror. She didn't want a repeat.

Her feet ached due to the elevation of her heels. It tended to curve them into an arch that was painful to sustain. She twisted and pulled at her wrists held up above her, not in an attempt to free them. She would never do that again! It was just habit forming to try and turn them and use them, just to remember that she held some power over them, that they were still hers.

The unforgiving nature of their bindings made a sourness pass through her. "Oh god, oh god, oh god…" she moaned inwards. It was so awful to be tied so firmly like this, to be so powerless. Outside of their little cabin, millions, billions of people were going about their daily lives free of terror, free of physical oppression. Even criminals in their prisons had the right to walk about, if only within their cells. The man had undoubtedly had that freedom but yet had no compunction about imposing a more dismal confinement on her than he had ever endured. It was so unfair that every time she thought of it she felt like she might get sick. And the fact that it was all going to end in darkness, utter, final and permanent darkness, made it all the worse.

Was there a life following this? This issue had lost all of its academic character. It was all too real now. She had to believe that there was. The other was too terrible and unfair to contemplate. So much of people's lives was made up of work and worry and pain that it was difficult to see the worth of life unless some better, friendlier, happier world was waiting.

She would see her father. It was hard to remember his face. But she remembered his gleeful eyes, his strong arms that had held her, his powerful, resonating voice. She remembered the warmth she felt whenever she saw him. If suffering what she was suffering meant that she would be with him soon, then she could see some worth in it. She could almost accept it with resignation and peace. If only she had some sign, that some voice within her would send her a message that that was true. But no message came. All she had were the cruelty of her bindings and the sure knowledge that sooner or later, the man would inflict more suffering upon her.

Jack came out of the bathroom refreshed. He saw the girl squirming slightly at her bonds. It made her ass wriggle invitingly. He walked over to the table. The Jim Beam was still sitting there. He unscrewed the top and took a nice mouthful. It burned nice going down. It made his body trill. He took another. That felt even better. He looked again at the girl. His cock twitched. He was ready.

Shucking off his shorts and t-shirt, he approached her. He heard her issue a whine as he came near and he realized that she sensed his closeness. That was okay. She would know it for sure soon enough.

He studied her body for a while. Her back was graceful and her hips just wide enough to give her torso a slight hourglass shape. Her compressed thighs were firm and smooth. There were slight dimples in her taut, appealing rear mounds. Red stripes colored her from her neck to virtually her ankles. They stood out nicely from her pale flesh. Her red hair made her seem exotic. It was almost like someone had whisked away the blond girl he had been holding and had replaced her with this similar but definitely different one. A more exciting model.

His lust was growing. He stepped closer. Her breathing had become more intense, heavier, as if she knew what was coming. He reached out his hands at waist level and gently placed them on the cheeks of her inviting ass. Her flesh shuddered at his touch. It was hot, as if she had burning up with desire for him. He knew that she detested his use of her and that the idea of her pining for his touch was just a fantasy, but it was a nice one and one which she had no power to dispel. He knew too that she had derived pleasure from their encounters and that she would from this one as well, knowledge that she undoubtedly shared. Hence that shudder of her flesh. She knew that once he took command of it, she was powerless to deny the efficacy of his caresses, the iron will of his cock.

He ran his hands over her hips and up her torso. She shuddered again. He pressed himself against her, circled her torso with his hands and took possession of her breasts. She issued a long, lustful sigh.

The pipe lay between her mounds and spread them slightly to the sides. He caressed and massaged them gently, thoroughly, playing with the nipples, squeezed them hard and then pinched the nipples harshly. She whined and squirmed. He laid his lips upon her soft, naked shoulders, kissing her, lapping at her skin with his tongue, reveling in the aromatic odor which the bath oils had given her.

He wanted access to her cunt. He leaned down and unhooked her ankles from the pipe and from each other. He didn't need to speak to her. He just insinuated his hands between her thighs and pushed them apart. She obeyed easily, even though her more widely spread legs put more pressure on her feet and hands. He dribbled his fingers across her coosh, enjoying the softness and plumpness of it and then dragged a finger down the length of her crevasse, nudging her love lips aside. She was already wet. He took some moisture onto the tip of his finger and spread it over her clit. She stiffened when he touched it, but then her body softened and she issued a pleasured moan.

He worked her pussy for several minutes. He didn't want her to come just yet, but he wanted her raging hot. She moaned and sighed and rotated her hips as he played with her sex. He kept one hand on her breasts, massaging and caressing each in turn, while he played with her love bud, ran his fingers in and out of her canal, teased the flesh all around it. He kissed her back and the exposed portions of her neck. He twisted her nipples. He ran his hand over her rear globes. Soon she was a quivering mass of inflamed flesh.

At that point, he unbuckled the chains from the probe in her rear. Crouching down next to her, he kept up his torment of her pussy with one hand while he slid the invader in and out of her distended hole. She shuddered and moaned and her hips rocked back and forth slowly to meet his efforts.

Carly thought that she might go mad. Her body was twisted into a huge knot that only an orgasm could relieve. The man kept her just on the brink of it. Part of her wanted to beg him to allow her to come, but she knew better than to talk. That and the shame she would feel at pleading with him to give her pleasure kept her silent except for the anguished moans and groans that she emitted that echoed loudly throughout her head.

The movement of the probe in her rear entrance accelerated her needs beyond the tolerable. She was powerless to stop it, but the thing of it was that that was not want she wanted to do. Its deliberate, almost torpid pace was excruciating. Faster! She wanted it to go faster! "Faster, please! Please! Please!" she thought deliberately. She recalled what had happened when she tried to dictate the pace of their fucking once before so she abjured from pistoning her hips. But she wanted to, needed to. She moaned loudly in her frustration.

Her moan told Jack that she was ready. He stood and slowly slipped the black plastic probe from her ass and put it aside on the floor. He forced her legs back together and then locked her ankles again to the pipe. He retreated from her for a moment, covering his cock with the lubricant, and then readvanced.

When the probe left her, Carly knew that it was only moments before she would feel the introduction of the man's hot, rigid pole. Her rear portal gaped in expectation. When he felt him press her legs back together, she knew that he was ensuring himself a tight fit. Despite the use of the probe, the presence of his cock would expand the opening and she would moan from the pain. But the pain would be, she also knew, a mere presage for the ecstatic pleasure that would follow and she resigned herself to receiving it. When the head of his instrument probed at her opening, she issued a moan of expectation. When it began its forward movement she groaned and whined as the pain of the splitting tissue tore through her.

He advanced his cock until it was fully within her. His chest was up against her back. His thighs were against the outside of hers. His hands crept around and took hold of her breasts. There was a long, excruciating moment of pause. She shuddered in anticipation of his movement. And then he began.

As before, the abrasion along her now widened circle of flesh came slow and steady. He was clearly in no hurry. But instead of being dead and remorseless, this invader was hot and alive. As it traversed her anus's ring, it delivered a wave of pleasure that reverberated throughout her body but more specifically in the depths of her cunt.

He went on and on. Her passion continued to build. His flesh was all around her, encompassing her, and she was held virtually perfectly motionless by her bonds. She could feel his cock's steady, rhythmic movements, the movement of his chest, the muscles of his thighs, the ministrations of his relentless hands on her breasts, his belly against her back, but she could not hear his labored breath or his grunts of pleasure. And she was in complete darkness. It was like being fucked by some alien creature, one that knew just how to torment her flesh and bring her irresistible streams of delight.

Her orgasm drew closer and closer. It was growing deep inside of her. It started at a spot deep in her belly. It grew like a giant balloon, expanding her consciousness of it. And like a balloon, it was stretching wider, wider, wider. It was only a matter of time before it burst. She had no control over it. His cock was like a pump, forcing more and more fevered air into it. She almost heard a loud, high pitched squeal of escaping air a moment before it blew.

And then it was upon her. Her pussy clenched hard on itself. She could feel her anal muscle grabbing hard at the relentless invader. She groaned and her body shook. Her mind became feverish and it felt like every cell in her body was vibrating adagio.

When the first intense, almost unbearable wave passed, her convulsions continued as the man's cock kept up its remorseless pace, his hands maintained their ceaseless explorations and deprecations of her breasts. She could feel her heart wildly pounding away. She bit down harshly on the gag in her mouth and her hands strained at their bonds.

For a moment, and it was only a moment, her body's rejoicing waned. It was just long enough for her to take in a deep, labored breath, just long enough for her mind to recall where she was and what was being done to her, just long enough for her to realize that the man's abrasions of her anal ring were going to continue despite her completion, and that there would come a time, a time which was rapidly approaching, that the pleasures she had been feeling would turn against her, that the pulses of electrical joy her body was feeling would become so strong, so imperious, that it would drive her mad with raging lust.

She panicked. "Mmmmmmmmm! Mmmmmmmmm-mmm! Mmmmmmmmmmmm!" she cried out in desper-ation. "Please stop! Please stop! Please stop!" her mind raged. But it was of no use. Even if the man could hear her, could understand her, he would have no inclination to spare her, to shorten by one instant his pleasures, to grant her even momentary respite. And it was too late anyway, for, in the very next instant her pussy exploded again and its mighty contractions sent her into delirium.

Jack was fully conscious of the torment he was delivering to the girl. It stoked his lust to no end. But he was in eminent control of himself and was enjoying too much the abrasions of her flesh on his cock to want to cut it short. Her body was sweating heavily and her musk commingled with the perfume of the oils of her bath to produce a mesmerizing odor. Her flesh was hot. Her breasts were firm and fluid and each time he squeezed them, his mind received a jolt of pleasure. Her body, although tied firmly down, was writhing and squirming against him. And when she came, her ring tightened again and again in time with her pussy's pulses, granting him fits of ecstasy.

He drew his cock back and forth slowly, steadily, letting the tight anal lips caress him the whole length. She was whining and moaning and squirming against him, struggling against her bonds as if someone had set her on fire. Suddenly, the urge to climax overwhelmed him. He began stroking faster and harder, pounding his belly against the rise of her mounds. He took her nipples in his fingers and twisted them viciously, making the girl howl. His need was building. He leaned his head back and issued a great growl. He released her teats and wrapped his arms around her torso, pulling her firmly into him. He felt the echoes of a new round of contortions from her pussy. It was all he needed.

His cock felt like it was jetting his balls directly into her. It jolted him with throb after thrilling throb. His cock danced as he planted it deep inside her again and again, banging her body up against the pipe, squeezing her thighs between his, making the little hole that was thrilling him as tight as it could be.

When his orgasm was spent, he leaned against the girl. She was moaning and whining. She began to cry and he took hold of her teats and twisted them. She stopped immediately. His chest was heaving and his heart was pounding. He slid his softening cock back and forth a few more times, enjoying a few post orgasmic twinges. "This keeps just getting better and better," he thought.

He slipped his limp but still blood engorged cock from her ass. She sighed as it exited. He ran his hands down over her shoulders and back in gratitude for the pleasure she had given him. Stooping down to the floor he picked up the black probe, spread her rear cheeks with his right hand, and pushed its head into the little hole. It gave a slight tug of resistance and then sank in. He buckled up the chains that held it in place and stepped back. The girl's body was covered with sweat and her body was still trembling. He rubbed her red, short haired head a couple of times, patted her in the ass, and stepped away.

For a moment, he just watched her. In the old days, the guys would be lined up right now, waiting their turn. They would keep the hole nice and greased so that the girl could go all night. After everybody had had their first turn, then, during the rest of the party, guys would sidle up as the need arose and get off again. But since the other whores would be around, not too many took second licks. Mostly the girl just had to stand there silent and in silence waiting for some anonymous prick to stuff her again. They didn't always have new girls at their parties, so the current clubhouse sluts would draw rubber balls out of a hat. Whoever got the black ball took her turn at the pipe for the night.

She wasn't exactly crying, but he could see that she was doing the next best thing. Her body was shuddering and her breathing was still coming deep and heavy. As long as no actual weeping came out of her, he would cut her some slack.

He went into the bathroom and washed himself off. Back in the kitchen area, he rounded up some snacks and a glass of juice. He took them, his smokes and the ashtray over to the bed. After redonning his boxers, he set himself up on the mattress and flicked on the TV.

Carly had heard him moving back and forth. She was striving at her most intent not to cry. Her backside still hummed from her fucking. The reinsertion of the black probe seemed to be keeping it going as if she expected the plastic instrument to start moving back and forth inside her at any minute of its own volition. She wanted so much just to curl up into a ball somewhere and close her eyes, put all of this behind her for a little while.

It was hard to believe that less than an hour or so ago she had been relaxing peaceably in the tub. Now she was back in fierce isolation, unable virtually to move a muscle. It was so awful not to be able to move your hands and legs. And to have her mouth distended and stuffed, it was like his prick was continuously within her. Waves of deep, chilling despair and fear passed through her, enough to make her want to scream out loud, to shake and squirm her body, to pull and tug frantically at her bonds.

It made her belly sour. Her mind felt like it was revving at a high speed, constantly flitting back and forth between resentment, sorrow and anger, whining like some high pitched electric motor given a task well outside its design specs, straining to do the job, knowing that at any moment it could erupt into a fatal frazzlement and explode. "Please! Please! Please! Someone rescue me! Please! Please! Please!" she begged of the universe, the one outside their little cabin, the one that was so indifferent to her sufferings.

Her pussy was still humming too. She couldn't believe that she had come so hard so many times from being fucked in her ass. In her previous life she had thought the practice dirty and disgusting and demeaning to women. Maybe it was all those things, but it had introduced her to a sensuality well beyond what she had ever imagined. It would be, she knew, if she ever got free and did it again with Randy or with some other guy, tied inextricably to her time with her tormentor. She would be able to recreate the thrill and terror and excitement that being fucked by him brought. It would be like a magic button that could be pushed, bringing her back to this place, this room, this pipe she was tied to.

She wondered what time it was. She had relatively only a few more hours to undergo his abuse yet today. In an hour or so it would be nightfall, if it wasn't already. And then a few hours after that sleep. Tomorrow they would be back on the road with whatever that brought.

Part of her, a part she thought degraded and shameful, rued that fact that her time ensconced here in their little pleasure cabin was soon to be over. Part of wanted to spend an eternity at that peak of passion that he brought her to, that moment of sartoris where nothing else existed except the thrusts of his mighty cock, the strength and callousness of his hands on her breasts, the heat of his remorseless mouth and tongue, kissing her or on her cunt. She shuddered just thinking what he had done to her and what he undoubtedly was going to do again and again until their time together ended in blackness for her.

She wondered if he would think of her. Was she among the memorable of his copulations or just another pleasant, compliant body? When he got where he was going, and by now she had figured out that Mexico was his probable destination, and she was sure that he would get there, he was too smart and ruthless to fail, when he was fucking his little senoritas, filling their mouths like he filled hers, taking possession of their holes, like he possessed hers, working his violence on their bodies as he had worked it on her, would his mind go back to their few days together and feel even a little remorse at having had to get rid of her?

But then, again, he would have two women to remember. There was the innocent blond girl who he had captured and despoiled. She was already gone. And then there was the firecracker of a redhead who thrilled at being used by him, yearned for his prick, wanted nothing more than to be devoured by him. Which one would he remember best? Which one was her true self?

The thought of what he had made of her brought on a suffusion of tears. She held herself back from sobbing. He would hear that and beat her again. But she couldn't stop the wetness from flowing behind her eye mask. She couldn't help the powerful feeling of loss that came over her. And there she was again. She couldn't help wanting to scream and rage and struggle and call out her hatred of him and all he was.

Jack was enjoying the show. It was one of those courtroom things with the lady judge making assholes out of everybody. A fat lady was suing her former boyfriend because he stole her engagement ring and gave it to another broad. The question was whether the ring actually belonged to the girlfriend or was it given to her on condition that they marry.

It appeared that an old boyfriend of the fat lady had shown up and the fiancé had caught them balling in their house trailer. Jack imagined the dumb fuck coming home and seeing the flimsy trailer rocking back and forth as the fat lady and her old flame got it on. She was wearing this tight white, stretchy blouse that held her huge tits tight. You could see her nips as big as thumbs sticking out. The fiancé was as skinny as a string bean with long, floppy, black hair and a gold tooth.

The lady judge ruled that the engagement ring was not given on the condition that they get married because the fiancé could have frustrated that purpose just by calling the whole thing off. But it was, she said, conditional on the fat lady keeping herself pure and all that shit. So by fucking her old flame she lost the right to the ring.

After, the fat lady and the skinny guy posed for the camera. The fat lady was hopping mad. The skinny guy was grinning. Just after he announced his engagement to his new girl friend, the fat lady reared back and clocked him right in the jaw. He went down like a dead man and all hell broke loose.

Laughing, Jack changed the channel. He went through a couple of cop shows, what looked to be a soap opera, a game show and then he was on the news channel once again. He lit a smoke and decided to watch it to see if there was any more on about the fire in Wausau at the old clubhouse.

First he had to sit through a lot of political news. He grabbed a handful of nuts and started chewing them. He hated politicians more than cops. At least cops you knew couldn't be trusted. They had bought a couple of politicians in the old days. They liked it swell when he handed them their cash or let them into the motel room where the obedient whore was waiting for them. But when the shit hit the fan, they all disappeared.

There was a large earthquake in some Arab country, demonstrations in some Asian place, a feature story about some sports guy helping children, a couple of commercials and then more national news.

The second story was about the shootout in Wausau. Three cops had been killed. The fire department had hosed down all the flames and they were still picking through the wreckage. Everything inside had been burned to ash. The Chief of the State Police and the Attorney General and a bunch of other cops stood around a microphone all pitying and sorrowful for the young girl who had been killed, but telling the public that everything was a net good since they had gotten rid of so many bad guys. The broadcast cut away to some stock footage of his trial, the prison where he had done his 12 years, pictures of the two guards he had cut open in his escape, a picture of the girl looking young and innocent. He knew better.

The pretty and earnest young woman who was making the report finished it up by saying that "…One thing is for sure. The people of Wausau will sleep better and safer tonight. Back to you John."

Jack laughed. The people of Wausau had their heads up their asses if they believed that. The Ruffians, a younger, tougher, more ruthless new club had been itching to expand in the Wausau area for years. Jack got all the reports in jail. They were probably on the move as he sat there, rolling up the Rogues' storefronts, taking over selling locations, sweeping up their whores. A few of the Rogues would fight back, but they would be outnumbered now and would either be forced to retreat to another chapter somewhere else or die.

The one thing that made him nervous was that there had been no statement from the FBI. He knew that they were no fools. The fact that there had been no FBI statement told him that they weren't buying the burnt up in a terrible conflagration story. Somewhere out there were G-men looking for him. Oh, and yeah, G-ladies now too. He could spot an FBI guy right off. They ran them through a machine there at Quantico that made them all the same. He imagined that the ladies would be that way too. Kind of like those guys in Dragnet, "just the facts, ma'm." They would be cool and calm and hard. And they would be like hound dogs that never let go of a scent.

He looked over at the girl. She had just issued a loud whine. He knew that the stuffing in her ears made it difficult for her to know how loud she was moaning so he didn't get mad. If she kept it up though, he would have to do something about it.

He decided to get up and make some coffee. He went to the stove. The pot was clean from the morning and all he had to do was fill it with water and coffee. It was so great to be able just to get up and get things. Anytime he wanted. And real coffee was a thousand times better than that watered down, stale shit they got in stir.

Once he had it on the stove, he turned on the gas and started to heat it up. He stepped back. The girl was standing only a few feet away from him. He realized that she had undoubtedly sensed him coming near. She looked like she had tensed up and she was squirming a little. He stepped over to her. He could not resist running his hands up and over her hips, up over her shoulders and down her back. He squeezed her ass and gave the probe in her ass a little jiggle that made her squeal. Reaching around her torso, he took hold of her tits and squeezed them. He could still smell the aroma of the bath oils he had put in the tub. They were just a little tinctured by the smell of her sweat. It smelt funky and he liked it. Her skin was so smooth and soft. He loved running his hands over it.

The coffee pot began to boil and he went over and turned down the gas. He noticed the Jim Beam bottle on the table. He realized that he should put it away. It was too much of a temptation. He was getting to like the little buzz it gave him whenever he took a swig. When he picked it up, he unscrewed the cap and poured himself a mouthful. It burned good going down and gave him a rush. He put the cap back on and put the bottle back down on the table. He decided that he might want a snort later too. And then he remembered the joints the girl had been carrying. They had smoked 2 of the four. The last time, he had taken a toke or two and he had liked the effect.

He rummaged around in their stuff and came up with the girl's pretty, yellow handbag. It made him think of the skimpy, yellow dress she had been wearing when he took her. He still had that and the high heel shoes in one of the bags. He relished for a moment the little strip tease he had made her do. She had come a long way since her reticence to display her considerable charms before him. He looked over at her bound form. Yeah, even if he let her go now, she would never be the same. He had shown her the dark places in her soul. She could have resisted him, fought tooth and nail and preserved her pride, but she didn't.

The mere threat of violence had been enough to make her do what he wanted. He had shown her that her pride and all the veneer of culture that had been painted on her animalistic nature was worth less than her life. She had bartered her dignity for the smallest increment of additional life, an hour, a day. She couldn't be sure how long her surrender had purchased for her. But even one instant weighed more in the scheme of things than those things she had undoubtedly until the very moment that she had seen him in her car thought sacrosanct. The first blow of pain had washed them all away.

He removed the joint from the tin and stuffed the tin back into the little, yellow pocketbook. He saw her wallet. He pulled it out. He went over to the bed, propped up the pillows and lay back against the headboard. He fired up the joint and took a long, deep toke. The delivery of pleasant wooziness came right away. "First the booze and now dope," he thought.

12 years in prison had changed him, that's for sure. Years ago, he wouldn't have come near anyone smoking a joint. His mind was sharp and ambitious. You couldn't run a gang of outlaws if you were fucked up half the time. He had built a little empire. Money and pussy had poured in. Now he would be content with a little piece of the world. He wanted just to lay back and mellow out. He couldn't wait to get to Mexico.

He leafed through the wallet as he smoked the joint. He looked at her driver's license. She was smiling in the picture. It was a carefree smile, one he hadn't seen since he had taken her.

He knew that there was no way she would have voluntarily given him the time of day in the real world. Her life was light and breezy, full of sunshine, days at the lake, going to the movies, enjoying the simple things. She would have been repelled by his dark mien. Hers was a side of life he had never known. He had sometimes wondered how he would have turned out if he had been born into one of those 'normal' middle class families, with a father who didn't spend most of his time in prison and a mother who wasn't a drunk and a whore.

His father was dead. He had died in a motorcycle accident when Jack was just 9. He was drunk and high, of course. From then on, there was a long line of circulating men in his mother's life. They used her and slapped her around when she became a pain or just for the fun of it.

Jack had tried to intercede once. The guy, a truck driver for a logging company, a big, bruising guy with a heavy red beard and arms as big as tree trunks, had laughed and then knocked him into the next week. When he came to, the guy was gone and his mother was curled up, passed out in her bed, a bottle of vodka by her side, blood all over her face and torn clothes. There were three twenty dollar bills on the bed. It was pretty much from that moment that he had promised himself two things. The first was that he would never let anybody fuck with him again. He learned to use a knife and hardened himself. The second was that he would never let himself get emotional over a cunt.

But if things had been different, he could have dated a sweet, young thing like this girl. He looked over her name. Carly. Carly Walker. He made a vow to remember it, whatever happened. He recalled the picture of her boyfriend. He was clean cut and looked eagerly pleasing. He flipped to it in her picture section. He was blondish with short cut hair. Not a hint of a whisker on his face. It was a head and shoulder shot, maybe a high school picture. That meant that the girl had been seeing him for a long time. She had been over to fuck him the night Jack had grabbed her. She smoked dope with him and probably sucked his cock with loving care.

He felt a pang of jealousy that this twerp had possessed a part of the girl he would never see. He would never see her laugh or smile like that in her picture. She would never dress up in sexy finery for him, not voluntarily anyway, nor paint her toenails, or smile when she saw him or anything like that. The thought of it gave him a pain somewhere he usually never felt it. It made him feel lonely and bitter and angry at what the world had made him become.

The bottle of sour mash was still on the kitchen table. He got up and took possession of it and brought it back to the bed. He took a long pull and then a strong toke of the joint. He felt like getting a little mindless tonight. He needed to make that pain go away.

He knew that he was torturing himself, but he continued his tour through the girl's life. There was a picture of an older woman, probably her mother. She was nice looking and well preserved. Not like his mother at all. She had been all worn out at 32. She had developed a smack jones after he had left her at 14. He had seen her a couple of times. It made him feel like crushing her between his hands, squeezing the life out of her. Why did she keep on living if she was so miserable? Why hadn't one of her dirt bag boyfriends done her a favor and put her out of her misery?

She had shown up at his trial one day. He had become enraged at seeing her. Later, in the holding area, one of the sheriff's officers had said something to him and he had leapt at the guy, trying to tear his throat out. He spent the rest of the trial in shackles.

He flipped past the picture of the girl's mother. There was a picture of the girl with two of her girl friends. Nice pieces of ass. They were all laughing and smiling in their tiny, little skirts and revealing tops. The picture looked like it had been taken at a county fair or something. It was definitely a warm summer night. A merry-go-round was behind them and people were walking past them in the background.

The only times he had gone to county fairs was to sell skag or to scout for girls who might be potential recruits for their operations, girls who looked lonely and beat down, who might accept an invitation to go for a ride on his chopper. They would never come back. Sometimes the papers ran pictures of them if somebody missed them. Often nobody did and the girl would disappear into a new life as an owned whore.

There was no way he would have considered recruiting the girls in this picture. It was clear that they had lives where someone would make a big fuss if they vanished. They would have brought a good price though. They were prime meat on the hoof, young and pretty and virtually untouched. Their innocence just begged to be destroyed.

There were no more pictures. There was a membership card in some gym, a AAA card, a medical insurance card, a library card. All accouterments of normal life. Well, she would never go back to it.

A wave of self disgust passed through him. He had destroyed this girl's life. It made him think of all the terrible things that he had done. His was a life of evil manifest. He took another toke of the joint and a swig of the Jim Beam. "So what!" he thought. Life hadn't been fair to him, why should it be fair to anyone else? He had no right to regret who he was and who he had become. He had chosen it. And it was not one of those choices you could just go back on. He had made a deal with the devil and he had to play it out. He tossed the wallet across the room.

The coffee was ready. He had forgotten about it. He got up from the bed, took another toke of the joint and dropped the still considerable roach into the ash tray.

Walking across the small room, he felt a little woozy. It was an unfamiliar sensation, but not totally unwelcome. He turned off the gas under the coffee pot and let it settle. The girl must have sensed him moving about, because she squirmed a little and issued a little whine.

He stepped over to her. Her body was so enticing. She jumped when he placed his hands on her, running them up and down her sides, over her hips and her ass. It made his lusts stir in him. If he had chosen a normal life, he wouldn't be standing here now, this girl's flesh at his command, he thought. He would never have felt the thrill of ownership of a piece of tail. He would never have fucked the maybe two hundred pussies he had done, maybe more. He would never have had them plead and squeal and whine for mercy, never seen the abject terror in their eyes, never have received their utter and complete subservience. He would have fallen in love with one of them and she would have crushed the life out of his affections, just like his mother had poured shit all over him as a kid.

No, he had made the right choice. And if this girl was paying the price, that was too bad. She had no right to her safe and happy life when he was angry and hateful. She had no right to be smiling and laughing, carefree, ignorant of the real ways of the world, when he was knee deep in it. She was his for the taking, and if her life was to meet a bitter end, she at least had had the other part to compensate her for it. It was more than he ever had.

He reached around her torso and squeezed her tits. He played with their nipples until they were stiff. He leaned over and sucked at her neck and shoulders pressing his naked back against hers while he mashed and kneaded her two beauteous orbs. He ran his hand down her sweet belly and toyed with the crux of her thighs which, with her legs together, squeezed her sex between them.

His cock was hard again, but he wasn't ready for another bout with her. He had just wanted to remind her of who owned her, reestablish his proprietorship. She was fine as she was for now, put away, stored for future use. She deserved everything she got.

He took a step away from her. He reared his heavy right hand back and gave her a vicious slap on her buttocks. Then another, and another. The sound of skin marring skin reverberated through the room. She whined and moaned in reply and issued a deep sob. His hand had left bright red prints on her alabaster ass. He thought for a moment in his haze of taking the whip to her beautiful, vulnerable back. What right did she have to the life she led when his had been all shit!

But then he calmed himself. Her back was already striped with the evidence of his harshness. She had done nothing wrong. Wasn't spending her last few days as his slave enough punishment? He recalled his resolve to avoid unnecessary cruelty to her. "Okay, okay," he thought. "Enough of this." He turned back to the stove.

After pouring his coffee he returned to the bed. On the way, he pulled out a book from one of the bags. It was a spy thriller, one he hadn't read yet from an author he liked. In his stories, beautiful spy girls were always getting their comeuppance. The hero was a guy a lot like him who didn't give a shit about anybody. It was fun to watch the body count rise as he fucked his way through the novel, discarding the women afterwards as if they were tissue he had wiped his ass with.

Carly was holding back her tears. The blows to her buttocks had been fierce and unexpected. She couldn't think of anything she had done wrong. How could she have when for the last hour or so she had been standing stock still listening to nothing except the sound of her own breathing, seeing nothing but the absolute blackness in front of her, unhappily shifting and moving her body in the minute range of motion her impediments allowed? Her emotions oscillated between misery, boredom, terror and rage at how cruelly and irremediably she was bound. In her dismal agony she tried to generate some psychic force that would blast her cruel impediments away, yearned piteously to move her hands, her feet, to be free of the heinous implantations installed in her body.

The ball in her mouth was the worst part of it. It was as if he had installed himself as a permanent part of her. His iron, cruel will had been thrust into her mouth. It was the clearest and starkest proof of his ownership of her, of her reduction to an implement of his pleasure, the stilling of her voice. She could sedate her mind into believing that somehow she wasn't here, that this was all part of some horrific dream she would awaken from, but her attention was constantly drawn back to the forced expansion of her jaw, the depression of her tongue, the thick presence of the offending object in her mouth.

The time dragged on and on seemingly interminably, but she knew that sooner or later he would untie her and fuck her some more. That was better at least than standing around in a totally black world with no outer sensations other than the pipe pressing up between her breasts, the aching in her feet and the tight binding about her wrists. At least while he was fucking her she could think of something else besides what was going to happen to her.

She had never wanted to live more than she did now. You went about your life thinking it would go on forever and then all of a sudden, without warning, you were confronted with losing it. She was afraid of what would come after the bullet to her brain, if he was at least kind enough to do her that way.

When she was younger she had always had this phobia that when you died you stayed in your body until it disintegrated from decay and that your soul was trapped in a lifeless form unable to communicate, unable to move, just able to think and suffer the loneliness of being dead. As far as everyone knew that was at least just as possible as going to heaven or finding absolute nothingness. Or maybe your soul wandered the earth pining for life, mingling with other tortured souls until your spirit finally dissipated. You could last for centuries. Wasn't that what some American Indian religions believed?

And she couldn't help mourning for the life she had lost. She hadn't fully appreciated it when she had it. She should have married Randy like he wanted and had babies. If she had, she wouldn't have been in that gas station that night. Or if she had only given in to Randy's plea that she stay the night. She loved him, of course, but staying over his place made her feel that she was becoming one of his belongings, his property.

Men didn't understand how much freedom women lost when they were in a relationship, how much they gave up when they married and had children. They became wholly different people, at least in the eyes of society. They were supposed to keep a home, cater to their man's needs, give up any residue of wildness they might have. For men it was different. They kept on being exactly who they were. They were expected to cut loose once in a while. Even relationships outside the marriage were treated differently. For men, it was a cry for liberation, for women it was the destruction of their very home.

But now she would never get the chance to marry Randy or anyone else. She would never have children. She wouldn't ever see her friends again, or her mom who she loved despite everything. Standing here so motionless, with no stimulation from outside of herself, she could think of nothing else.

Or rather, almost nothing else. What she also thought about, and she fought these thoughts off as determinably and as futilely as she did her thoughts of death, was how obsequious and degraded she had become. She sucked the man's cock and it made her hot. His tongue and lips made her scream with pleasure. His cock ruled her, possessed her like she had never been possessed. She hated and cursed herself for it. And for the fact that when he touched her again, the same feelings of raw need would overwhelm her.

Just now, his hands had driven her to distraction. When he manhandled her breasts, she felt her pussy begin to burn. Her skin tingled wherever his hands roamed. His hot lips on her skin had made her knees tremble. It was with great disappointment that she had felt him step away. And then he had struck her brutally, dashing her hopes that he would unbind her and take her in his arms, reminding her that the most important part of his enjoyment in the ownership of her was the pleasure he received from degrading her, reminding her that she was just a lowly animal to him, not a person at all.

The presence in her rear, the thick, black phallus he had locked into her, a presence she had tried, without success, to ignore, was a stark reminder of the callousness with which he treated her. She felt the tears coming again. She bit down on the offensive presence in her mouth and fought them off.

Jack had dozed off after the second chapter of his book. He awoke with a start, not knowing where he was. He had kept the pistol near him and he instinctively grabbed for it. He was a hair's breadth away from putting a .45 caliber slug through the door opposite the bed. His heart was racing and a chill had run through his body. It took a little bit for him to calm down.

He got up from the bed and looked at the clock. It was 20 minutes after 7. The room had become dim, lit only by the light from the bathroom which he must have left on. Opening the blinds a smidgeon, he saw that it was dark out. There were two floodlights in the motel parking lot. The snow had stopped except for a light flurry. The wind had died down too. No one had crossed the parking lot since the lady manager had come and delivered the venison earlier.

The parking lot looked like a scene from Dr. Zhivago, sparkling from the glare of the lights. The car was barely visible. Jack knew that it would take a huge effort to dig it out. Also, he would have to wait until the parking lot was cleared to leave. He hoped that the place got plowed early on or, if he was in luck, during the night. Maybe that's why the lights are on, he thought.

He turned towards the girl. His little idyll with her here would soon be drawing to a close. He decided that he would get some more enjoyment out of her while he had the time. The pot and the booze had made him feel a little randy. His mind was in a good place, easily able to fend off any of the bad thoughts he had been having.

She jumped when he placed his hands on her again. He couldn't resist rubbing her fine ass and hips. He reached around her and squeezed her breasts. He hadn't really realized how much he had missed the feel of a good pair of tits until he had taken hold of hers the other day. Now he couldn't get enough of them. He took hold of her nipples between his thumbs and forefingers and squeezed them hard. The girl squirmed and whined. He was leaning up against her and her ass rubbed against his turgid cock as she wriggled in place, the only response available to her. He released her breasts and then reached up and unfastened her wrists from the pipe above her and from each other. Her brought them around her back and fastened them there.

Squatting down, he freed her ankles. Then, rising, he disconnected her collar from the pipe. He took hold of the little skein of hair he had left uncut at the back of her head and led her over to the bed.

Before bringing her down there with him, he scooted off his shorts. He got on the bed, pulling her behind him and sat up against the headboard. He draped her over his thighs, face down. He adjusted her until she was just right. Her breasts were dangling over his thighs on his left and her rear end was plumped up on his right, her smooth, taut belly on his thighs. He made her spread her legs so that he could have access to her sex.

The Jim Beam bottle was just beside the bed and he took time out to scoop it up and take a swig or two. It burned nice going down and warmed his body. He picked up the zapper from the TV and surfed the channels until he found one, way up at the 500's, that just played classic country music. An old Glen Campbell song came on, one of Jack's favorites. The guy in the song sounded so sad and lonely out there on the wires, pining for his lady. It always caused a little ache in Jack when he heard it. It reached a place in him that was mostly missing. Sometimes he wished he could muster the kind of passion that guy and all those country boys had for their lovers. But he knew he didn't have it in him. Anyway, they were just songs, about the way things maybe ought to be. Not about how they were.

He spread his hands over the soft skin of the girl's back, causing her joined wrists to rise. It felt so good on his fingers and palms. He ran his right hand over her plump, rear mounds and over her distended thighs. His left hand crooked under her chest and took hold of a breast.

Jack took the next 40 minutes or so enjoying his buzz while he explored the girl's flesh. He closed his eyes and let his hands do the seeing. He stroked and massaged and squeezed and played with her breasts with his left hand, alternating between them, pinching them from time to time until her squeals grew loud and insistent.

His other hand swam the great sea of her lower half, caressing her proffered rear orbs, her thighs, playing with her velvety, engorged coosh. The feel of his thumb or fingers deep within her slippery channel enthralled him. Several times he caressed her little nubbin, spreading her pussy juices over it, until her body squirmed with need. And then he would withdraw his ministrations, caressing the insides of her thighs or her buttocks, enjoying the visible and audible exhibition of her frustration, her long, anguished sighs, her deep moans, the shuddering of her thighs, the deep, labored breathing. Or he would just lay back, drinking in the familiar, twangy tunes from the TV while he slowly caressed her vortex of desire, keeping her on a low but steady burn.

Carly felt like she might go mad. She was still locked into a world of darkness by her blindfold, and the only sounds were her heavy breathing or her moans and sighs. The man's hands were tormenting her. He had never seemed so god like as now, his hands emanating from somewhere, invisible, empowered to wander her body like obsessive prospectors in search of a lost mine.

When he had untied her from the pipe she had been grateful. She had fully expected that he would bind her hands behind her and bring her to the bed. She had hoped, though, that he would remove the barriers to her full presence in the world of the real. But she was still condemned to exist in the limbo into which the man had thrust her.

The hands, the hands, the hands, they just wouldn't stop. His touch was as delicate as a girl's when he wanted it to be. At times, she could barely feel his fingers on her flesh, instead experiencing what seemed like a product of her imagination as they circled her breasts.

He would place the point of her nipple in the palm of his hand and then engulf her breast with his five fingers, spread all about them, barely touching her electrified skin. And then he would slowly draw the fingers down, easing his palm away, until his digits converged on her tit's taut tip, squeezing it lightly and then harder and harder and then harder until she had to issue a complaint of pain. She tried not to. It was against the rules to make too much noise. And twice, when her squeals became too loud, he viciously twisted the end of her breast and gave her buttocks a fierce blow, making her howl for real.

And on the other end, well, that hand was much, much more evil than the other. It brought her to the edge of climax again and again, denying her satisfaction each time. It kept up a voracious siege of her pussy, probing it, rubbing it, pinching it, pressing her outer labia together. Then it would, temporarily, abandon its post to wander aimlessly over her sensitized flesh.

Yet again, he was proving to her how powerful he was and her total lack of it. She yearned for even the minutest break in his assault on her, for some moments of peace. Her hands yearned to take hold of the hands that were tormenting her, but they were bound and totally useless to her. She was tempted to try and bring her legs together, or to twist and turn her body until it fell out of his reach, but she knew the terrible price that would be paid for even the slightest resistance to his pleasures.

And yet part of her wanted the delicious sensations that he was bringing her to continue. She wanted his hand on her pussy, his hand on her breasts. But she wanted too to be allowed to bring her lusts to completion, to feel that agonizingly pleasurable contraction of her purse, the shuddering of her body, the fierce electrical signals shooting through her brain's center of pleasure.

She had no idea that she could be kept on the burn for so long. His activities seemed to proceed in cycles, with long periods of desultory caresses, to frenetic manipulations of her body. She knew that sooner or later he would penetrate her. He would tire of his games and pierce her body with his remorseless cock. But when? It seemed like he could go on for hours. And where? He kept playing with the cock like object in her rear. He had disconnected it from the belt and every once in a while he would start sliding it in and out of her. The sensation was so exquisitely pleasurable that she had to curl her toes and clasp her hands together to avoid screaming into her gag. Despite the pleasure it gave her, she still considered it rude and perverse and she was ashamed of what it did to her.

Or he could use her mouth. In some ways that was the best of the three possibilities. She felt the most control over what was being done to her that way. She got to actively please him in a way that might make her seem more human to him. And, the best part, she got to have the evil presence in her mouth removed. To be able to spread her lips, to move her tongue, to have even a moment's freedom where her mouth was empty of all invaders, that was a beneficence indeed.

But if she had to be fucked, and she made it clear to herself that her preference was for no fuck at all, or, to put it another way, for freedom, but since that goal was all but unattainable, and being fucked was completely unavoidable and out of her control, she wanted to do it the way that brought her the most fulfillment. Sucking his cock could be thrilling and it made her pussy burn to have his meat in her mouth. Being fucked in the rear, she could be made to come that way, he had proved that to her, but it was a different kind of an orgasm, her pussy clamping down on itself, empty, ignored and, she had to admit, forlorn. For when she came with his cock raging inside her cunt, his steel bar running rampant over her tender tissues, abrading her button of pleasure, his hips slamming against hers, it sent her pussy into paroxysms, moved the earth beneath her, sent her to a place far, far, far away.

He had been relatively docile for a while, limiting himself to soft caresses, gentle touches, a slow, lazy penetration of her pussy that kept her sexual engines idling expectantly. She had smelled the joint when he smoked it and realized that his torporous behavior could be chalked up to its effects. Then, the hand on her breasts began to become more insistent. The finger in her crevasse began to move more rapidly. It was joined by another. A thrilling pulse of pleasure went through her. Something was happening. Her lusts began to rise. "This time! This time! Please! Please!" she thought desperately. When his fingers began to trace a line around her clit and then settled on it, lightly at first, rubbing in little circles, and then harder and harder, her thighs began to tremble.

It wasn't so much that Jack had gotten bored with his little playtime with the girl. It was just that his cock had been getting insistent. He could have gone on for a much longer time. But his cock was hard and his balls were beginning to ache a little bit. He wanted her at the height of her excitement though before he let her up and so he continued to play with her clit, running his fingers every few moments or so into her steaming chamber and giving her some hard strokes.

She was panting and moaning when he finally took hold of the little skein of hair at the back of her head and forced her to raise herself. Her breast and chest were covered with sweat. Her breath was heavy. This was how he liked to see her, all worked up. He reached behind her head and loosened and then removed the ball gag she had been wearing for the last couple of hours and tossed it down on the bed. She stretched and licked her lips, her mouth turned down in an unhappy frown. Her eyes were still covered. He pulled her back from him, her knees shuffling, and then bent her over. He hovered her face over his loins while he took his cock in his left hand. He slowly guided her mouth to it. When it brushed against her lips, she opened her mouth obediently, circum-navigated it with her lips, and began to suckle.

A wave of pleasure passed through him. It was a lazy kind of pleasure, one that matched his marijuana/Jim Beam buzz. In fact, while he guided her head slowly up and down over his prick, he took hold of the rapidly emptying bottle of mash, unscrewed the top with one hand, and took a mouthful. He shivered as it went down. It burned good. His head swam just a little more.

The sizable roach was still in the ashtray and leaning over, while holding the head of the girl still, his cock jammed into her throat, he fished it out. He lit it up and took a deep hit. A wave of euphoria passed through him along with a tingling in his skin all over his body. His cock felt like it was reverberating in the girl's mouth. He had heard the guys many times describe with enthusiasm the beneficial effect of being high for fucking, but he had never tried it. It seemed like they were right.

He took another deep toke and, closing his eyes, held his breath for about 30 seconds and then let the remnants of the smoke out. Dimly, he heard the girl whining and her head was exerting a slight upwards pressure on his hand. He looked down and realized that she was probably on the borderline of an oxygen emergency. He couldn't have that and so he eased the downward pressure of his hand and allowed her head to rise to the point where she could take a deep breath. He let her recover for a moment or two and then put her back to work.

Slowly, he caused her head to rise and fall. Her tongue was artfully arduous and she exerted a satisfying suckling action on his prick. There was a sad song on by some lady singer remorseful about jilting a lover who she now wanted back. As far as he was concerned, the bitch got what she deserved. But when the Patsy Cline song came on, the one about walking after midnight, a little bit of the singer's forlornness sank home. It was a good reason not to ever get connected to anybody. They all screwed you in the end. But something about Patsy's heartache felt good inside. It wasn't a happiness that she was suffering, just a bittersweet feeling that someone might feel for someone else that way, but not him.

He looked down at the girl servicing his prick. The room had grown even darker now. He could just see the dark form of her head. He leaned over and turned on the table lamp beside the bed so he could see her better. He held her head still for a moment. She had been on an upward stroke and her lips were pursed around his shaft, her cheeks slightly bulged. He liked the look of her new, reddish hair. And the short cut he had given her made her seem elf like.

He decided that she needed some more stimulation of her passion. Holding her head still, he reached over to the side of the bed and found the stone egg he had been using on her. The zapper was next to it. He started the egg vibrating and then, releasing her head, transferred it to his right hand. Her body was perpendicular to his so her took hold of her thigh and forced her to shift to more of an angle so that he would have access to her cunt. Her mouth remained obediently in place. When he ran the vibrating stone along her pussy lips, she issued a little moan of unhappiness that reverberated on his cock. It felt good, so he did not punish her for it.

When he slipped the stone inside her, she released a little squeal. He let it go. He pressed the stone in deeply. Placing his right hand again on her head, he put her back into motion. When he was satisfied she had a good pace, he released her hair. She was smart. She realized without him telling her to keep going. He leaned back, placed his right hand on her ass and closed his eyes, reveling in the delightful sensations.

Jack let her go on and on. His head was swimming pleasantly. His cock seemed hyper sensitive. He imagined its bulbous head flowing back and forth in the girl's mouth. She would give a little squeal from time to time or a moan, but otherwise she was silent. With his hand on her ass, he could feel her body quivering as the effects of the vibrating egg raised her lusts. When he began to move back and forth the probe that spread her anal ring, her moans became more intense. He had to be careful since he didn't want her coming yet. She was right where he wanted her, teetering on the brink of orgasm, all thoughts run out from her brain except the cock in her mouth and the humming in her crevasse.

Finally, Jack decided that the girl had reached her apogee of arousal. He reached down and, probing her slice with his fingers, slipped out the vibrating egg. He removed the thick probe from her anal ring. Reaching behind the girl's head, he took hold of the little tail he had left there and eased her off of his cock. He pulled her head up towards him and to his left. The girl moved obediently, although she gave out a whine of unhappiness. He kept pulling her until she was forced to throw her leg over his. He had her then where he wanted her.

He shifted his hold to under her chin and lifted her head so that she had to sit erect and then raise herself on her knees. When she was in the proper position, he used his left hand to guide his prick to her cleft. When it was properly aligned, the roundish helmet just probing the inner flesh, he lowered his right hand. The girl slid down, encapsulating his prick in her gushing chasm. She gave out a long, deep groan.

Carly knelt stock still. Having the man's prick inside her was like the answer to a prayer. She wanted desperately to move her hips, to slide his rigid bar along her fevered chamber. But she didn't know if she had permission to move. Even so, having been granted at last the benefit of his cock meant that soon her torment would be over and she would be able to come. The vibrating stone had just about driven her over the edge. And to have his cock in her mouth at the same time made her passion go off the scale. She knew she would curse herself for her lustful abandon later, but for now she was going to let herself go, to let herself enjoy every second of her monumental arousal.

She felt the man's hands on her hips and he urged her into a gentle motion. She moaned as his pole abraded her tender interior. She leaned over slightly, her hands still bound behind her back and was able to bring her clit into contact with it. The feeling of his cock riding over it made her swoon.

She didn't know when the man's hands left her hips, but she understood that he wanted her to do the work. It was yet another step in her degradation. She would be fucking him. She turned away that thought. She would deal with it later. All she knew was that she was finally in control of something and riding his cock back and forth felt so good that there was no way she would stop unless he made her.

She groaned with pleasure, the sound echoing in her ears. It was so strange to be fucking a man without seeing him. It was like some spirit had come to possess her, a god transformed into a cloud or the wind, taking form only at the contact point of her loins. She sensed that the man wanted her to maintain her easy, laconic pace. That was okay with her. It felt so good that she almost believed that she could go on forever.

After a short while, she felt the man's hands on her arms. He pulled her torso down. She felt him reaching behind her and then unlocking her hands from each other. She exuded joy as she felt them liberated. It was easier to fuck the man's cock if she could lean forwards, her hands on him, and she tentatively placed them on his chest. He in turn reached up and took hold of her breasts, squeezing them hard. He pinched her nipples, sending an electric shock through her system. Something snapped in her and she began her motions again.

She was totally in control now. She gave his cock long, purposeful strokes. Each one seemed to send a torrent of intense lust through her body. Her pussy felt set to explode. Her motions came faster. The man was gripping her thighs. Her orgasm was looming over her, ready to subsume her. She spread her hands on the man's chest. It felt so good to touch him. Since she didn't have to look at his face, she could imagine him as anyone, maybe a lover, a man she had met that day. They had gone back to his room to fuck. She was fucking him. He felt so good. He had his cock in her. It scoured her insides and abraded her clit. Faster, faster she went. "Ohhhhhhhh!" she moaned. "Ohhhhhhhhh!" She wanted to scream out her joy. She knew that words were forbidden so she bit her lip and groaned deeply.

And then it came. Her pussy clenched down on the man's steely pole. Her body felt like it had been surrounded by an intense electronic field that was energizing every part of her. "Ohhhhhhhhh! Ohhhhhhhh!" she screamed. "Ohhhhhhhhhh!"

When her orgasm began to lose steam, she faded for a moment, enjoying the aftermath of her pussy's rapture. She knew that the man hadn't come, so before he could punish her for slacking, she picked up the pace of her motions again. Her lusts started building up right away. It felt so good. She bent over, succumbing to a swoon. She could smell the man's sweat.

Her lust turned feverish. She lowered her head and began kissing his chest. "It isn't him," she thought. "It's my lover. We're fucking. We just met and we're fucking, we're fucking." His skin was salty and hot. She slipped over to a nipple and took it into her mouth. She suckled it wildly. Then she did the other. She kept up her motions. His cock felt soooooooo good! "Oh, god! Oh, god! Oh, god forgive me," she thought. "I'm a whore! A slave! A slut! But it doesn't matter! It doesn't matter! It feels so good! So good!"

The man's hips were matching her movements. His hands were running frantically over her thighs, her hips. She moved her hands forward and found his face. She lifted her head and brought her lips to his. She thrust her tongue in his mouth. The hotness of his tongue made her squeal. She kissed him hard and long. Her climax was coming again. She was pumping furiously on his cock. "Come for me! Come for me! Come for me!" she thought madly. His hands tightened on her hips. He began to thrust up hard at each downward stroke. "Yeah! Yeah! Yeah!" she thought. "Give it to me! Give it to me!"

His grip grew even tighter and his motions became faster and harder. She could feel his body tense. His upward strokes became urgent. It was all she needed. Her pussy exploded with joy. She pressed her lips even harder against the man's. She could feel her pussy gripping his cock. Each contraction sent a violent pulse throughout her body. She sensed the hot splash of his cum. She gave a violent groan and then was spent.

CHAPTER EIGHT

She lay there against him. His chest was rising and falling quickly. Her pussy was still trilling. Once, twice, three times, she experienced a body shuddering aftershock. His cock was softening, but still blood filled and he was moving his hips slowly, drawing to himself a few last spasms of pleasure. His large, meaty hands were on her back and their heat radiated through her. She could feel her heart still beating heavily.

All she could hear was the echo of her deep breaths. Darkness still surrounded her. It felt so good to be lying atop him. It wasn't the man, of course. It was that lover she had met, the one who had swept her off of her feet and induced a soul shattering passion in her. She nuzzled her head in between his neck and his shoulder.

Her hands were gathered under her chin, her folded arms pressing against the sides of her breasts. They were free for the first time in a long while. Her mouth was empty and her rear was unassailed. It felt so good to be free of all bonds and invaders.

If only the man would let her stay like this. She would do whatever he wanted, obey every command. She knew that escape was fruitless and she promised, in her mind, that if he allowed her to stay free, she wouldn't attempt it.

But she was not allowed to talk. She could not convey to him her promises. Maybe if she stayed lounging on his chest, his strong, solid, warm chest, he would receive her message. In any case, she did not want the spell of her suffusion of contentment to dissolve.

She felt him stirring beneath her. She slipped her hands from underneath her and brought them to his face. No, not his face, her lover's face, the face unimagined, but the gentle, caring soul real in her mind. She caressed his cheeks, gently flitted her fingers over his brow and his eyes. She shifted herself forward and probed for his lips with her mouth. When she found it, she kissed him, a soft, full kiss. She spread his lips with her tongue and entered his mouth. His arms tightened around her. Their tongues intermingled, slowly, languorously, sending a message of warmth through her body.

Jack's mind was overwhelmed with sensations unfamiliar. No one had ever kissed him like this. He realized that the girl was exposing to him the essence of her inner nature, soft, giving, warm, affectionate. It was the real thing. He tried to remember her name again. Not Carol. Not Christine. What was it? He cursed himself for not remembering. He knew that she deserved more than anonymity. He caressed her back. She was soft, so soft. His cock had slipped from her crevasse. He tried to recall how many times he had fucked her today. Six? Seven? He was outdoing himself. His balls were stirring again and he knew that he had at least one more in him. He wanted to save it.

His hands slipped down to her ass. She moaned in his mouth, a moan of contentment mixed with pleasure at the contact. For an instant, a vision flashed through his mind. They were lovers. They had just finished making love in a little cottage he owned overlooking a mountain lake. Soon, they would cook and eat the trout he had caught earlier that afternoon. She would put a flower in her hair. They would kiss and hold hands and watch the sun go down over the mountains. And then, they would make love, long and passionate. She would call his name, pledge her troth, cure his hurt, restore his soul.

But it was just a passing moment. The reality of who he was and what he was, the world that he belonged to, came rushing back. The weight of her recumbent body began to stifle him. The turgid emotions that were leaching from the cracks she had forced in his armor were toxic to him. They reeked of despair, revulsion, sorrow, longing and loneliness. He became infused with the need to strike out at her, to punish her for what she represented, for all she stood for. He took hold of the spate of hair at the back of her head and forced a parting of their lips. He felt her body stiffen atop him. The urge to strike her, to pummel her, to destroy her raged through him. He looked in her face. He could not see the terror in her eyes, but he could see her quivering lips, their downward turn.

He felt the intake of her breath. And it stilled him. No, he had promised himself that he would not harm her more than was necessary. She was guilty of no more than being who she was. She could not help that any more than he could.

He released her hair and instead gave her head a gentle, soothing stroke. He rolled over, bringing her beneath him. He kissed her lips softly three times and then each delicate nipple once, giving them brief, warm suckles. Her body seemed to relax. Her mouth slackened. Peace was restored.

He climbed off of her and gently brought her to her knees. Taking hold of her wrists, he slowly brought them behind her back and connected them. He brushed her hair twice with his hand and kissed her again.

Carly had shuddered with panic when he took hold of her hair. She realized that she had violated one of the tenants of his dominion over her: she had expressed her humanity to him. And that was verboten. She cringed in fear, expecting some vicious blow. But then she sensed that he had somehow changed his mind. Something had come over him, something that was different than before.

She cooperated when he brought her to her knees. She did not resist as he brought her arms behind her back. With a 'click' he had restored the balance between them. She was back to who she was, what he had made her. A wave of sorrow went through her. The kisses that he gave her, kisses which bespoke tenderness, and which she, to her chagrin, welcomed, did not make the sorrow dissipate. She felt him get up from the bed. He returned a few moments later.

He sat on the bed next to her. His lips met hers once more and he stroked her chin. Then his hand gently forced her jaw down, causing her mouth to open. Acrid tasting leather crossed her lips and she felt the faux penis glide over her tongue to the back of her mouth. He connected the gag behind her head. He gently urged her to her stomach. His hands ran down her back, over her arms, over her buttocks and down her thighs. They stopped at her ankles where she felt him join her ankle bracelets together. Slowly, as if not to cause her strain, he raised her legs and connected them to the bindings on her wrists. He stroked her head again three times, planted a kiss on her and then rose from the bed.

She turned her head to the right, away from the living area of their little cabin. The urge to cry swept over her. For a short while, not more than a few minutes ago, she had been away from her dismal prison. Now she was back. She was once again ensconced in her sightless, soundless cocoon. She was once again the less than human creature the man had reduced her to. A surge of sorrow and helplessness and despair ran through her. She stifled a sob and sank back into a dreadful gloom.

Jack restored his boxer shorts and stepped to the side of the bed. He retrieved his dwindling pack of cigarettes, the ashtray and the much reduced bottle of Jim Beam. Sitting down at the table, he took a big swig of the sour mash and lit a smoke. He sat watching the girl. Reducing her to harsh bondage was meant to reestablish the distance between them. Slowly, he began to recover his edge. She was just a piece of ass, after all. Having her bound and helpless made it easier for him to objectify her.

The room was mostly dark except for the circle of light from the bedside lamp. It was as if someone had put a spotlight on her. Although bound into immobility, she was never perfectly still. He could see her sides expand and contract as she breathed. Her fingers from time to time did a little dance. Her wrists squirmed, testing her bonds. Her back arched as she tried to stretch herself into a more comfortable position.

He was trying to put her out of his mind, but he was finding it difficult to do. There was a little closet on the other side of the small stove. He considered stowing her in it so that he could forget her presence for a while. Or he could put her in the tub and close the bathroom door. But a part of him desired her presence. Soon enough, maybe a little more than 24 hours or so from now, he might be parting from her forever. That was time enough to purge her from his thoughts.

He stood and flicked on the overhead light. It splashed the room with brightness. The clock said it was 10 minutes past 8. He realized that he was hungry. He had bought a nice, two pound, boneless sirloin yesterday.

He had intended to eat it at lunch time, but he had had the venison instead. He decided to cook it. Who knows, tomorrow might be his last day on earth instead of hers. He knew that the FBI was still looking for him. If they guessed that he had sought the cover of the snow storm to hinder their pursuit, they would be waiting on the other side of the mountains. It was still a long way to New Mexico. Anything could happen. There was no way he was going to let a good steak go to waste. Not after 12 years of eating shit.

He got up from the table and found his green combat pants and put them on. He donned a t-shirt. Getting dressed helped to widen the distance between him and the girl even more. People had clothes and got to move around; slaves stayed naked and remained where they had been put.

He got the steak out of the small fridge and got a broiler pan from underneath the stove. He would have preferred barbequing it, but that was obviously out of the question because of the snow. He placed the steak in the pan, salt and peppered both sides and put it under the broiler. From his bags of stores he drew out a can of peas. He opened it and dumped it into a pot.

While the steak cooked, he sat at the table and leafed through one of the motorcycle magazines he had bought. There were some outrageous bikes displayed throughout the pages. He slavered over them. One in particular, a vintage 1939 Indian Scout 640 with maroon fenders and the trademark golden Indian chief logo on its gas tank. It was 750 c.c's and in cream puff condition. As a relic of yesteryear, it was a great prize to whoever owned it, but it would not do for the rutted and unpaved trails of Mexico.

Back in the classifieds he found a 2003 Big Daddy BMC chopper for sale for $14,000. It was cut way back with dual exhausts and black gas tank and fenders with cherry red flames painted on them. That he could see himself on as he traveled the back roads with his chippie on behind. He thought of the girl and wondered what she would think about having that power between her legs. He could almost feel that raw, hot wind whipping through his hair and hear the deafening sound of its engine. No helmet laws in Mexico, he was sure of that. And to think that something like that was just within his reach. Days away.

The broiler was crackling and the aroma of sizzling meat was punctuating the air. He got up, opened the broiler and flipped the steak. The peas were boiling and he turned them down. He got out a plate and glass and silverware and set them down on the table. He only let the steak cook for a few moments longer. It liked it nice and red inside. He pulled out the broiler pan and set it down on the stove. The meat was still sizzling. He flipped it onto the plate on the table and then, after draining them, tumbled out a large pile of peas. There was still some orange juice in the fridge and he got it out and poured himself a glass.

It was a fabulous meal. The meat was done just perfect. It seemed to melt in his mouth it was so tender. He made sure to cut just medium sized pieces so he could savor the rich, fat laden meat. He chewed each piece until he had eked out the last spurt of flavor. He had picked out a good marbled slab after going through the entire stack they had at the supermarket. The whole trip was justified just by this. Fuck the girl, fuck Mexico, fuck everything. This was a steak to die for. It was the steak that he had been dreaming of for year after year. If he had a piece of meat like this back in the joint, he could have sold it for $1000. It would have been worth every penny.

There had been only a few guys who could have afforded it. Big Benito Marquez, a Chicano from LA who had been caught with 2 pounds of cocaine and 3 dead bodies outside of Milwaukee. Or Shabazz White, the leader of the Blood faction, or, for that matter, Lamar Johnson, the Crips' captain, both doing life bids for gang slayings. There was a Chinese guy called Charlie Wang, who had been caught running in 8 kilos of heroin from Canada, good Thai blonde. He was actually doing a Federal bid, but the Feds had broken up his Tong gang in Lewisburg. They didn't have enough federal maximum security joints to spread them all out so some were sent to state facilities. Somehow, Charlie lived a life of luxurious ease. He always had plenty of cash.

It was definitely something worth dying for. The savory flavor made his stomach purr. The peas weren't bad either, but they were just peas. 2 pounds of meat was a lot to eat, but he did a good job of it. It was nice and thick and he had browned it on the outside just right, so that what fat there was around the edges was turned delectable.

In the end, he couldn't finish it. He leaned back in his chair and gave out a long, satisfied belch. There were a few bright green peas left and he picked at them as he luxuriated in his full belly. It had been, all in all, a quite delightful day. In fact, there wasn't a single thing that had happened that he would change. The girl had been wonderful. Karen, was that it? Her name? He knew it was something like that. "Well, Karen, you are a delectable morsel, if I have to say so myself," he thought. She was still lying hogtied on the bed, of course. He bet that she was hungry.

He was back to the same dilemma he had had earlier in the day. Should he give the rest to her or not? She probably deserved it for being such a good fuck and all that. But the prospect of steak and eggs in the morning was pretty tempting. He still had some bacon, but nothing beat steak and eggs.

There were still a couple of cans of beans in one of the bags. He had decided not to inflict unnecessary pain on the girl, unless he couldn't help it, like if she got out of line again, but that didn't mean that he had to baby her. She probably ate like a lord compared to him over the last 12 years. Beans and maybe a few peas would be good enough.

But not yet. A smoke seemed like a good idea, and maybe a swig or two of Jim Beam. And there was that joint to finish off. He looked at the clock. It was 5 to 9. He had been told to expect the call from his Rogue brothers between 10 and 11. There was plenty of time to relax a bit and then feed the girl. And if there wasn't, well, she could go hungry for all he cared.

Everything he needed was already on the table. He fished the roach out of the ashtray. He fired it up and took a long toke. He let it suffuse into his bloodstream through his lungs and then released what was left of the smoke. His head grew fuzzy. He took another toke and held that in too. The room seemed to pulse as the THC entered his brain. "Whoa!" he thought. He waited a little bit before taking the next toke. He had always hated the smell of burning pot, it reminded him of it how fucked up it could get you. He found that he didn't mind it now. The roach had gone down to the bitter end. He held the tiny thing between his thumb and forefinger and took the last hit. It burned his fingers a little, but he didn't mind. When he was done, he popped the remnant into his mouth, snuffed it out with his saliva and swallowed it.

The room seemed a really friendly place. His body felt mellow and relaxed. His balls tingled a little bit. Maybe he had two more go rounds in him, he thought. He wasn't sure he had the time to fuck the girl and feed her, so he would have to choose between the two. He took a swig of Jim Beam. Its effect blended well with the THC high. He took another. He swirled the bottle. There was maybe 3 ounces left. He would have to save it.

He looked at the girl. She looked real good from where he was sitting. Her shoulders were strained backwards and her arms stretched out to meet her ankles. Her head was bent down and pressed into the bed. She was trying to suppress her whimpers.

There was one thing about being hogtied, you couldn't forget about it for a single second. It was a good way to emphasize his total control and ownership of her, to teach her all about her new, lowly status. She had no right to anything without his say so, even down to the ability to move a single muscle. It was 8:30 now and she had been that way for about 20 minutes. Back in the day, he would leave a recalcitrant girl like that for a couple of days. She was willing to do anything you said after that. The girl was obedient, but she still lacked the utter devotion to obedience that was needed for a real good slave. It was too bad he didn't have more time to break her in.

He would use her ass again once more before the night was through, he thought. But he wanted to take his time just in case he couldn't get it up again. If he waited until after the call, he could make it his grand finale before he knocked off for the night. And he wanted to hear her scream with passion one more time before lights out. "Okay, so I'll feed her," he decided.

Retrieving a can of baked beans from the grocery bag, he opened it and poured it into the pot that held the rest of the peas. There was no sense in cleaning two pots if he didn't have to. Besides, it all went in one stomach anyway. He turned the heat on low and put a lid on it so that it wouldn't burn.

Carly had smelled the steak cooking. She hadn't realized she was hungry until then. She wondered how long she would have to wait until he decided that she should eat too. She had been laying there for a long time. Maybe an hour. All the usual things had been going through her head. So much so that she had grown tired of it. But every time she had the unbearable urge to move her hands or put her legs down, which was pretty much all the time, she was reminded of how hopeless her situation was and her chest ran cold.

She was doing her best not to cry, but every once in a while, no, more than that, more like every few minutes, the terrible fate that had overtaken her became too much to bear and she would be overwhelmed with dismal emotions. The only consolation was that the day had to be almost over. And the fact that the man had to run out of gas sometime.

She had done her best to ignore the feelings of self reproach she had for her passionate display just a while ago. It didn't help much. She knew she would never be able to explain it to anyone if she somehow survived her ordeal. First of all, she would be too ashamed to reveal it. And no one would ever be able to understand it anyway.

She didn't understand it fully, even though she rationalized it as a survival mechanism.

When she smelled the smoke from the joint, she realized that she had at least a bit more to wait to eat. She knew that he had been drinking too since she had tasted it in his mouth when she had kissed him. She still had the fear that he would get wildly drunk and commit terrible acts of violence on her. Not that he hadn't been cruel enough when he was sober. But if he could beat her without remorse, in fact with enjoyment, because she knew that he enjoyed it, when he was sober, then he was surely capable of much worse when he was drunk. His violent assaults on her so far had been measured, limited in scope. If he was drunk, he might lose that control. She trembled when she thought of it. It was yet another source of rabid fear for her.

She couldn't feel the vibration of his footsteps while she was on the bed, so the first thing she knew when he came to get her was when he put his hands on her bindings and released her ankles from her wrists. He slowly lowered her legs, freed them, and then took hold of the bit of hair on the back of her head. He pulled at it forcefully and she did her best to rise in obedience, but she couldn't prevent a squeal of pain erupting in her throat. He immediately gave her a fierce slap on her buttocks. And then two more. Her eyes filled with tears and she emitted little sobs, but she otherwise held her reactions in. It burned where he struck her.

He took hold of the small clump of hair again and pulled on it once more. This time it was even sharper and harder. She strained to hold her squeal of pain in and she rose to her knees as fast as she could. He pulled her to the edge of the bed and held her in place while she moved to put her feet on the floor. Once on her feet, he moved her in the direction of the bathroom. He forced her to sit on the toilet and pee.

When she was done, he wiped her and then made her stand there for a minute or so. It didn't take much imagination to realize that he was probably pissing too. When she felt his hand on her hair she knew he was done. He walked her out a few steps from the bathroom and then, with one hand still in her hair and the other on her shoulder, forced her to her knees. Once there, he made her bend over until her forehead was on the floor. Then he released her. She felt him step away.

It was only a little while that he was back again. He pulled on her hair, a little less hard this time, and brought her to an upright position. When he removed her blindfold, she had to blink several times to get used to the sudden light. It was like being popped back into the world. Like magic, the room had reappeared. He was behind her so she couldn't see him. She hadn't seen him for several hours, not since he whipped her. She didn't want to see him if she didn't have to. She had half forgotten how evil he looked, how harsh his face was, how his eyes bored into her and the hardness behind them. Her stomach went queasy as she reexperienced her dreadful fear of him.

Her head jerked as he unfastened the gag from behind. He slipped it out of her mouth. She stretched her lips and moved her tongue. It felt good. He took hold of her hair again and forced her to look down. There was a bowl of steaming beans in front of her with what looked like peas all mixed in. A bowl of orange juice sat next to it. No steak.

A tide of resentment and anger swept through her. It was yet one more insult. "You motherfucker," she thought angrily. "You bastard! Fuck you! I'm not eating that crap!" She thought it, but she didn't say it. Her anger had not turned into bravado. But when he pushed her head back down, forcing her to spread her knees so that she could get low enough, she didn't lower her face into the bowl to eat. She just closed her eyes and mouth and stayed where he had left her. There was a deadly pause. It only took a moment for her fear to produce the bile in her belly. But she had had enough. She would rather starve than eat that mush. Not when he had had what smelled like a juicy steak. "Fuck you!" she thought. "I'm not eating."

The pause went on. Carly trembled as she awaited the man's reaction. Her mind was filled with hatred for him. Then, she felt him crouch down beside her. He leaned over and took hold of the back of her neck in the vice-like grip of his left hand. She panicked. Her eyes sprang open. "I'll eat! I'll eat!" she thought desperately. All her resolve had disappeared like a drop of water in a hot frying pan. She tried to move her face down, but his hand held her head still. She felt him loosening the chains that held the thick probe in her rear. He pulled it out.

A second later, he struck her rear with the flat of his mighty right hand. It jolted her body and a fierce pain radiated through her. It was followed rapidly by a second and a third, a fourth and a fifth. Each one seemed to strike her harder than the last. She couldn't help it. She screamed. "Owwwwwwwww! Owwwwwwwwwww! Owww-wwwwwwwwwwww!" She started to sob. His grip was digging into her neck. She could feel his anger. He had never hit her this hard. "Mmmmmmmmmmmm! Mmmmmmmmmmmmm!" she cried out, trying to beg him to stop.

She didn't want to use words, dared not use them. She wanted frantically to tell him that she would obey. He struck her again, and again and again. She howled from the pain. And then a fourth and a fifth. Her rear cheeks felt like they were on fire. "Ohhhhhhhhhhh! Ohhhhhhhhh! Ohhhhhhhhh!" she cried out. Two more followed in rapid succession. She couldn't hold her silence any more. Ohhhhhhwwwwwww! Ohhhhhhhwwww! I'll eat! I'll eat! Please stop! Please! Please!" Five more blows fell. She shrieked and cried. "Oh! Oh! Oh! Oh! Oh! Pleeeeease! Pleeeeease stop! I'll eat! I'm sorry! I'm sorry!"

The blows stopped. His grip did not relent from her neck. Her body was wracked by violent sobs. He let her go on for a few moments. She felt him fiddle with her ear. He removed the plug. She heard his voice for the first time in hours. It was gravelly and harsh. There was a fearsome iciness to it. He imposed her sentence. "Five more for talking."

"Mmmmmmmmmmmmm!" she moaned unhappily, pressing her lips together so no more words would escape. The blows came like rapid-fire, fierce, body jolting blows. She screamed and sobbed uncontrollably. Her voice echoed throughout the small room. Then they stopped once more.

He turned his body and shifted hands on her neck. A moment later, she found her face plunged into the hot beans. They smeared all over her face. "Eat!" he commanded. She tried and she tried, but between her sobs and her face being squished down into the bowl, she couldn't get any into her mouth.

"Eat!" he said louder. She finally got a small mouthful in and started chewing. He lifted her head. She chewed rapidly, desperately. She could feel her face smeared with sauce. When she swallowed, he pressed her face down again. She scooped up as much as she could. He raised her head again. Her mouth was turned down in a dismal frown, but she was chewing. He released her neck and stood up, looming over her. She felt his eyes burning into her and she leaned over, her legs spread wide, and she sucked up another small mouthful of beans and peas. While she chewed, she turned her head and looked up at him dourly, tears still flowing from her eyes. He stooped, picked up the earplug he had removed, and stuffed it back in her ear.

Jack looked at the girl. Her ass was beet red. "Well, that's what she gets," he thought. The anger had run out of him. But he was still annoyed. She had a lot of nerve pulling a stunt like that. He would decide later whether to punish her some more. She definitely deserved it.

He went back to the table and rooted in one of the bags for another pack of cigarettes. He pulled one out, opened it and drew out a smoke. He noticed that his hands were shaking. She had really gotten to him. She was lucky that he didn't choke the life out of her right there and then. He went to all the trouble of getting her something to eat, heating it up no less, and she did that. It was typical of a female to be so ungrateful. He sat down to watch her eat.

She finished quickly, licking the bottom of the bowl, making sure she got it all up. Then she moved to the bowl of orange juice and lapped that up as well. When she was done, she knelt up and sat back on her heals. She kept her head pointed downwards, not looking at him.

Jack took a swig of the sour mash and got up from his chair. He wetted a paper towel and went over to the girl. She flinched as he approached her. Her face was smeared with the brown sauce. It had run down over her jaw line onto her neck and chest. A pea was stuck in her right eyebrow. She looked like a mud woman. It almost made him laugh. He plucked the pea out and held it in front of her. She dutifully nibbled it from his hand.

He needed three towels to finish the job of cleaning her up. When done, he tossed the dirty towels into the garbage and picked up her blindfold and gag. He put the blindfold on first. When he installed the gag, he pulled it tighter than usual. She moaned but didn't squeal. He pushed her over and reinserted the black probe in her ass, reaffixing the chains that held it in place. He had decided what to do with her.

He forced her to lie on the floor face down. After hooking her ankles together, he retrieved one of the short ropes he had been using. Releasing her hands from one another, he tied one end of the rope to her right wrist. He drew both of her arms up high behind her back. She squirmed and moaned in discomfort. Running the rope through the ring in back of her collar, he connected her left wrist to it. Her wrists were hauled up just above the middle of her back. It was high enough to cause her extreme discomfort, but not high enough to tear any ligaments or pull any muscles. He tripled knotted the rope and then fixed her wrist bracelets together. Due to the angle of her wrists, it would be impossible for her to reach the knots to try and loosen them. And even if she did, they were tied so tight that it would take more than her mere fingers to untie them.

She moaned from the pain. Her fingers wriggled helplessly. The rope was pulled taut by the downward pressure of her wrists. If it was uncomfortable, it was meant to be.

He took a longer length of rope from his supply and double knotted one end around the joinder of her ankle bracelets. He picked up her feet and dragged her, breasts down, over to the corner of the room where she had been tied up earlier that afternoon. She wriggled and twisted her body in complaint. He looked at the pipe up near the ceiling. Then he looked at her. In his estimate, she weighed about 110 lbs., maybe 115. It would hold her. He drew the free end of the rope over the pipe and gave it a good pull. Her ankles rose into the air. He pulled it again and her knees and hips were off the ground. She was moaning unhappily. Giving it three successive yanks and he had her whole body in the air. Her head was about a foot from the floor. He tied off the free end of the rope to her ankles, making sure it was tight and would not pull loose.

"There," he thought. "See how you like that for a while."

He crouched and played with her breasts, pinching and slapping them hard while she moaned and cried. Then he stood up, twirled her so that her ass was facing him and gave it two forceful blows. She gave out sounds of her pain. Her body swayed back and forth. Two was enough. He needed to do the dishes.

Carly moaned and bit down on her gag. He body stayed swaying. Her shoulders ached terribly. "Please don't leave me like this! Please! Please!" she begged in her mind. The blood was rushing to her head, making her dizzy, and it was a strain to breath, especially since she had only her nose to breathe through. When she twisted and pulled at her hands, it hurt even more, so she stopped that right away. "Ohhhhhhhhhh!" she moaned. "Ohhh- hhhhhhhh!"

She was overwhelmed with remorse for her little rebellion. Look what it got her. And her ass still burned where he had pummeled it. She realized that until then the man had been pulling his punches with her, holding back his strength. This time he had let it all out in a fit of rage.

She wriggled her body in frustration and unhappiness. It made her body sway and that made her full stomach queasy. "Please don't leave me like this! Please! Please!" she repeated in her mind. She was so overwhelmed with grief at her dismal predicament that every cell in her body seemed to turn sour. "Oh, god! Oh, god! Oh, god," she ranted silently. She wanted to scream, beg, plead. She wanted to do anything to be restored to contact with the earth. Her weight was stretching her legs to the utmost and she could feel the strain in her knees. How long he would leave her like this worried her intently. He had made her sit bound to the chair for hours. She had stood at this very same spot for what seemed like hours too. "Please! Please!" she thought desperately. "Take me down! Please! Please! I'll be good! I'll be good! I promise!"

She broke into sobs. She knew that he would leave her this way for a long time. She didn't think she would be able to stand it. She might go insane. And then the thought occurred to her. Was he done with the punishments? His rabid attack on her buttocks had been out of anger and to get her to comply with his demands. Hanging here like this was certainly part of the punishment phase. But would he be satisfied with it? Or would he get out the switch again, lash into her helpless form again and again? She prayed that he wouldn't. She prayed and prayed. It was all so unfair! How could God have let this happen to her? When would it ever end?

After this, what new degrading, hurtful plans did he have for her?

She realized that her current predicament was all because of the final residual of her pride and for the want of a piece of steak. How foolish it seemed now. She wriggled and struggled and pulled on her bonds again in agonizing frustration. All it did was make her feel worse.

Jack was too busy cleaning up the kitchen to pay her much mind. It was just as well to have her out of the way. He scoured the broiling pan, an act that reminded him how good the steak had been. He washed and dried the dishware and the utensils. He wrapped the remnants of the steak in a paper towel and put it in the fridge with the last of the orange juice. He saved the pot for last.

When done, he sat down and had a smoke. He had heated up what was left of the coffee and had poured himself a cup. It was 9:35. There were 25 minutes before he could expect his call. He didn't want to miss it. The phone was in one of the bags and he got it out, checking to make sure that it was on. It was, and he had 3 bars of reception, good considering where he was and the storm an all. Now that he was sure that the girl wouldn't see it, he left it on the table where he could be sure he heard it ring.

After his smoke, he rooted around in the bag for some more of the chocolate. There was about a quarter of the large bar left. He looked at the girl. It was too bad for her. He had planned on giving her some after she ate, but she wouldn't get any now. She was letting out a slow, steady whine like one of those tones they put on the radio to let you know it was an emergency broadcast test. He didn't like that. He lifted his foot and gave her shoulder a hard shove with it. She was only a few feet away from the table.

Her body described a four or five foot arc. Her breasts jiggled and her head gyrated in unhappiness. He ate the chocolate while he watched her body swing back and forth like the pendulum to a clock. It slowly came to rest and then he set her back in motion just for the fun of watching her sway.

When the chocolate was gone, Jack eyed the dregs of the Jim Beam. It wasn't enough to restore his buzz, but there was another joint. He fished around in the girl's yellow pocketbook and came up with it. He noticed a folded up piece of paper that he had missed previously. He pulled it out. It was an unfinished letter in beautiful cursive scrawl. The paper was beige with a bough of pink and yellow daisy like flowers at the top. It began, "Dear Mom."

He brought the letter over to the table and sat down. He fired up the joint. After letting the first, ceremonial toke out of his lungs, he unfolded it and began to read.

"Dear Mom,

I am sure you will realize how hard this letter is for me to write. I am so sorry about our disagreements and how my anger at you has kept us apart for the last year. I realize now that you meant the best for me when you argued against me getting my own apartment. You were worried about how safe I would be. And, I also realize now, how lonely the house must be with both me and Dad gone.

I hope that you realize how important this move was for me. I really needed the space to become my own person. It has been lonely for me at times too even though I have Randy for company a lot of the time. Still, it has been good for me and I feel so much more a complete person now.

Work is going well. I think that I may be getting a promotion soon. Randy has been just great. I really love him. He asked me to marry him last Saturday but I told him that I am not ready for that.

Someday soon, I hope that we can get together. You could come up to see my apartment. The cat..."

That was where the letter ended. Jack took another hit off the joint. "See," he thought, "girls should listen to their mothers." If she had, she probably wouldn't have been where she was when he captured her. Well, that was too bad. And it was too bad for old Randy boy too. He would have to put his hook back in the pond. Jack was sure that there would be a host of girls looking for a nice, stable guy like him.

He wondered why she stopped writing it. There was always the possibility that she was writing it at a point when time was short and didn't get to finish it. But then there was that next to last line about coming up to see her. Maybe the girl decided that she just wasn't ready for reconciliation yet. Family problems are a bitch, as he well knew. He looked over at the girl. Her swaying had stopped and the only noise coming from her was some sniffling. She could cry if she kept it quiet, he decided.

Going back to the letter, he wondered what he should do with it. It might do the old bag some good to know that her deceased daughter had had some thoughts for her shortly before she bit the big one.

On the other hand, how was he supposed to ever get it to her? He couldn't very well write "Mom" on an envelope and drop it in a mail box. He could send it to the girl's address, it was on her driver's license. But where would he send it from? The whole point was for the cops not to be able to trace his tracks. Wherever he mailed the unfinished missive the postmark would be a dead giveaway. And besides, it would get the old bag all bent out of shape to get the letter when they hadn't even found the body yet. For he knew that the Rogue boys in New Mexico would have a safe and secure spot for her. Some excavator from the 23rd century might find her bones.

Maybe it was better to burn the letter so that it never surfaced. He took another deep toke of smoke and looked at the girl again. He wondered how she would feel about him going through her things. Probably not very good. But it wasn't like she had revealed any deep dark secrets. He probably knew more about her inner nature than that fucking Randy ever did. That putz had never seen her under stress like he had. And the way she fucked. Randy probably didn't know anything like that. He was probably a once a nighter. A little foreplay then lay on top and hump away. He doubted that he had ever fucked someone in the ass, and he was sure he had never fucked the girl there. She had been too surprised at it.

No, he had seen the girl at her extreme. She was smart and resourceful. She had patience. She took pain really good. And she had balls. Refusing to eat was probably the bravest thing she had ever done. Now that it was all over and the punishments and such had been worked out, he conceded that he had been surprised at her temerity. Yeah, she had spunk.

And the fact that she had declined to marry that dork showed she had sense. No way would Randy old boy be ever able to hold down those smoking desires that lay under her surface. She would have been fucking the mailman within the year.

He looked up at the clock. It was 9:47. The call would be coming in soon. He put out the joint. He lit the burner under the coffee pot. He realized that he didn't have any paper to write down any directions. He got up and looked in the drawer to the nightstand. There was no paper, but there was a pen. He looked in the kitchen cabinet. No go. Then he looked at the table. The girl's letter was still there. That would do nicely. He would write the instructions on the back. It looked like he was keeping the letter after all.

He poured himself some coffee. Now it was a waiting game. At the joint you did a lot of waiting. Mostly for the screws to open doors. They liked to make you wait. It reminded you who was boss. It was degrading. So he learned to wait. But now, he was all on edge. Maybe they wouldn't call. He might be overplaying his hand at this brother Rogue bit. Maybe the chapter president would consider it safer to deal him to the cops than to take the risk of a conflagration like they had back in Wausau. Maybe he would pick up the phone and a battalion of Arkansas State Rangers would come piling in their guns a blazing.

The gun was on the nightstand. He went over and got it. If the cops broke in, he wanted to get the first couple before they got him. They would be wearing their bulletproof vests, so he would go for head shots. He put the gun on the kitchen table. He looked at the clock: 9:49. The clock was sure moving slow. He sipped his coffee and lit a smoke. Everything depended on this phone call. Freedom was on the other end of it. He was sure his brothers would find a way to get him into Mexico. And they probably had some pretty good connections south of the border. They could hook him up. He just had to make it there.

When he finished the cigarette, it was 9:53. He had smoked it really fast. Nerves, he guessed. He took a sip of coffee. He watched the clock. The red hand went around slowly. He checked the phone again. For a second, he panicked. Didn't these phones have buttons where you could turn off the ringer? Was the ringer on? He looked at it. There was the number pad, a couple of buttons on the top of the pad on either side. One said 'Call'. The other said 'Options'. Would it be under Options? He hit the button. A screen came on with choices. Ring Tones was one of them. That had to be it. But how did you make the little white thing go down so you could select it? He couldn't figure it out. "Shit!" he shouted. The girl would know. Stupidly, he had kept the phone a secret from her. He should have made her show him how it worked.

He could do it now. All he had to do was remove her gag and blindfold. But what if she wouldn't tell him? She had guts and if she realized that using the phone was so important to him, she might just refuse to help him. He had a feeling he could beat her raw and if she had really determined to dig in and resist him, she wouldn't give it up.

And what if he got the little white thing down to where it said ring tones, what then? He might fuck it up. He might end up turning the ringer off instead of on. He tried to think. Wouldn't the company that sold them have them preset with the ringer on? That would make sense. It had to be on. He was getting his shorts in a knot for nothing. He put the phone down. He looked up. It was 9:58. Two minutes.

He watched the clock the whole time. The red hand took its sweet time running around the numbers. He didn't realize that 2 minutes could be so long. 90 seconds left. 60 seconds left. 45 seconds left, 30, 20, 10. And then he started a mental countdown, 10, 9, 8, 7, 6, 5, 4, 3, 2 ,1. He looked at thc phone. It remained silent.

There was a whole hour to wait. Between 10 and 11 the man had said. "Shit!" he thought. "Now what the fuck am I going to do for a whole hour?" There was no way he could read and he didn't want to watch television. He poured down the rest of his coffee. He could probably drink a gallon of it in an hour, he thought. The rest of the doobie was in the ashtray. He was tempted to pick it up. But smoking dope seemed to make the time go longer. And he didn't want that. And, besides, if he was too fucked up he might not take down the instructions properly.

He heard a whimper behind him. He turned to look at the girl. Now that was something he could do for an hour.

He turned his chair to her and snuck it up close. Even upside down she was a decided piece of ass. Even with only her dainty little nose showing on her face she was alluring. Reaching down, he took hold of her nipples and playfully shook her upside down breasts so that they rippled. He ran his hands up the sides of her torso, over her hips and her thighs. Her body was warm and soft. Just an inch or so of her slit was showing through her jammed together thighs, but it was the right inch.

He placed his finger between her thighs and rubbed it gently over her clit. He could penetrate her slice only just a mite, but after a short while it was enough to draw out some of her moisture and slicken her bud of joy with it. Her body shivered several times as he agitated softly her center of pleasure. He leaned forwards, holding her still by the hips, and insinuated his tongue, lapping on the edges of her labia, running it back and forth over her now stiffened nubbin.

After she had emitted a few good moans, he leaned back. He kept his finger gently irritating her clit while he looked down at her face, or where her face should be. Her nostrils were flaring and her breath was heavy. He patted her on the hip. "Let's get something straight, little lady," he said to her jocularly, "this thing here is about me, not you." He knew that she couldn't hear him. But that was okay. He enjoyed the joke.

Her head was at just the right angle, as if he had planned it. He reached around her head and unfastened her gag. Before removing it, he slid the cock like leather plug back and forth in her mouth, just so she would get the idea of what was coming next. Leaving it in for the moment, he got up and took off his pants and boxers and drew off his t-shirt. His prick had stiffened. "Good boy," he said. He sat back down on the chair and, after drawing it back and forth a few more times, slipped the plug out of her mouth. He tossed it on the table next to him. He looked at the phone. It was dark. He looked at the clock: 10:10.

Returning to the girl, he slipped himself forward in the chair and then reached around to the back of her head and grabbed the tassel of hair there. He pulled her head forward and, with his other hand, directed his rampant tool towards her mouth. She had closed her mouth when the gag left it and her lips were compressed closely together as if to deny him entrance. He bumped the bulbous head of his thick cock up against them. She hesitated for a second. He was about to give her tits a vicious slap when the lips opened and he eased himself in.

The girl made a perfect, hot tunnel for him. It just showed what a little firmness did. She didn't want his prick in her mouth. In fact, she had an idea to refuse it. Like a computer, her mind had gone quickly through all the variations of what would happen if she kept her lips closed. It only took a second. She realized immediately that this was not the time, nor was she in a position to make a stand. And so, open sesame!

Jack closed his eyes and reveled in the moist heat on his prick. Obedient to a fault, the girl was suckling on his tool pleasingly and washing it with her tongue. It was a little strange to have it on top of his prick rather than underneath it, but the net effect was the same, a garden of delight.

He pushed and pulled her head back and forth slowly. His other hand was teasing her clit, not too much, but just enough to keep her on the burn. From time to time, the girl moaned. Jack would reward her for the vibrations on his cock by bringing his hand down and massaging her breasts, toying with her rock hard nipples, squeezing and pinching until her moans became more troubled. Then he would return it to her nest to renew his assault.

Jack lost track of time. That was the whole idea, wasn't it? The girl only faltered once when he playfully gave her clit a twist and she issued an unhappy howl. Two hard slaps across her breasts got her started again, with alacrity.

Suddenly, he noticed a buzzing sound. It was repetitious, starting and stopping. He wondered what it was. Then, like an explosive bullet, the realization shot through his mind: it's the phone! He jumped to grab it. His cock vacated the girl's mouth like a locomotive leaving a tunnel. He picked up the phone. For a panicked second he couldn't figure what button to push. He finally figured it out and put the phone to his ear. "Hello!" he shouted.

"Hey man, I almost gave up on you. Were you sleeping or something?"

"No," Jack answered. "I was getting a blowjob."

The voice at the other end of the phone laughed. "That's the way, bro," he said. "That's the way."

"So what's up?" Jack asked, anxious to get to the business purpose of the call.

"Man, did you see that fire up there in Wisconsin? It was a real blow! Three cops killed. Not a bad day's work."

"Yeah," Jack responded sullenly. He noticed that the girl's mouth was empty and she was licking her lips. With the phone held against his ear, he reached down and got the penis gag and pushed it against her lips. She opened them obediently and he rammed it home.

"They think you dead man. You and the chippie," the voice went on. "No one's looking for you any more."

"You can't be too careful," Jack countered. "Listen," he continued, "I gotta know how this is all going to play out."

"Easy! Easy man! Don't you worry. We're going to bring you right in. You got a map?"

"Yeah," Jack answered. "Hold on a minute."

He put the phone down. He glanced at the girl and saw that the gag had worked its way half out her mouth. He leaned over and shoved it back in harshly. Then he buckled it behind her head. He gave her body a shove, causing it to swing in a wide arc. "We're going to New Mexico, baby!" he shouted. "We're gonna make it!"

He rummaged in the bags until he found the interstate atlas he had bought. He turned the pages until he got to New Mexico. Right there in the center, down by the bottom was Alamogordo. It looked beautiful. He went back to the phone.

"Got it!" he said.

"You see how Highway 70 comes southwest from Mescalero and then makes a sharp right at Tularosa?"

Jack looked for it for a moment or two. Then he saw it.

"Yeah!" he said enthusiastically.

"Just about a mile and a half after that turn there's a bar called Pete's. It's on the left hand side. It's a small joint so you have to look close for it. But it's well lit."

Jack had the pen and paper out and wrote down the name of the bar and how far out of town it was.

"Okay," Jack said.

"When do you think that you'll be by?"

"I figure we leave tomorrow at 6 or 7 depending on when they get the roads clear. If we drive right through we'll be there late tomorrow night."

"Well, the bar closes at 2. If you're going to be later than 1, wait until the next night. Anytime after 9. I'll be there. I can't give you directions over the phone to where

I'll be taking you. It's too complicated. I'll have to lead you in."

"How will I know you?"

"Ask anybody for Moondog. They'll know me."

"Okay, thanks," Jack replied.

"Hey, good luck, man. Watch out for those Texas rangers. They'll stop you as soon as look at you. We don't want no heat to come down on us. If you get into a shootout, just keep going."

"Got it," Jack replied.

"Ooooooooooweeeeee!" the voice on the other end of the phone yelled. "We are proud of you boy. You're going to get the grand reception!"

"Thanks," Jack answered. He wasn't sure he wanted a grand reception. He wanted to keep his visibility low.

"Okay then, see you late tomorrow or the next night."

"Yeah, see ya," Jack replied.

"Don't bother calling this phone number. It's a disposable and I'll be getting rid of it right after this call. You should do the same."

"Right!" Jack confirmed.

The phone went dead. He looked at it. He couldn't believe it! It was going to happen! Freedom was just around the corner. He would make it there by tomorrow night or die trying, he thought.

He was so excited, he couldn't sit. He stood up and gave out a great "Whoooooooooop!" He did a little dance. He saw the bottle of Jim Beam and for a moment had the urge to finish it off, but he decided against it. He would have a use for it later.

He felt like a bolt of electricity had shot through him. He was all energized like that battery bunny on TV. He felt like he could last a hundred years. He needed to celebrate. He looked over at the girl. Her body was still swaying slightly from when he had given it a shove. He decided he would finish his blowjob.

Carly realized he was back when he put his hands back on her breasts. Something had happened. She just knew it. He had pulled out of mouth like his cock had been on fire. And then he had jammed the gag back in without buckling it closed behind her head. Something was going on that he didn't want her to know about.

She prepared herself for the ordeal of servicing him. Her shoulders ached from the contorted positions of her arms. The blood was pounding in her head. She had rued a hundred times her little rebellion. She still expected him to whip her and her heart dreaded it.

When he had put his cock in her mouth before, she had immediately decided to do her best to pleasure him. It made good sense seeing how if she didn't please him he could easily make her horrid predicament a thousand times worse. But it also went with her strategy of making her seem human to him, or, at least seem valuable, worth the trouble of keeping around. No matter what he did to her she had to remember that he could turn on her in an instant. Twice now she had felt herself at the edge of extinction. The first had been when she was tied up in the bathroom of the first place they stayed at. He had actually turned on the water while she was in the tub and from the way he had bound her the water only had to rise a few more inches before she have would started drowning.

The second time was yesterday when he had put the gun to her head. Every time she thought of that her blood ran cold.

Tomorrow they would leave the cabin. Although he had taken steps to minimize the chances of anyone recognizing her, she knew that if anyone did, or if he thought they did, she was a goner. And if he got just a little nervous, if he reconsidered the risk of capture he was taking just by having her with him, he might change his mind. They would drive down another lonely country road. He would dig another hole. And this time he would probably go through with it.

So, she needed every edge she could get. The slightest memory of how well she gave him pleasure might mean the difference between life and death. The slightest bit of humanity he saw in her might save her life. Until then, she would look for her chance to escape. He had to make a mistake sometime, didn't he? Didn't he?

She felt his hands on her belly. He rubbed it up and down and then descended to her breasts. His all powerful hands, the hands to which she could deny nothing, began a slow caress, massaging and squeezing them. Her pussy tingled. It wasn't so much from the sensations themselves, it was more the fact that she knew where he was going. You would think it hard to feel sensual bound the way she was, but it wasn't the sensation of having her mammaries probed and squeezed that set her off. It was the very fact of her lack of power to stop it.

Some place, way, way down in the substrata of her being, from deep in some bottomless crevasse, a strange, soul eating spirit had arisen and taken control of her. It fed on her unhappiness, her pain, her despair. It whispered in her ear, "Yes, yes, this is who you are! You are a creature of the darkness! You exist to be degraded. Find joy in your abasement, crave to be profaned!" The devil had found her out and stripped away her pretensions of purity, dignity and honor. "Revel in your true nature!"

the demon whispered. "Receive the humiliations you deserve! For there lies true ecstasy!"

She knew that she was fighting desperately for her sanity. While she was alone in her silent, dark world, she rued her cruel bonds, the inability to exercise the slightest act of volition. Every time she thought of how unfair and callous it was to treat her this way, thoughts that she vainly tried to fight off, a chill went through her body and she felt an ache so deep in her psyche that she thought she might dissolve into nothingness.

She tried to will herself into another place, another dimension. She pulled fruitlessly at her bonds. She tried to stoke her rabid hatred of the man so that that became her driving emotion. She tried to fool herself into thinking that somehow things were going to turn out all right. But none of it worked. She kept coming back to her unhappiness, her sense of inevitable, impending doom, the shame of her powerlessness, her weakness, her helplessness.

And then, when he touched her, the puzzle was solved. Her mind was seemingly programmed, like the voice kept telling her, to need, want, crave the things he was doing to her. Her powerlessness, her weakness, her utter helplessness stoked the fire lit by that dark demon and pushed aside everything else.

His hot hands left her breasts and flowed up over her hips to her thighs. They reached around and caressed her buttocks. Lust followed them wherever they went. While one hand held her still by the hip, the other slithered between her joined thighs and found her hungry slit. Just the contact alone sent a wave of passion through her. And when the fingers began to stroke her bud of pleasure, gently, rhythmically, incessantly, she could not help squirming her hips, her breath becoming labored, her breasts becoming taut.

When she moaned, he removed his hand from her quim and his hands found the buckle to her gag at the back of her head. He slipped the leather faux penis out. She had only a moment to enjoy the restoration of her mouth's liberty. Mere seconds later, the soft hardness of his cock pressed between her lips and replaced it.

His one hand had hold of the hair behind her head. He tilted it back slightly so that his upward impending member could find an unstrained path. He moved her head slowly back and forth. His cock was hot and hard. It filled her consciousness completely. It seemed huge, larger than life. It became the center of the world.

And then his free hand crept back up to the crux of her thighs. His fingers slipped into the edge of her engorged chasm, abraded her clit, stoked her lusts.

The creature which had ascended from the subterranean levels of her being took charge. It was as if she were possessed. A rabid fever coursed through her. "Ohhhhhhh, yeah! Ohhhhhhh yeah! Ohhhhhhh yeah!" her mind kept repeating. She suckled the invasive meat with abandon, slavered it with her tongue, pursed her lips and contracted her mouth so that the holy cock would achieve the maximum of contact with her soft interior, receive the adoration it deserved.

Jack matched each forward stroke of the girl's head with a forward thrust of his hips. Her mouth was hot and soft. Each traverse of her lips along the stem of his crank sent him a thrilling message of pleasure. "Oh, yeah! Oh, yeah! Oh, yeah!" he kept repeating. He was so overwhelmed with relief and joy at the connection he had made that he could barely control his excitement. He knew that he should make it last, but his body yearned to be taken to the heights of revelry. He abandoned her clit and took hold of the girl's head with both hands. He held it still, poised at the perfect angle and he thrust into her mouth mightily again and again. His crisis loomed. He couldn't ignore it. His mind rejoiced as his cock burst into a series of hard, jolting spasms. "Oh yeah! Take it! Take it! Take it!" he yelled. "Take my cum! Take it!"

He slowed his thrusts as his ejaculations waned. His whole body felt suffused with warmth. "Oh, that was beautiful," he thought. He gave the mouth a few more thrusts, until his cock softened. He withdrew it and patted the girl on the cheek. "Good job," he told her, although he knew she couldn't hear.

The gag was nearby on the floor and he reinstalled it right away. He rubbed her furry, red head and gave her body a gentle shove, sending it into motion once again. The girl was mewing behind the gag. He took hold of her teats, stilling her for a moment, and gave them a warning twist. The sounds stopped. Then he put her into motion once more.

Carly felt shamed at her display. She was such a whore! She had no pride anymore. The taste of his cum was still in her mouth. She had been dismayed when the gag had been restored so quickly after he was done. It emphasized that the main purpose of her mouth hole was to satisfy his prick. When that was accomplished, it was put back into storage. All she got for thanks was a pat on the cheek.

Her pussy still burned with need. She squeezed her thighs in miserable frustration. She had begun to issue pleas to be freed from her dismal posture when he had taken hold of her nipples and squeezed them hard. She knew what that meant and silenced herself. It was hard. She felt more sobs coming on and fought them off. "Please let me down! Please! Please!" she thought piteously. She strained and pulled at her bonds as she swayed back and forth and cursed herself, cursed the man, cursed God who had abandoned her.

Jack stretched his back and arms. It had been a great day! Now it was time to make preparations for tomorrow. He wanted to be able to get out as quickly as he could so he started packing their shit. He got out the clothes they would wear. She would wear one of the t-shirts he had gotten from the army navy store back in Wisconsin and her denim miniskirt. No underwear, of course. He wanted to be able to play with her pussy while they drove. He hadn't gotten any for her anyway. All she had to wear on her feet were the sandals he had lifted. That would be tough in the snow, but she wouldn't be out of the car for more than a minute. Once they got to Texas all the snow would disappear.

He made sure all the garbage was put in the trash, put his book and magazine away, emptied and cleaned the ash tray, swept the floor. He set up the coffee pot for the morning. He put his boots with a fresh pair of socks in them by the door. He used the bathroom, brushed his teeth.

He would make sure they he had a good breakfast. He wanted to make as few stops as possible. He took out the peanut butter and made a few sandwiches. There was still some soda left. They could drink that.

It took about 20 minutes to tidy up. When he was done, he stopped and looked at the girl. It was time to get her down. She had been punished enough, although it had been convenient to have her put away. He went over to her and untied the rope from the pipe, gently lowering her to the floor. She gave a loud moan of relief tinctured by what sounded like a sob. Taking hold of her feet, on her belly like before, he dragged her to the center of the room. He let her lie there, recovering from her ordeal while he had a smoke.

It was a little after 11. It had been a full day and he wanted to get to sleep early. But looking at her lying there, all bound and naked, he knew he wasn't finished with her. He wondered if he was up to the job. He was still naked too and he took hold of his cock and gave it a couple of pulls. According to his calculations, he owed her an orgasm from before when he got himself off in her mouth. It wasn't that he felt sorry for her that she didn't get off. It was just that he was a strict punishment and rewards kind of a guy and she had done a good job on the blowjob under very difficult circumstances. Besides, he just liked to see her in the throws of passion. It was exciting and fun.

When the smoke was finished, he got up and loosened her ankles. Taking hold of the hair on the back of her head, he guided her to her knees and then to her feet. She swayed unsteadily. He made her spread her legs. He removed the blindfold and the plugs from her ears. She looked at him warily. She looked tired and beaten, worn. It was not surprising. He guessed that she wouldn't refuse any more orders to eat. In the end, he had decided not to whip her. An hour and a half or so of dangling by her heels was enough.

Stepping behind her, her loosened her gag and pulled it from her mouth. He even unfastened the thick, black plug from her nether hole and slipped it out. He left her standing there while he took it into the bathroom and washed it. He washed off the ear plugs and the gag as well.

He brought her into the bathroom and made her use the toilet. She hadn't shat in 2 days and he had been wondering how he was going to take care of that, but she did it for herself. He was relieved from having to stick a bottle up her ass and give her an enema. He didn't want her to get all cramped up on the road and be forced to have her use a bathroom, or what was more likely, take a shit in the woods somewhere. You had to be practical about stuff like that.

While in the bathroom, he brushed her teeth.

Back in the main room, he tapped a spot on the floor with his foot. Obediently, she sank to her knees, spread them, and put her forehead on the spot he had demarked. Filling a good sized bowl with cold water, he brought it over to her and set it down. He sat in his chair and snapped his fingers twice. She looked up. He pointed to the bowl.

She edged herself over to it and lowered herself to drink. He got a kick from watching her. Her breasts flopped and swayed. Her hands were still way up on her back and her fingers wiggled. She finished it all like a good girl. When she was done, he snapped his fingers again and motioned for her to stand facing him. She had trouble getting up from her knees and almost fell over, but she did it. He snapped his fingers again, indicating that she should spread her legs and she complied dutifully.

He sat watching her for a few minutes. He wanted to firm up in his mind his vision of her. She was one he would remember all right. She had just about a perfect body, and her heavy breasts, still with the firmness of youth, rose at their ends in a perfect, presentation angle. He loved the red hair. Her luscious mouth, something he hadn't looked at much since she had been gagged most of the time, was down turned but still looked inviting. It really was a shame he couldn't take her to Mexico. And it was a shame what the boys in Alamogordo would undoubtedly do to her. Maybe it was better that he find a nice spot for her way out in the desert. Some place with a nice view of the sunrise. He wouldn't even make her watch while he dug the hole; he would make it quick.

The girl kept her head pointed down like she didn't want to look at him. He didn't like that. "Look at me," he ordered.

Her head rose and her eyes tentatively took him in. Her body shuddered as if she was repulsed at what she saw. You couldn't blame her really. But he wanted to see her eyes. They were beautiful, blue and starry. They kept flitting away from him, but she dutifully brought them back each time. There was a long pause. She looked like she was on the verge of tears. He spoke to her.

"Tomorrow, we're going back on the road. Don't get out of line. Understand?"

Carly understood all right. She nodded. His question didn't call for speech. It was mostly rhetorical anyway. She didn't know where they would end up tomorrow night, but she knew that she wouldn't be safe until they got there. Anything could happen on the road. There were a thousand little dirt roads he could take her down. She trembled at the thought.

She knew he had ordered her to look at him, but she couldn't tolerate the view of him for more than a few seconds at a time. She was so afraid of him that watching him watch her, theorizing all the time about what cruel thing he planned to do her next, made her body feel sour. She wanted her blindfold back. With that on, he was less real, more a force of nature than a man. A force of nature just is, good or bad. It did what it did because of its nature. But a man, that was different. Only in man does maliciousness grow. Only man hurts for pleasure. Only man takes joy in the degradation of others.

And this man was among the worst. If the soul is what makes us human, makes us feel kinship to others, gives us sympathy and compassion and love, than this man did not have one. Science need look no further for an explanation. Men like him were born without a soul. They were proto humans, human in form only. Nothing could be done about them except, as far as she was concerned, to put them down as you would any rabid animal.

Jack caught the fierce flashes of hatred the girl had for him. It didn't bother him one bit. It made no difference to him. She could think whatever she wanted about him as long as she obeyed him literally and completely in everything he said. And as long as she continued to be a sexual convenience. No, more than that, a sexual engine he could rev up at will. If she were a mere convenience, she would have eaten dirt long before this. She was much more. Underneath her beauteous mien was a creature of rapacious lust. He had proven it many times since he had come to own her. It fascinated and excited him. His cock stirred now, just looking at her.

He got up from his chair. The girl flinched. But she didn't move. She knew better. He turned off the overhead light so that the only light in the room was the soft light from the bedside lamp. It gave the room an eerie aura, as if he had snapped his wizard's fingers and whisked them off to his dungeon. He took hold of the Jim Beam bottle and the 2" roach from the ashtray and brought them to the girl. Removing the top from the bottle, he put it to her lips. He made her drink it a little at a time. When it was empty, he made her tilt her head way back so that she would get all the last drops. When he removed it from her lips, there was still a drop or two. He wetted his whistle with them.

When he had put the bottle down on the floor, he lit the joint. He made her smoke it. She dutifully filled her lungs each time, held her breath and then released her air. Only a small puff of smoke came out. He took a few hits too, getting his buzz back on.

When she was done with the joint, he made her eat the tiny roach remnant. He then picked up the bottle and placed it in a bin marked 'recycling'. He turned to look at her. Her eyes were glazed. Her face sagged a little bit. "Good," he thought.

He advanced on her and walked around her slowly. Her body stiffened as if she expected some blow. Her bound hands, high up on her back, fluttered nervously as if they were creatures of her psyche and not of her will, like the tail of a dog or a cat.

When he had started his second course around her, he stopped at her back. He stepped close to her and put his hands on her hips. He felt her shudder. He let his hands drift up her sides and then down, softly, gently. He ran them over her rear and the outside of her thighs. He slid them back up slowly. He was pressing himself up against her back. His breath was on her neck. When he took hold of her breasts, her body seemed to soften and she moaned. That was what he liked to hear. It was exactly what he had been talking about.

He massaged her breasts and pinched her nipples. His chest was pressed up against her bound arms and his cock, which had to his delight hardened, lay against the divide between her rear cheeks.

When he pinched her nipples hard, the girl moaned and her knees weakened. But she did not resist. He ran his right hand over her belly, down to the sweet slope that led to her mons while the other hand continued its assault on her mammaries. Without bending her over, he was just able to touch the very northern edge of her pussy. He gave it a caress and she trembled.

He moved to her right side. His right hand lowered. He dragged a finger along the traverse of her slit, bottom to top, and then, on the return journey, slipped it deeper between them. She was well lubricated and his finger moved easily. The next time, he used 2 fingers and probed deeper still. He was watching her face. When he slipped his fingers along the line of her outer labia, she closed her eyes and bit her lip. When he let his fingers rise and circled them softly around her clit her knees turned soft again and she moaned.

His left hand took hold of the hair behind her head and tilted her head back a few degrees. He leaned over and placed his lips on her mouth. She uttered a groan between her tightly pursed lips and then opened them. His tongue entered and, within seconds, hers was joining it in a little dance.

He continued kissing and caressing her for a while. She was moaning and kissing him back almost desperately. His cock was rock hard and he intended to fuck her, but he wanted to complete his mission here first. He kissed her for a long time, agitating her pussy, making it dilate and fill with the blood of her needy passion. Then he stopped kissing her. He ran his left hand over her breasts and stepped back. Their only point of contact now was his hand and her pussy. It was slippery and hot. Her mouth was open and she was exhaling the heat of her passion through it. Her eyes were still closed and he told her to open them and to look at him.

Carly was cursing herself for her display. Her head was spinning from the joint and the alcohol. The hand in her pussy was dexterous and able. It plunged its fingers inside her, it agitated her clit. It laid over her slit and massaged it. Every time she got used to one manner of stimulation, it seemed to shift, causing her to try and build up her defenses all over again in another sector of her mind. She didn't want to come for him. It was like he was exhibiting to her what a slut he had made of her. No kisses, no caresses, no hot body in tangent with her own, just the well skilled hand doing its job, causing her lust to build higher and higher.

When he ordered her to open her eyes and look at him, she almost burst into tears. He was going to leave her nothing. She yearned again for the darkness of the blindfold. His eyes were intent, black and sinister. His face had an amused, satisfied look, like he was pleased that his experiment was working. Yes, he could make her come any time he wanted. She would perform for him like a well trained pet.

Everything about what he was doing to her made her lust go off the scale. Helpless and bound, forced to endure his caresses, being under the watchful gaze of her master, her lord, her virtual god, standing naked and so open to him, his nakedness, her nakedness, the memory of everything that had happened to her in this small room, caused a torrent of passion to rush through her body. She felt her orgasm building. The residue of herself that was still present in her brain rebelled and began to push against it. But its resistance was feeble, doomed.

She was trying to stand straight up as he had commanded her, but the force of the waves of pleasure flowing through her caused her knees to buckle. She bent forward; her breath was pouring in and out of her open mouth. She moaned, deep and loud. She felt his hand pressing on her pussy, forcing to regain her posture. She felt her thighs shaking. She felt the urgent need to cry out her lust, scream and shout her passion. She could sense that that was what the man wanted. It was why he had removed her gag. He wanted her to display her wantonness in an irremediable way, in a way he could store in his brain and recall forever. This is what he would remember her for.

She didn't want to do it, but when her pussy began to contort and contract upon itself in heavy, shattering pulses, she let out a scream. "Ahhhhhhhhhhrrrrrghh!" And a shout, "Ohhhhhhhhhhhhh!" And another "Ohhhhhhhhhhhhhhh!" And another, "Ohhhhhhhhhhh-hhhhh!" Then she released a series of loud, staccato grunts, each one timed with a convulsion in her pussy. "Urrgh! Urrgh! Urrgh! Urrgh! Urrgh!"

Her eyes had closed momentarily, but she opened them again right away, her fear of retribution piercing her ecstatic reverie. He was grinning. She had never seen him grinning. In the dim light, he looked like a rugged goblin ready to put a captive in the oven.

Suddenly, he moved towards her. The hand in her pussy pushed her towards the bed. She pedaled backwards until she hit it and fell over on her back, crushing her arms and causing pain to shoot through her. He kept pushing on her pussy until she scrambled backwards to the center of the bed. He got on after her and insinuated himself between her knees. She knew what was coming and she dreaded it with all her heart. He was leaning over her, the grin still on his face. She felt the round helmet of his cock slip along her crevasse and then, without ado, slide inside her.

She groaned loudly. He lay atop her, his forearms pressed into the mattress on either side. He started pumping away. His hand ran over her head, skipping through her short, reddish hair. He bent down his head and took her lips. She greeted his tongue. Delirious with passion, she felt the demon in her arise and take over. It would be doing the driving. She was just along for the ride.

Jack was fucking her with long hard strokes. "What a great cunt! What an ever loving great piece of ass!" were the thoughts raging in his mind. He kept repeating them. His cock was rejoicing, his balls were tight. He knew that he could go on a long time. He wanted it to last. "Oh, what a fucking great cunt! Oh, yeah! Oh, yeah!" he thought madly.

The girl came again and shouted her ecstasy into his mouth. Her pussy squeezed his prick hard again and again. He was overwhelmed with a rabid lust. He pounded his hips against hers. Her legs were crossed against his back and she was thrusting right back. She shouted her lust into his mouth. After a while, she began to sob and blubber, but her legs still pulled down on him tightly, her hips rose to meet each one of his mighty thrusts. He felt his crisis coming. "Not here!" he thought. "Not here!"

He slipped his cock free of her needy hole and circled his arms under her thighs. He pressed them back against her chest. Her ass rose. Holding her ankles in place with one mighty hand, his other guided his cock to her dainty rear hole. When the head of his cock entered, the girl inhaled deeply. Her body was shaking. He pushed himself in slowly. His cock was covered with her juices and slithered through the small aperture easily. She gave out a groan as her membranes were stretched. Once sunk to the hilt, he drew himself back and forth a few times to assure himself that the going was easy. He ran his free hand over the undersides of her thighs. Then he renewed his assault.

His need was upon him and the pace of his thrusts reflected it. He looked down at the girl. Her eyes were spread wide, her mouth was open. She was looking at him as if she was seeing him for the first time. Her face was red, her chest sweaty. When her orgasm came, her face scrunched up tightly and her lips compressed. But only momentarily. Then she groaned loudly and long, "Urrrrrrrrrrrrrrrrrrrrrrrrrrrrrrrgh" Her eyes rolled back, her face became slack. She let herself go completely.

That was all Jack could take. His cock exploded into a series of powerful spasms. His groan was like hers, only deeper and louder. He was thrusting away furiously. It seemed like his crisis could go on forever. He could feel the muscles in his perineum contracting with each spurt of his cum. Then the last one came and he groaned and collapsed.

The room was filled with the sounds of their gasps for air. Carly felt her heart pounding away. When her pussy's aftershocks came as the man unconsciously slid his softening but still hard manhood back and forth, she closed her eyes and shuddered. Slowly, they wound down. The man was laying heavily on her. Her thighs were still pressed up, her knees at her breasts. As he finally slipped from her throbbing tunnel, he released them and let them fall to his sides.

A wave of unhappiness flowed through her. It had happened again. She knew that she should be inured to it by now, but she could not forgive herself for her frantic, delirious, unrestrainable lust for the man's touch, his lips, his cock. Wherever he put it, her mouth, her ass, her pussy, it drove her to heights of lust she had never known existed. Tears came to her eyes and she turned her head away so that she wouldn't have to look at him. In her passionate state, she had ignored the strain on her arms underneath her, but now the intense discomfort of lying on them came back. She knew she couldn't move until the man did, he was lying heavily atop her, and even then only when he decided to let her.

It was several minutes before the man stirred. He rose up from her and shimmied himself off of the foot of the bed. As his hands passed her ankles, he locked them together.

She heard him washing himself in the bathroom. Then he came back. He motioned for her to roll over. With some difficulty she managed it. He took hold of the hair in the back of her head and brought her to her knees. He had the gag in his hand. He presented it to her lips and she absorbed it unquestioningly. Once he had it buckled in place tightly, making her squeal, he got on the bed behind her and made her touch her forehead to the mattress. She felt the anal probe being restored. He attached it to the chains that led to the belt around her waist.

He went to the bathroom again and she heard him piss. When he came back to the bed, he tied a rope around her ankles and affixed it to the frame at the foot of the bed. He lifted her head and tied the end of a rope to the ring in the front of her collar. He made her lie on her belly and tied the other end taut to the headboard. He got in the bed next to her. The bedside lamp was still on. He leaned over her and put it out, plunging the room into darkness. He ran his hand slowly down her back and groped her ass. Then he pulled the bedclothes over them and laid his head on his pillow facing her. Within a minute his breath was coming deep and slow.

It took Carly a lot longer to fall asleep, time spent in abject misery. Sometime in the night, she felt the man's hands on her, drawing her to her side, facing away from him. The rope to her collar had been untied. He made her bend in half, thrusting her ass towards him. He stroked her pussy lips from behind until she was wet and then slipped himself in. Carly groaned with pleasure and unhappiness as he fucked her.

To be continued.

www.ingramcontent.com/pod-product-compliance
Lightning Source LLC
Chambersburg PA
CBHW050419260626
47156CB00003B/1069